LOST

in a

PYRAMID

And Other Classic Mummy Stories

LOST

in a

PYRAMID

And Other Classic Mummy Stories

Edited by

ANDREW SMITH

First published 2016 by
The British Library
96 Euston Road
London NW1 2DB

Introductory material copyright © 2016 Andrew Smith

'The Mysterious Mummy' by Sax Rohmer reprinted
courtesy of the Society of Authors and the Authors'
League of America as the Sax Rohmer Estate.

Cataloguing in Publication Data

A catalogue record for this book is
available from the British Library

ISBN 978 0 7123 5617 6

Typeset by Tetragon, London
Printed in England by TJ International

For Matthew Cheeseman and Paul Bareham

CONTENTS

INTRODUCTION

This collection consists of short stories published between 1869 and 1910, a period which represented the heyday of the mummy story, for quite specific historical reasons, which it is helpful briefly to outline here. The critic Ailise Bulfin has noted that the mummy story first became popular during the construction of the Suez Canal, which was built between 1859 and 1869. The canal enabled ships to move between Europe and South Asia without having to undertake the extensive detour around the African coast, but the building of the canal was to have far-reaching consequences for British colonialism. In 1875 the British Prime Minister, Benjamin Disraeli, purchased a number of shares in the Canal Company, which ensured that Britain had a strong economic interest in the area, one which was consolidated when Britain gained military control of the canal in 1882. The canal became internationally recognised as a neutral zone, although one which fell under British protection, from the late 1880s. From that period Britain found itself playing a role in Egyptian economic and political affairs in what became known as the "Egyptian Question". Egypt would gain its independence in 1922, but Britain maintained an interest in the area until the Suez Crisis of 1956.

The period during which the tales in this collection were published also witnessed the excavation of many key Egyptian sites, such as the tombs of the Valley of the Kings. These excavations had begun in earnest in the early nineteenth century and had stoked a British fascination with all things Egyptian, which influenced the design of jewellery, crockery, and even buildings – including the iconic Egyptian Hall designed by Peter Frederick Robinson for the collector and antiquarian William Bullock, which stood proudly in Piccadilly from 1812 until its demolition in 1905.

These events – the British protection of the Suez Canal and the continuing excavations of Egyptian tombs – together provide both a context and an explanation as to why so many mummy tales were published during this period. Bulfin claims that around 100 of them appeared in the periodical press between 1860 and 1914. Bulfin has also noted that around two-thirds of these tales could be classed as "curse narratives" and the remainder as romance tales. There are a number of curse narratives in this collection, and it is important to note that they tend to express ambivalence towards both the military occupation of Egypt and the consequences of tomb excavations. The justification for both of these activities seemed to many at the time to be morally questionable, and the idea that one might be cursed as a result of political and economic interference (combined with what looked suspiciously like tomb raiding – indeed, a type of grave robbing), to indicate that British colonialism was being subjected to the type of attack that it deserved. This politically liberal approach is touched on, often obliquely, in some of the tales reproduced here, including Louisa May Alcott's 'Lost in a Pyramid, or the Mummy's Curse' (1869) and Eva M. Henry's 'The Curse of Vasartas' (1889). Other tales are much more confident in asserting a sense of British entitlement, in which ancient Egypt is effectively demonised via explicit links to the popular form of the Gothic. In these stories, eradicating such monsters from the world constitutes a moral imperative – 'The Story of Baelbrow' (1898) by Katherine and Hesketh Prichard (writing as E. and H. Heron) is the clearest example of this impulse in this collection. There are other tales which represent ancient Egypt as a place of freedom in which young female mummies, conjured as semi-erotic visions, seem to provide an antidote to Victorian notions of middle-class probity. Tales such as Grant Allen's 'My New Year's Eve Among the Mummies' (1879), Justin Huntly McCarthy's 'Professor Petrus' (1884) and Julian Hawthorne's 'The Unseen Man's Story' (1893) can be seen as part of this strand. Many of these tales also reflect anxieties about Egypt by focusing on what happens when either mummies or their artefacts seemingly come alive in Britain and play out their revenge upon the nation which has taken them from their tombs – as witnessed by Sir Arthur Conan Doyle's 'Lot No. 249' (1892) and W. G. Peasgood's 'The Necklace of Dreams' (1910).

Understanding the historical context is one way of approaching these tales, and anyone interested in exploring such ideas further would do well to read Roger Luckhurst's insightful *The Mummy's Curse: The True History of a Dark Fantasy* (2012), which examines in depth the cultural contexts of the time. However, as interesting and important as these contexts are, the organising principles behind this volume were twofold: to find tales which have not been heavily anthologised before, and to create a collection that is eminently readable. Around half of the tales have not been in print since their original publication. The unrivalled archives of the British Library have proved an essential resource for finding these stories, which were often written by now-forgotten authors. Other tales have appeared in previous anthologies, although not with regularity – with the notable exception of the long tale by Sir Arthur Conan Doyle, 'Lot No. 249'. This is included here in part because it is critically regarded as a canonical example of the form, but also because of the quality of the writing (although in the interests of including some rarely published tales the same author's 'The Ring of Thoth' [1890] has been omitted). Many tales were excluded on the admittedly subjective criterion of readability. The quality of tales found in the periodical press (from which the majority of the stories in this collection are derived), is decidedly variable. Length was another consideration. 'Lot No. 249' is, clearly, the longest, and the others were around ten to fifteen pages long in their original formats. Other tales were deemed too short for the collection; some are only three or four pages long and lack the necessary narrative drive to be sufficiently arresting.

I would like to thank Robert Davies, Managing Editor of British Library Publishing, for suggesting this volume and for helping me to track down a copy of a particularly rare story. Whether you are reading this volume for entertainment or with an additional eye on the history of the form, I hope that you will have as much enjoyment reading the collection as I did in assembling it.

ANDREW SMITH,
University of Sheffield

FURTHER READING

Ailise Bulfin, "The Fiction of Gothic Egypt and British Imperial Paranoia: The Curse of the Suez Canal" in *English Literature in Transition, 1880–1920*, Vol. 54, no. 4, pp. 411–43.

Roger Luckhurst, *The Mummy's Curse: The True History of a Dark Fantasy* (Oxford: Oxford University Press, 2012).

'LOST IN A PYRAMID, OR THE MUMMY'S CURSE' (1869)

Louisa May Alcott

Louisa May Alcott (1832–1888) is best remembered today as the author of bestselling literature for children such as *Little Women* (1868) and *Little Men* (1871). However, there was another, darker, side to some of her writings, which she often published under the nom de plume of A. M. Barnard. These included her long short story 'The Abbot's Ghost, or, Maurice Treherne's Temptation' (1867) and a novel about a Gothic Faustian pact, *A Long Fatal Love Chase*, which was written in 1866 but not published until 1995. Her sensational *A Modern Mephistopheles* was published in 1877.

'Lost in a Pyramid, or the Mummy's Curse' was published in *New World* in January 1869 and is regarded as one of the first Egyptian curse stories – if not *the* first. The tale focuses on the negative consequences of raiding and desecrating an Egyptian tomb. This has ramifications not just for those who carried out the raid, but also for their loved ones. The curse is developed in an unusual way as we see the protagonists from the modern world sickened by the apparently beautiful and exotic. A seemingly innocent memento from the tomb proves to be their undoing.

I

"And what are these, Paul?" asked Evelyn, opening a tarnished gold box and examining its contents curiously.

"Seeds of some unknown Egyptian plant," replied Forsyth, with a sudden shadow on his dark face, as he looked down at the three scarlet grains lying in the white hand lifted to him.

"Where did you get them?" asked the girl.

"That is a weird story, which will only haunt you if I tell it," said Forsyth, with an absent expression that strongly excited the girl's curiosity.

"Please tell it, I like weird tales, and they never trouble me. Ah, do tell it; your stories are always so interesting," she cried, looking up with such a pretty blending of entreaty and command in her charming face, that refusal was impossible.

"You'll be sorry for it, and so shall I, perhaps; I warn you beforehand, that harm is foretold to the possessor of those mysterious seeds," said Forsyth, smiling, even while he knit his black brows, and regarded the blooming creature before him with a fond yet foreboding glance.

"Tell on, I'm not afraid of these pretty atoms," she answered, with an imperious nod.

"To hear is to obey. Let me read the facts, and then I will begin," returned Forsyth, pacing to and fro with the far-off look of one who turns the pages of the past.

Evelyn watched him a moment, and then returned to her work, or play, rather, for the task seemed well suited to the vivacious little creature, half-child, half-woman.

"While in Egypt," commenced Forsyth, slowly, "I went one day with my guide and Professor Niles, to explore the Cheops. Niles had a mania for antiquities of all sorts, and forgot time, danger and fatigue in the ardour of his pursuit. We rummaged up and down the narrow passages, half choked with dust and close air; reading inscriptions on the walls, stumbling over shattered mummy-cases, or coming face to face with some shrivelled specimen perched like a hobgoblin on the little shelves where the dead used to be stowed away for ages. I was desperately tired after a few hours of it, and begged the professor to return. But he was bent on explor-ing certain places, and would not desist. We had but one guide, so I was forced to stay; but Jumal, my man, seeing how weary I was, proposed to us to rest in one of the larger passages, while he went to procure another guide for Niles. We consented, and assuring us that we were perfectly safe, if we did not quit the spot, Jumal left us, promising to return speedily. The professor sat down to take notes of his researches, and stretching myself on the soft sand, I fell asleep.

"I was roused by that indescribable thrill which instinctively warns us of danger, and springing up, I found myself alone. One torch burned faintly where Jumal had struck it, but Niles and the other light were gone. A dreadful sense of loneliness oppressed me for a moment; then I collected myself and looked well about me. A bit of paper was pinned to my hat, which lay near me, and on it, in the professor's writing, were these words:

"'I've gone back a little to refresh my memory on certain points. Don't follow me till Jumal comes. I can find my way back to you, for I have a clue. Sleep well, and dream gloriously of the Pharaohs. N N.'

"I laughed at first over the old enthusiast, then felt anxious, then restless, and finally resolved to follow him, for I discovered a strong cord fastened to a fallen stone, and knew that this was the clue he spoke of. Leaving a line for Jumal, I took my torch and retraced my steps, following the cord along the winding ways. I often shouted, but received no reply, and pressed on, hoping at each turn to see the old man poring over some musty relic of antiquity. Suddenly the cord ended, and lowering my torch, I saw that the footsteps had gone on.

"'Rash fellow, he'll lose himself, to a certainty,' I thought, really alarmed now.

"As I paused, a faint call reached me, and I answered it, waited, shouted again, and a still fainter echo replied.

"Niles was evidently going on, misled by the reverberations of the low passages. No time was to be lost, and, forgetting myself, I stuck my torch in the deep sand to guide me back to the clue, and ran down the straight path before me, whooping like a madman as I went. I did not mean to lose sight of the light, but in my eagerness to find Niles I turned from the main passage, and, guided by his voice, hastened on. His torch soon gladdened my eyes, and the clutch of his trembling hands told me what agony he had suffered.

"'Let us get out of this horrible place at once,' he said, wiping the great drops off his forehead.

"'Come, we're not far from the clue. I can soon reach it, and then we are safe'; but as I spoke, a chill passed over me, for a perfect labyrinth of narrow paths lay before us.

"Trying to guide myself by such land-marks as I had observed in my hasty passage, I followed the tracks in the sand till I fancied we must be near my light. No glimmer appeared, however, and kneeling down to examine the footprints nearer, I discovered, to my dismay, that I had been following the wrong ones, for among those marked by a deep boot-heel, were prints of bare feet; we had had no guide there, and Jumal wore sandals.

"Rising, I confronted Niles, with the one despairing word, 'Lost!' as I pointed from the treacherous sand to the fast-waning light.

"I thought the old man would be overwhelmed but, to my surprise, he grew quite calm and steady, thought a moment, and then went on, saying, quietly:

"'Other men have passed here before us; let us follow their steps, for, if I do not greatly err, they lead toward great passages, where one's way is easily found.'

"On we went, bravely, till a misstep threw the professor violently to the ground with a broken leg, and nearly extinguished the torch. It was a horrible predicament, and I gave up all hope as I sat beside the poor fellow, who lay exhausted with fatigue, remorse and pain, for I would not leave him.

"'Paul,' he said suddenly, 'if you will not go on, there is one more effort we can make. I remember hearing that a party lost as we are, saved themselves by building a fire. The smoke penetrated further than sound or light, and the guide's quick wit understood the unusual mist; he followed it, and rescued the party. Make a fire and trust to Jumal.'

"'A fire without wood?' I began; but he pointed to a shelf behind me, which had escaped me in the gloom; and on it I saw a slender mummy-case. I understood him, for these dry cases, which lie about in hundreds, are freely used as firewood. Reaching up, I pulled it down, believing it to be empty, but as it fell, it burst open, and out rolled a mummy. Accustomed as I was to such sights, it startled me a little, for danger had unstrung my nerves. Laying the little brown chrysalis aside, I smashed the case, lit the pile with my torch, and soon a light cloud of smoke drifted down the three passages which diverged from the cell-like place where we had paused.

"While busied with the fire, Niles, forgetful of pain and peril, had dragged the mummy nearer, and was examining it with the interest of a man whose ruling passion was strong even in death.

"'Come and help me unroll this. I have always longed to be the first to see and secure the curious treasures put away among the folds of these uncanny winding-sheets. This is a woman, and we may find something rare and precious here,' he said, beginning to unfold the outer coverings, from which a strange aromatic odour came.

"Reluctantly I obeyed, for to me there was something sacred in the bones of this unknown woman. But to beguile the time and amuse the poor fellow, I lent a hand, wondering as I worked, if this dark, ugly thing had ever been a lovely, soft-eyed Egyptian girl.

"From the fibrous folds of the wrappings dropped precious gums and spices, which half intoxicated us with their potent breath, antique coins, and a curious jewel or two, which Niles eagerly examined.

"All the bandages but one were cut off at last, and a small head laid bare, round which still hung great plaits of what had once been luxuriant hair. The shrivelled hands were folded on the breast, and clasped in them lay that gold box."

"Ah!" cried Evelyn, dropping it from her rosy palm with a shudder.

"Nay; don't reject the poor little mummy's treasure. I never have quite forgiven myself for stealing it, or for burning her," said Forsyth, painting rapidly, as if the recollection of that experience lent energy to his hand.

"Burning her! Oh, Paul, what do you mean?" asked the girl, sitting up with a face full of excitement.

"I'll tell you. While busied with Madame la Momie, our fire had burned low, for the dry case went like tinder. A faint, far-off sound made our hearts leap, and Niles cried out: 'Pile on the wood; Jumal is tracking us; don't let the smoke fail now or we are lost!'

"'There is no more wood; the case was very small, and is all gone,' I answered, tearing off such of my garments as would burn readily, and piling them upon the embers.

"Niles did the same, but the light fabrics were quickly consumed, and made no smoke. 'Burn that!' commanded the professor, pointing to the mummy.

"I hesitated a moment. Again came the faint echo of a horn. Life was dear to me. A few dry bones might save us, and I obeyed him in silence.

"A dull blaze sprung up, and a heavy smoke rose from the burning mummy, rolling in volumes through the low passages, and threatening to suffocate us with its fragrant mist. My brain grew dizzy, the light danced before my eyes, strange phantoms seemed to people the air, and, in the act of asking Niles why he gasped and looked so pale, I lost consciousness."

Evelyn drew a long breath, and put away the scented toys from her lap as if their odour oppressed her.

Forsyth's swarthy face was all aglow with the excitement of his story, and his black eyes glittered as he added, with a quick laugh:

"That's all; Jumal found and got us out, and we both forswore pyramids for the rest of our days."

"But the box: how came you to keep it?" asked Evelyn, eyeing it askance as it lay gleaming in a streak of sunshine.

"Oh, I brought it away as a souvenir, and Niles kept the other trinkets."

"But you said harm was foretold to the possessor of those scarlet seeds," persisted the girl, whose fancy was excited by the tale, and who fancied all was not told.

"Among his spoils, Niles found a bit of parchment, which he deciphered, and this inscription said that the mummy we had so ungallantly burned was that of a famous sorceress who bequeathed her curse to whoever should disturb her rest. Of course I don't believe that curse has anything to do with it, but it's a fact that Niles never prospered from that day. He says it's because he has never recovered from the fall and fright and I dare say it is so; but I sometimes wonder if I am to share the curse, for I've a vein of superstition in me, and that poor little mummy haunts my dreams still."

A long silence followed these words. Paul painted mechanically and Evelyn lay regarding him with a thoughtful face. But gloomy fancies were as foreign to her nature as shadows are to noonday, and presently she laughed a cheery laugh, saying as she took up the box again:

"Why don't you plant them, and see what wondrous flower they will bear?"

"I doubt if they would bear anything after lying in a mummy's hand for centuries," replied Forsyth, gravely.

"Let me plant them and try. You know wheat has sprouted and grown that was taken from a mummy's coffin; why should not these pretty seeds? I should so like to watch them grow; may I, Paul?"

"No, I'd rather leave that experiment untried. I have a queer feeling about the matter, and don't want to meddle myself or let anyone I love meddle with these seeds. They may be some horrible poison, or possess some evil power, for the sorceress evidently valued them, since she clutched them fast even in her tomb."

"Now, you are foolishly superstitious, and I laugh at you. Be generous; give me one seed, just to learn if it will grow. See, I'll pay for it," and Evelyn, who now stood beside him, dropped a kiss on his forehead as she made her request, with the most engaging air.

But Forsyth would not yield. He smiled and returned the embrace with lover-like warmth, then flung the seeds into the fire, and gave her back the golden box, saying, tenderly:

"My darling, I'll fill it with diamonds or bonbons, if you please, but I will not let you play with that witch's spells. You've enough of your own, so forget the 'pretty seeds' and see what a Light of the Harem I've made of you."

Evelyn frowned, and smiled, and presently the lovers were out in the spring sunshine revelling in their own happy hopes, untroubled by one foreboding fear.

II

"I have a little surprise for you, love," said Forsyth, as he greeted his cousin three months later on the morning of his wedding day.

"And I have one for you," she answered, smiling faintly.

"How pale you are, and how thin you grow! All this bridal bustle is too much for you, Evelyn," he said, with fond anxiety, as he watched the strange pallor of her face, and pressed the wasted little hand in his.

"I am so tired," she said, and leaned her head wearily on her lover's breast. "Neither sleep, food, nor air gives me strength, and a curious mist seems to cloud my mind at times. Mamma says it is the heat, but I shiver even in the sun, while at night I burn with fever. Paul, dear, I'm glad you are going to take me away to lead a quiet, happy life with you, but I'm afraid it will be a very short one."

"My fanciful little wife! You are tired and nervous with all this worry, but a few weeks of rest in the country will give us back our blooming Eve again. Have you no curiosity to learn my surprise?" he asked, to change her thoughts.

The vacant look stealing over the girl's face gave place to one of interest, but as she listened it seemed to require an effort to fix her mind on her lover's words.

"You remember the day we rummaged in the old cabinet?"

"Yes," and a smile touched her lips for a moment.

"And how you wanted to plant those queer red seeds I stole from the mummy?"

"I remember," and her eyes kindled with sudden fire.

"Well, I tossed them into the fire, as I thought, and gave you the box. But when I went back to cover up my picture, and found one of those seeds on the rug, a sudden fancy to gratify your whim led me to send it to Niles and ask him to plant and report on its progress. Today I hear from him for the first time, and he reports that the seed has grown marvellously, has budded, and that he intends to take the first flower, if it blooms in time, to a meeting of famous scientific men, after which he will send me its true name and the plant itself. From his description, it must be very curious, and I'm impatient to see it."

"You need not wait; I can show you the flower in its bloom," and Evelyn beckoned with the *méchante* smile so long a stranger to her lips.

Much amazed, Forsyth followed her to her own little boudoir, and there, standing in the sunshine, was the unknown plant. Almost rank in their luxuriance were the vivid green leaves on the slender purple stems, and rising from the midst, one ghostly-white flower, shaped like the head of a hooded snake, with scarlet stamens like forked tongues, and on the petals glittered spots like dew.

"A strange, uncanny flower! Has it any odour?" asked Forsyth, bending to examine it, and forgetting, in his interest, to ask how it came there.

"None, and that disappoints me, I am so fond of perfumes," answered the girl, caressing the green leaves which trembled at her touch, while the purple stems deepened their tint.

"Now tell me about it," said Forsyth, after standing silent for several minutes.

"I had been before you, and secured one of the seeds, for two fell on the rug. I planted it under a glass in the richest soil I could find, watered it faithfully, and was amazed at the rapidity with which it grew when once it appeared above the earth. I told no one, for I meant to surprise you with it; but this bud has been so long in blooming, I have had to wait. It is a good omen that it blossoms today, and as it is nearly white, I mean to wear it, for I've learned to love it, having been my pet for so long."

"I would not wear it, for, in spite of its innocent colour, it is an evil-looking plant, with its adder's tongue and unnatural dew. Wait till Niles tells us what it is, then pet it if it is harmless.

"Perhaps my sorceress cherished it for some symbolic beauty – those old Egyptians were full of fancies. It was very sly of you to turn the tables on me in this way. But I forgive you, since in a few hours, I shall chain this mysterious hand forever. How cold it is! Come out into the garden and get some warmth and colour for tonight, my love."

But when night came, no one could reproach the girl with her pallor, for she glowed like a pomegranate-flower, her eyes were full of fire, her lips scarlet, and all her old vivacity seemed to have returned. A more brilliant bride never blushed under a misty veil, and when her lover saw her, he was absolutely startled by the almost unearthly beauty which transformed the pale, languid creature of the morning into this radiant woman.

They were married, and if love, many blessings, and all good gifts lavishly showered upon them could make them happy, then this young pair were truly blest. But even in the rapture of the moment that made her his, Forsyth observed how icy cold was the little hand he held, how feverish the deep colour on the soft cheek he kissed, and what a strange fire burned in the tender eyes that looked so wistfully at him.

Blithe and beautiful as a spirit, the smiling bride played her part in all the festivities of that long evening, and when at last light, life and colour began to fade, the loving eyes that watched her thought it but the natural weariness of the hour. As the last guest departed, Forsyth was met by a servant, who gave him a letter marked "Haste." Tearing it open, he read these lines, from a friend of the professor's:

DEAR SIR—Poor Niles died suddenly two days ago, while at the Scientific Club, and his last words were: "Tell Paul Forsyth to beware of the Mummy's Curse, for this fatal flower has killed me." The circumstances of his death were so peculiar, that I add them as a sequel to this message. For several months, as he told us, he had been watching an unknown plant, and that evening he brought us the flower to examine. Other matters of interest absorbed us till a late hour, and the plant was forgotten. The professor wore it in his buttonhole – a strange white, serpent-headed blossom, with pale glittering spots, which slowly changed to a glittering scarlet, till the leaves looked as if sprinkled with blood. It was observed that instead of the pallor and feebleness which had recently come over him, that the professor was unusually animated, and seemed in an almost unnatural state of high spirits. Near the close of the meeting, in the midst of a lively discussion, he suddenly dropped, as if smitten with apoplexy. He was conveyed home insensible, and after one lucid interval, in which he gave me the message I have recorded above, he died in great agony, raving of mummies, pyramids, serpents, and some fatal curse which had fallen upon him.

After his death, livid scarlet spots, like those on the flower, appeared upon his skin, and he shrivelled like a withered leaf. At my desire, the mysterious plant was examined, and pronounced by the best authority one of the most deadly poisons known to the Egyptian sorceresses. The plant slowly absorbs the vitality of whoever cultivates it, and the blossom, worn for two or three hours, produces either madness or death.

Down dropped the paper from Forsyth's hand; he read no further, but hurried back into the room where he had left his young wife. As if worn out with fatigue, she had thrown herself upon a couch, and lay there motionless, her face half-hidden by the light folds of the veil, which had blown over it.

"Evelyn, my dearest! Wake up and answer me. Did you wear that strange flower today?" whispered Forsyth, putting the misty screen away.

There was no need for her to answer, for there, gleaming spectrally on her bosom, was the evil blossom, its white petals spotted now with flecks of scarlet, vivid as drops of newly spilt blood.

But the unhappy bridegroom scarcely saw it, for the face above it appalled him by its utter vacancy. Drawn and pallid, as if with some wasting malady, the young face, so lovely an hour ago, lay before him aged and blighted by the baleful influence of the plant which had drunk up her life. No recognition in the eyes, no word upon the lips, no motion of the hand – only the faint breath, the fluttering pulse, and wide-opened eyes, betrayed that she was alive.

Alas for the young wife! The superstitious fear at which she had smiled had proved true: the curse that had bided its time for ages was fulfilled at last, and her own hand wrecked her happiness forever. Death in life was her doom, and for years Forsyth secluded himself to tend with pathetic devotion the pale ghost, who never, by word or look, could thank him for the love that outlived even such a fate as this.

'A NIGHT WITH KING PHARAOH' (1869)

Baron Schlippenback, KSL

The precise identity of Baron Schlippenback may never be known. It is unlikely that he was the minor German poet Albert von Schlippenbach (1800–1888) or the Russian naval officer and some-time naturalist Baron Alexander von Schlippenbach (1828–?). Schlippenbach is an old noble European name that has its origins in the fourteenth century, and it is probable that its near likeness was chosen simply as an unusual and exotic-sounding nom de plume. A further tale, 'The Incumbent of Bagshot', appeared under this name in the 1869/70 issue of *Belgravia*.

'A Night with King Pharaoh' is a double-cross story in which two adventurers are betrayed by their guides, but are saved by an unusual figure who looks like a mummy but is actually from closer to home. The tale includes some uncomfortable racial stereotypes and the character of Donovan seems like a parody of an explorer. However, the tale's focus on religious fervour provides an alternative image of spirituality and salvation, which complicates some of the more two-dimensional elements of the story. The tale also makes reference to the notable Italian explorer of Egyptian sites, Giovanni Battista Belzoni (1778–1823), and on the second page the reference to "Irving" is to the famous Scottish clergyman Edward Irving (1792–1834). That our explorers are not really much more than tourists is suggested when one of them refers to the popular Murray's *Hand-Book for Travellers in Egypt* (published in 1847) to identify a tomb.

HIRING A DRAGOMAN

"How I do envy you men!" said Mr McBaine, the bluff, pleasant English Consul at Cairo, throwing himself back in his chair, and purring away for a moment or two after he spoke through the cool rose-water in the vase of his narghilé, as he looked at me and Masters. "Bubble, bubble," went the water with a sleepy pleasant sound. I almost fancied myself sitting beside a fountain in Damascus, reading the love-verses of some Persian poet. "Here am I" (for the oracle, slowly withdrawing the bright amber mouthpiece, spoke again after a short interval of silence), "here am I, poor devil," he went on, "chained to my desk, signing papers, squabbling about contracts in Arabic, running backwards and forwards to Alexandria to see the Pasha – never a day to myself; and here are you, young, rich, enthusiastic, going off to explore tombs, climb pyramids, wade through desert-sands, copy cartouches, follow the very footsteps of Herodotus; in fact, as the Americans say, 'see the whole elephant'; while I am to be left plodding on at Cairo like an old mill-horse that I am. Isn't it desperate hard, Miss Shepherd?"

The worthy Consul, half an Arab in tastes, here stretched out his gaunt legs, assumed an aggrieved look, and rubbed his stubbly grey beard as if it was a talisman against trouble.

Miss Shepherd, one of three sandy, masculine, clever sisters about to visit Thebes and the First Cataract, replied that she only wished the Consul would accompany them; how delightful it would be! On which all three sisters turned up their eyes simultaneously and raised their hands.

We were a party of English travellers that night at the Consul's, all about to start for the First Cataract. We were going at different times, and in three different boats. Ramsay and Erskine, two enthusiastic young Scotch missionaries, first; next Masters and myself; lastly Mrs Shepherd and her delightful daughters.

The Consul's large, dim, semi-oriental room had pierced lattices instead of windows, and its two large coloured Chinese lamps scarcely shed more light than was just sufficient to observe the singularly pale, absorbed face of Erskine, the younger of the two Scotch clergymen, who sat with his eyes fixed intently on a string of tasselled ostrich-eggs that hung from the ceiling in the Arab manner.

I think I had never seen anyone who so much resembled that eloquent enthusiast, Irving: the same handsome features, the same silken flow of long black hair, the same fine exalted expression, and all spoiled too by Irving's great defect, a cast – must we say it? – a painful squint, that gave a sinister and almost crazed look to the whole face.

"When do you two gentlemen start?" said Mrs Shepherd, a good-natured fussy woman, addressing Erskine and Ramsay; "and can you tell us how much money we ought to take, as I and Laura here differ on the subject?"

"My dear mamma," said the eldest and rather soured Miss Shepherd sarcastically, "how can you tease Mr Erskine with such questions? You know Murray lays it all down, – twenty pounds for each person for the three months; and Murray is always right."

"You might just as well ask Erskine, Mrs Shepherd, what horse to bet on for the next Derby," said Ramsay, laughing. "The prophecies about Egypt and the future of the Turk are all Davy here cares for. – Well, so you've hired your boat, Barclay – good one – how much?"

"My friend Donovan, the commission agent," I replied, "is coming tomorrow to draw up our contract with Shoolamei. Wonderful creature, Donovan – a real Irish Samson, up to every move. Our boat is one-hundred-and-fifty ardebs burden, and is to cost forty pounds the month. We shall be second up the river."

"Yes; we start tomorrow, God willing," said Erskine, suddenly leaping into the conversation. "We shall be the first to hear the song of Memnon. O, there is a great work to do in Nubia!"

"And we," said Mrs Shepherd, "shall be third, I suppose. But pray, sir, who was this Mammon? Who was Mammon?"

"How can you, dear mamma, make such awful mistakes?" said the amiable Laura Shepherd. "Why, Memnon was one of the Pharaohs, of course. – Mr McBaine, will you play us one of those extraordinary Arab airs on that curious sort of lute you have? O, do."

The Consul was delighted; he took down a huge Egyptian lute, and began an excruciatingly plaintive air, full of remarkable and subtle inflections not over-pleasant to English ears.

"Very singular, most remarkable! O, thank you, thank you!" chorussed the three Miss Shepherds.

"What a hideous row!" whispered Masters to me, with a sour look of hatred at the unconscious Consul, who kept humming Arabic songs. "Here, I'll give 'em something."

Masters went to the piano, as if at my request, and instantly broke forth into that sprightly charming Welsh air, "The Bells of Aberdovey".

"Slight, but cheerful," said the Consul patronisingly. "It wants the tenderness of our oriental music. – Mr Erskine, do you play?"

"O, yes, he plays delightfully," said the Misses Shepherd.

"I am fond of music," said the young clergyman, gravely rhapsodising; "but I fear my taste is an exceptional one. I like only old church-music, and most especially the hymns of our early church. They seem to me like the voices of denouncing angels; they fill the air with prophecies of sorrow and doom; they speak loudly of coming wrath to the persecutor, to the good of beatitude ineffable. While I play, legions of the accursed appear to march and battle round me, till presently one bright note, like a sunbeam, glances across the turmoil, and then at once there rises before my mind the green calm of an unfading paradise."

"He played at Malta four hours without stopping," said Ramsay. "But I tell him it is dangerous for him, for he is not strong; and besides, he is working much too hard just now at his Arabic and Armenian."

"Evidently a tile loose," whispered Masters to me, touching his forehead as he spoke; "he's always at high pressure."

By this time Erskine had seated himself at the piano and begun to play that grand hymn, the *Dies irae*. He thundered out its warnings; he shot lightnings of swift-flashing notes across the deeper undercurrent of its threatened judgements; he clashed out screaming sounds as if of souls in torture; he struck the keyboard as if it had been an anvil – sparks seemed almost to fly forth as he hammered at the bass; he played till the hot drops beaded on his forehead (Mrs Shepherd slept through it all); he then, I suppose, began to improvise, for no natural piece of music could ever have been so long, and gave us what must have been warnings of a new crusade, for there was oriental battle-music in it, and charges of horse, French and English marches, file-firing and sabre-clashing; lastly, he performed what he called "the Resurrection of the East". On, on he went, it seemed hours, till all at once his fingers relaxed, his eyes glazed, and he fell back senseless on the floor. He had fainted, as I had feared he would.

"Mad as a March hare!" said Masters scornfully, spirting a fusee as we went out of the Consul's door. "I wouldn't be in Ramsay's shoes for a couple of hundreds. I can't think how that mad duffer could let those Shepherd women egg him on to such a crack-brain display of himself. Suppose I'd gone on with "The Bells of Aberdovey" all night; why they'd have had me in the madhouse long before this. By the bye, how Ramsay carried on with that younger Miss Shepherd – decent girl, but not my sort; and didn't old McBaine scowl when I talked too loud! Hang me if I darken his doors again, the old Turk! But look, there are Erskine and Ramsay crossing the corner of the Usbeekeeh; he is spouting, I do believe, even now. Look at him – only just look at the man."

I turned to look, and saw Erskine standing, a tall dark figure, waving his hand at the great moon, that, large and bright, shone out with a lustre and purity only to be seen in the East. Ramsay was urging him forward.

"If old McBaine ever gave anybody anything stronger than sherbet, I should call that fellow half-seas over," said Masters. "That's just the sort of man who would throw up a good living in England to go out and hobnob with cannibal idiots 2000 miles off. He'll be trying to convert the Pasha next, or denouncing polygamy in the Sultan's harem. He actually longs to lose his head. I do think he'd try and turn the Pope out of St Peter's with his own hands. O, there's a tile off, no doubt of it. I never did see such a queer fish, such an impracticable mad lot in all my life. I suspect those Nubians will bring him to grief. He's sure to go preaching about alone. He talks of stopping with them; they'll kill him for his gold watch, or his teeth, or his studs, and there'll be an end of him. For heaven's sake, let's slip into Zech's first, or we shall have him sitting up jawing all the blessed night over his lemonade about founding a Christian empire in Nubia, or making Rothschild Emperor of Jerusalem. How I do hate that sort of irrational man, with theories no person on earth can understand! Look out, double up, they're turning the corner now."

"O, you're far too hard on Erskine, Masters," I said, as we entered Zech's hotel, and ascended the staircase together *en route* to our bedrooms in that enormous caravanserai. "He is a fine enthusiastic fellow, and of the true Peter-the-Hermit type. Such men often convert whole nations, and reform the centuries in which they live. If Erskine's health holds out, he will be a great religious reformer."

"Well, I don't like the kind of man, that's all I can say; but we won't quarrel about it, old fellow. Take that chair, light a cheroot, and let's settle our kit on paper, before that amusing wild-beast of a fellow, Donovan, comes. He'll be on us like a typhoon tomorrow early, depend on it, and I want you to see my new Westley Richards."

I awoke at midnight; someone was singing. It was Erskine, two rooms off, chanting passages from the *Stabat Mater*.

Bang, rap, bang, went a slipper at his door. Bare feet paddled down the passage.

"For heaven's sake, Erskine," cried an agonised and angry voice that I knew to be Masters's, "do get to sleep, and let other people. I hear groaning all down our corridor; go to sleep, man; you've had singing enough, surely, for one night."

Erskine replied diffusely; but what he said I did not hear, for I fell asleep.

A tremendous burst at the door awoke me the next morning; great feet trod the matted floor, a giant's hands shook my bedclothes roughly, and tore aside my mosquito-curtain; a huge coarse red face, not over-clean, crowned with a red tarboosh, glowered on me. It was Donovan, who, drawing a packet from his paletot-pocket, slapped it on the table, and then drank at a draught half a bottle of claret we had left from the night before.

"There's my luggage," he said, in his astoundingly deep voice; "slippers, shirt-collar, and revolver. Came from Alexandria, my boy, by the night-train, and devilish hungry I am. Do nothing without my steak – shall eat two this morning. Get up, you spalpeen; here's the contract in Arabic for you to sign."

"But, Donovan," I moaned, wistful of sleeping, "there's no hurry; wait for the dragoman."

"*Wait for him!*" roared my persecutor, rushing to the door, and shouting in Arabic twice as loud as a bull. "Why, the fellow's downstairs, and the captain too – brought them both an hour ago. Great rogues; but they're afraid of me. Everything's ready; I never delay things. Flags, powder, shot, wine, biscuits, ink, charcoal, will all come from my store by next train – save you forty per cent. Saw the Pasha yesterday, by the bye, about the right to excavate at Memphis. There was a dirty little Frenchman tried to get a prior permission, just to stop you. He boasted of it as I was going up; so I kicked him out of the palace for his impertinence. The moment the Pasha saw me, 'Donovan,' says he, 'my boy, what the devil have you been doing, kicking this Frenchman? This is a breach of the peace, Donovan,' says he."

The mode of putting the Pasha's remonstrance was so Irish and so intensely absurd that I could restrain myself no longer. I laughed till the bed shook again. Donovan looked amused and sobered for a moment; then he dipped his hand in a side-pocket and drew out an enormous flat-headed monitor-lizard, which he thrust in the face of a German waiter, who just then came in to say our dragoman was below.

The German turned pale, shuddered, and fled, much to Donovan's cyclopean delight.

"I've got a vulture and a young hyaena coming for me today," he said; "I suppose you can give them a shakedown here. They are presents. I bought them for a friend at Malta. You should have seen me the last time I was here, riding full tilt down the Usbeekeeh with a parrot on my shoulders. Every now and then the little dodger would fall off and hop after me. To see the Arab fellows stare! O, I sha'n't forget it. – Now then, you duffers" (here he opened the door and roared down the corridor), "Abou Hoosayn Shoolamei and Ali Reis."

I prayed for mercy. Couldn't he wait until I was dressed, and had had my bath?

"Not a moment," said the Whirlwind. "Business is business. What did I come for but to manage the contract for you?"

A sneaking tap at the door, and a mean fat-faced fellow in a turban thrust in his head deprecatingly.

"Want dragoman, sir? Second Cataract – pound a-day – good testimonial – Sir Smith, Dr Dredger – Christian man, sir – no cheat."

Donovan snatched up my bootjack, and roared like a hurt lion. "I know you; you're Lezano – the fellow that two American gentlemen tied to the mast and flogged for stealing a bank-note. Vamoos quick, or I'll shy this. You dirty blackguard – get out of that!"

Sir Smith's dragoman had scarcely gone, when the door again opened, and two men presented themselves. The one was a short thin Maltese, with a long vulture nose and only one eye; the other, the Arab captain of the boat, – a tall, square-built, sullen fellow, with an air of authority, but evidently a satellite of the one-eyed dragoman, a little, subtle, thievish, hypocritical, servile fellow, with timid greedy eyes and a weak chin; who kept moving about a great gilt thumb-ring as he spoke, whenever he was not fumbling in the folds of his red sash for his bag of copper-change. They were both evidently nervously anxious to sign the contract.

"Anything gentlemen wished. All rait, Mr Donovan, as gentlemen wish. Stop where you like. No delay till reach Thebes, but two days for baking bread for the crew. All rait, sir – make all rait."

"No backshish to crew; boat to be sunk to kill rats before starting," roared Donovan, laying down each condition with a blow of the bootjack on the table. "Provisions to be first-class" (here Arabic to explain "first-class"), "beds clean, awning to quarter-deck, cat on board, fresh meat as often as possible, small boat to go on shore with, no unnecessary stoppages, crew not to absent themselves without leave, and mind you, Shoolamei, ballast enough, or I'll pull you up before the Consul, every man-jack of you: decks washed every morning – mind that, you fellow, grinning there – and plenty to eat, no starving, or I'll thrash you both the first time I meet you. Now, then, sign this. – Where's Masters?"

Out whisked the Whirlwind: in he came directly, leading Masters half-dressed, and a hairbrush in each hand.

The dragoman remarked that he could not write.

"You thief of the world," cried Donovan, "who ever thought you could? Come, no shuffling. You'd better treat these gentlemen well, or I'll kill you. Where's your seal? Come, out with it!"

As the dragoman proceeded to wet the seal with ink and stamp his cipher, Donovan became vituperative in Arabic.

"What's that all about?" said Masters, who had been eyeing the dragoman and his friend with a most sarcastic and suspicious look. "What does that amount to?"

"I told him," said Donovan, stroking his beard, "and swore by the heads of Hassan and Hoosayne, that if he defrauded either of you, or violated his contract, I would drag him before the cadi, and beat him with my own hands; and that when the criers had next to proclaim the daily rise of the inundation, they should end by proclaiming the shame and rascality of Abou Hassan Shoolamei of Cairo, and Ali Reis of Boolak."

Donovan winked fiercely at us as he repeated this rodomontade.

As soon as the somewhat sinister-looking men had left the room with many solemn oriental leave-takings, I asked Donovan calmly what he really thought of their probable honesty and fidelity.

Masters fixed his eyeglass steadily on Donovan, and paused for a reply.

"Well," said Donovan, "you fellows mustn't expect too much. I never yet did find an Arab I could rely on entirely; but I think these two will do, if you keep a firm hand. They're both rogues, like all these dragomans and captains; they'll of course pluck you a little. But they'll be on their guard, I've thrashed so many of them. I nearly killed one fellow, a Syrian, because he tried to burn my boat. I walked into him, you may depend on it. O, there's no fear from Shoolamei. Don't show your money, don't leave any trinkets about; it's a bad plan. They'll tell any lie. Above all, be firm, and don't trust them farther than you can see. As for Erskine and Ramsay, who are gone up the river, they'll have a nice time of it. Those rascals will pull their very eyelashes out. O, they want a firm hand, these Arabs. Ha! you fellows are like young monkeys; you've all your troubles before you. By the bye, did I ever tell you how I organised that revolt in Alexandria, when five thousand of my Italians, armed with knives, resisted the Austrians, who wanted to seize some refugees?"

I said, "No."

Masters began violently to brush his hair, and secretly groan; but at that moment the breakfast-gong beat, and we were saved an infliction. The Shepherds at the *table-d'hôte* eyed with profound astonishment that huge Irishman, with his fez cap and careless dress, his stupendous appetite, his leonine laugh, his loud declamatory assertions of his own sagacity and prowess, and his chivalrous scowls at anyone who stared at him!

We had been fourteen days afloat; the life was pleasant, but still, from the want of exercise, it must be owned, rather monotonous. Miles and miles of earth-bank, through which the great brown river had cut silently its irresistible way. Ramsay and Erskine were on before; the Shepherds followed us. I read Herodotus aloud, while Masters watched at the cabin-window for pelican or wild-duck. He never brought much to the bag, as we could not stop to pick up the birds, and the current ran fast; but still it amused Masters. Day by day we could not help observing that the crew got more sullen, the captain more silent, and the dragoman more insolent and dictatorial. My gravest suspicions were aroused, though I scarcely knew why.

We passed the monastery of Our Lady Mary, on the lower plateau of the Gebel-e-Dayr mountain. A true Egyptian sunset turned the cliff to a ruby colour. On the top of the cliff three black specks proved to us that the monks saw us, and were sending out their swimming emissaries; still none came.

As the sun set in ineffable splendour, we fired our usual evening gun, and in came the malign dragoman with a smoking tureen of our favourite lentil-soup.

"I wish those beggars had swum out to us," said Masters.

"Dirty rogue men," said Shoolamei. "No Christians – humbug men – all they do, scratch, scratch, beg, beg."

Just as he left the cabin we heard a furious splash in the water, angry shouts in Arabic, and cries of "I am a Christian, O hawajee (pilgrims)!"

We ran out, and there was Shoolamei, yellow with rage, beating with a heavy oar at a lean monk who floated on the water, buoyed up on a raft of inflated hide.

The monk, avoiding the blows, screamed and spat, writhed his thick brown body as if he was a water-snake, and shouted his war-cry of mendicancy.

"Why, what's up?' said Masters angrily.

"This up, this up – bad man – thief man!" said the dragoman, quite beside himself with hatred of the vociferous Christian.

"Lay down that oar!" I said.

"I'll kill him, as if was toad!" replied Shoolamei, striking harder, and inciting the crew also to strike.

"If Shooly doesn't stop, I'll tip him over," said I to the captain, who looked on sullenly.

Shoolamei still used the oar, but could scarcely reach the monk.

"Once! Will you stop? Twice! – three times!" I said, and with a strong heave of both hands, the dragoman still striking furiously at the monk, I threw Shoolamei over into the river.

The captain and men dropped their oars, and seemed inclined to make a rush on us. I drew my revolver.

"Fish that man up," I said, "or the monk will strangle him. Touch me, and I'll kill one of you."

Masters ran down for his double-barrelled gun.

The men still looked savage and threatening, but a whisper from the Reis, who was smiling with treacherous cunning, and pretending to laugh at the whole matter, calmed them, and pulling out Shoolamei and the monk together, they resumed their oars.

Shoolamei appeared vexed, yet contrite; but he muttered when Masters and I laughed at the draggled and miserable appearance he presented. A minute or two more and he was waiting on us and the poor monk with all the obsequiousness of a servant whose very existence depends on his master's pleasure. His one eye was turned almost benignly on us and on our gesticulating guest.

"Now that's what I call a good sort," said Masters, when Shoolamei saw the monk over the boat-side, and watched him swimming back to the monastery of Our Lady Mary – "bears no malice. I know I shouldn't have much liked the flying mare you sent him. What a cropper he did go, to be sure! I thought he was never coming up again. Well, he deserved it; for that last kid he bought had been kept far too long. I only wish you had sent the captain in too; for he's a surly beast, and makes a point of not understanding my Arabic, which is ungrateful, for I almost find the beast in tobacco. I believe that what Donovan says is right – the only way to reason with an Arab is to take him hard between the eyes, and then talk to him."

"We must keep them good friends," I replied, laughing; "but the lesson I gave Shoolamei will do him good, I'm sure. He fancies he is going to get the upper hand, but he isn't. Yet still, somehow, Masters, I don't like the man, and we must watch him closely."

Our first inquiry at Thebes was for Erskine and Ramsay. The latter had gone on alone to the First Cataract. Erskine had gone inland, in order to preach to the natives in some villages in the interior. We had had to tow nearly all the way, and forty days had passed in this tedious operation. The Shepherds' boat we had seen in the distance at Denderah.

"Just like Erskine," said Masters contemptuously; "anything to be singular. He'll turn hermit next, like – like what's-his-name, who preached the Crusades. – Now then, look here, Shoolamei, about these tombs?"

We had not been ten minutes at Thebes, and here was that excellent but inconsequential fellow, Masters, already proposing, with the true English spirit of business, to begin the tombs. Pleasure with an Englishman always assumes an air of business. It is to be done quickly, punctually, and, if possible, cheaply.

That night we spent at the Egyptian Consul's, in a room every corner of which was packed with mummy-cases. The Consul had some native dancing to amuse us, and discoursed on the splendour of Karnak. We talked of nothing but lotus columns, hieroglyphics, Belzoni's discoveries, obelisks, and the vocal Memnon.

As we rose to take leave, the Consul said to us carelessly: "Had you a good character with your dragoman?"

I told him he had been hired for us by Donovan; whom he knew well. That seemed to entirely satisfy him. I asked him if he had any reason for his question. He replied: "No; only watch him. There was a story or two against him at one time."

LEFT TO DIE

"Who is to go with us, Shoolamei, to the tombs?" shouted Masters through the cabin-door, the moment he had leapt out of bed the next morning, and fired off a salute at a passing flock of wild-geese.

A big Nubian helmsman and a little Arab sailor rose up from the deck, where they were feeding out of a great wooden bowl, and grasped their acacia-sticks and their water-bottles ready for a start. Shoolamei and the captain whispered together, then came forward to our cabin-door. They motioned the volunteers back to their meal, and took up the water-bottles and staves.

"We go to tombs – I and the Reis," said the dragoman, with one malign eye looking sourly into space, and one sound eye all benevolence. "We wish good sight to gentlemen in Thebes. We show No. 17 tomb, Belzoni's tomb, high-priest tomb, great tomb – all right off. Yes, better than boatmen – lazy fellows, know nothing. I and Reis show tomb – any tomb show yes – best. Get good donkey for gentlemen – English gentlemen like good donkey."

"O, that'll do," said Masters. "We know all about it. English gentlemen like good donkeys, and good dragomans like you; that's about it. Come, fire away with the breakfast, and put-up some grub for us – some limes, mind, and some figs, lots of that stewed-apricot stuff, some cold meat, and some hard-boiled eggs."

"How deuced civil that rascal is this morning, Masters!" said I. "I suppose he's afraid we shall have the Consul down on him, eh? He'll be wanting us to do all Thebes in a week. We've cured the fellow, sure enough."

"O, he be hanged! I won't move till I've seen the place from top to toe. We ain't at Thebes every day; and mind this, he sha'n't hurry me today; the more he hurries, the more I shall take it quietly; and if he gives us any cheek, down he goes, in the tomb or out of the tomb."

The heat had evidently upset Masters's liver. He was at bay against our lazy captain and our despotic sly dragoman. Shoolamei had better take care, I thought; for Masters, good-natured as he was, had his rough side, and could hit very hard from the shoulder.

We started directly after breakfast, mounted on donkeys; Shoolamei and the Reis taking our guns in case of a chance jackal among the sand-hills; a Nubian boy carrying our water-bottle, and running behind us, patient and untiring, with a great basket of provisions hanging over his swarthy shoulder. It was very hot even then, and the pure blue of the sky had turned to a sort of brazen glow and glare that only an eagle's eyes could meet with impunity. The sand over which we scuffled returned the glare with interest, and rose in a hot cloud around us if we ventured to urge our donkeys faster than their usual lazy uncomfortable amble. The boys, their drivers, chattered in Arabic, and ran after us in subservience to Shoolamei and his long javelin of acacia-wood.

I and Masters kept well in front, our bridles of blue beads jangling as we rode first, so as to be able to talk undisturbed. Shoolamei applauded our riding and our spirit, our steeds and our punctuality. He was all smiles. Even the stolid Reis relaxed into approving gestures, and uttered his favourite English phrase, "Yes – all rait – yes!" several hundred times.

"What a famous humour they're in!" I said to Masters. "Rather civil of them too, coming to save us a guide. I say, Masters, we must give Shoolamei and the others a sheep at the next place. I really thought the other day we were going to have trouble with the fellow."

"Hang his civility!" said Masters, turning round in his saddle and scowling at unconscious Shoolamei, who, by the bye, had now mounted a donkey, as also had the Reis; "some trick or other. I suppose he's going to ask us for more money in advance, or to reconsider the contract, or something of that kind. I don't like the fellow; he's a bad lot, that's my belief; and I shall tell Donovan so."

"Masters, you're a cynic."

"Well, I suppose I am; but I don't like dragomans, that's the fact. By the bye, did I tell you that yesterday, as I was counting out the sovereigns in my belt for my Syrian trip, I looked up and saw that one-eyed beast glowering in at me? When he observed me he began cleaning a cabin-window; but I don't think he had come for that. I almost wish, though, I hadn't left the belt in the trunk under my bed. I shall wear it again always, as I used to."

"Don't be so suspicious of poor Shoolamei," I said. "How could he help seeing your money? Of course he knows we have money. What of that?"

"Well, I don't know; but still I don't like the fellow, and I'd just as soon he had not seen me put the belt in that small valise."

As we were riding through the rank green fields that spread round the great statue of Memnon, a frightened-looking seller of antiquities from the tombs of the kings met us, and spoke in Arabic to Shoolamei and the Reis.

"What's up, Shoolamei?" said Masters; "the fellow looks as if he'd been bitten by a mad dog."

Shoolamei, who was of no religion, and believed in nothing, stared through his one eye, and said—

"There was a ghoul seen last week in the tombs of the kings; no guide will go there now." The fellow sneered as he told us this. "Perhaps hyaena, eh? – what say? English gentlemen afraid? Turn back – eh?"

"You be hanged!" said Masters furiously. "If you turn back, I'll have you before the Consul; remember that. – I should like to have a fair shot at a ghoul – new idea, eh, Barclay? – Come, push on, Shoolamei, or let me. – I say, Barclay, isn't it lucky we brought our white umbrellas! It's screeching hot; my brains are being regularly scolloped in the shell."

Presently we reached the burning Valley of the Tombs, with its cavernous rocks, and its wild, desolate scenery, bare, lonely, parched, and torrid. No weed grew there, nor any green thing; the quick brown lizards, glancing over the heaps of sand and broken white plaster, were the only living creatures that we saw, except once, when a scared jackal darted across a distant hill, and ran into a tomb where some Pharaoh had once rested.

We halted at a square dark doorway numbered 20. It was one, we observed, not noticed in *Murray*. Masters got out his red guide-book, and flew into a rage.

"Shoolamei," said he, "we want No. 17 – Belzoni's tomb. This is no use. Come, we will do as we like; you take us to No. 17 right off."

Shoolamei grew obsequious and argumentative.

"Not best first," he said; "no good. Belzoni tomb spoil all. Better see different sorts first – this very large, curious for first. *Englishmen never see it*. They're foolish."

"Well, so it is," said I, referring to *Murray*; "it's the high-priest's tomb, Petemunap (King Horus), eighteenth dynasty. Deuce of a long time ago. Three-hundred-and-twenty feet straight off to first deviation; eight-hundred-and-sixty-two feet altogether from entrance; area, twenty-three-thousand-eight-hundred-and-nine feet; occupies an acre and a half."

"The deuce it does!" said Masters; "like the cheek of those high-priests. What a pluralist he must have been!"

"Yes," said Shoolamei, "this priest too big, large, very large, tremendous room – much hieroglyph – men cooking – men rowing – everything. Better than Belzoni tomb – much fuss, Belzoni tomb – not so good – no."

"Well, I suppose we must see it," said Masters. "Give us the candle, Shoolamei, and mind and bring the rope, in case we want to go down anywhere, or the steps are bad. – Suppose, Barclay, we were to find a row of mummy kings, or a chest of papyri, with the lost books of Livy – eh? or a complete Ennius, or some find of that kind; that would be rather jolly, eh?"

There was a good deal of whispering between Shoolamei and the Reis. The Reis was afraid of the ghoul, so Shoolamei said, but at last he consented to go with us. He did so sullenly and almost savagely. The dragoman had some hold over that man that we never could understand, for the Reis always did as he wished, although often after a struggle.

Down we went slowly out of the light, down a broad, broken staircase into the darkness, our path strewn with broken plaster, and encumbered with thick soft sand, detritus, and powdered gypsum. The walls were covered with sculptures and hieroglyphics, brilliant in rich reds, blues, and yellows; kings seated with their fan-bearers, priests, ministers, and soldiers. Trains of slaves and bearers of tribute defiled along the passage, and seemed almost to move as we passed them with our flickering lights. Passages, doorways, more staircases, then oblong chambers, mysterious pits, pillared halls, and intricate nests of small rooms, filled with sculptures representing all the phases of Egyptian life a thousand years ago; glass-blowers, saddlers, curriers, carpenters, chariot-makers, fowlers, husbandmen, boat-builders. Myriads of brown faces had bent over this work, myriads of brown hands had toiled in those gloomy chambers, miles as it seemed away from the burning sunshine of the outer valley.

Sculptured room after room, sculptured passage after passage, sculptured ceiling after ceiling, cell after cell, centuries of careful records of the hopes, toils, ambitions, and vanities of generations of ages since passed to dust. Still unheeded, the silent figures performed their mimicry of life, and recorded the names and deeds of men immortalised, but only within this tomb. The darkness pressed upon us; it moved before us slowly as our candles advanced in solid masses, like huge doors of black marble slid back from the mouth of a sepulchre. As our light moved on, fresh troops of quaint red figures and hieroglyphics appeared, approached, and faded again into the darkness. It was a gigantic but useless effort of man's ambition thus to inurn his body; a stupendous effort of wealth, and of that almost supernatural tenacity of purpose that enabled the Egyptians to rival the Titans and to raise the Pyramids.

"Glad we came here," said Masters, with a great effort to keep his eyeglass steady. "Good fellow, that Shoolamei. This is a regular find. We'll write to the *Times* about this. I propose, Barclay, we do it thoroughly."

"We'll go to the very end, if it takes all day," said I; "though the air is very close. I believe there's never enough foul air to be dangerous in these tombs."

All at once the darkness seemed to widen round us, the ceiling to lift, and we found ourselves in a large hall, supported by six giant columns of barbaric shape.

"This very fine – this good," said Shoolamei, muttering in Arabic to the Reis, as he suddenly scrambled up a heap of dry palm-twigs, and set them on fire with his candle.

"How stunning!" said Masters. "By George, look, old man, this is something like!"

It was indeed an extraordinary scene; the blaze of flame lit up the huge hall, disclosing the colossal coloured figures of winged genii that adorned its four walls. On the ceiling a giant Isis and Osiris guarded the broken granite sarcophagus that still stood in the centre, on the edge of a great dark chasm, down which descended two broken staircases. Athor, Horus, and Anubis looked down on us from the vaulting, as the flame had brought them to life, but in the succeeding darkness they again melted away.

We all stood on the edge of the staircases, and looked down as into the entrance of Hades, dark, inscrutable.

"This not ghoul-tomb – that next tomb. Papyri there," said Shoolamei, pointing down; "perhaps treasure. I think king mummy there; perhaps sarcophage – eh? Try, perhaps find, eh? What think? Englishmen never here before. I hold rope safe round pillar; take plenty candle. Have lunch first."

As we lunched, Shoolamei and the Reis sat talking apart earnestly, and with side-looks cast at us.

"I'll go in for it," cried Masters, pouring out some wine; "here's to the two future Belzonis!"

"Belzonis – ha, ha! Very good. What think?" said Shoolamei, laughing in his sour dry way. "Reis here say you more sense than Belzoni; not afraid to go to end, and find king mummy. If you find, you give poor Shoolamei one guinea, eh?"

"Give you! yes, and my blessing too, you duffer," said Masters, as we finished our luncheon. – "I'll stick my candle in the brim of my wideawake; you do the same, Barclay. Come along. I'll go down first; the walls are quite steep, and I can work down with my feet safe enough to the first landing, wherever that may be."

The two Arabs secured the rope safely at one end, then let the other fall into the darkness.

Masters went down laughing; at about fourteen feet he stopped, and shouted up lustily. The two Arabs laughed together, and I laughed.

"All right, Barclay; come along! There's another staircase here to the right, and we shall have a great find yet. Now, man, come. The hieroglyphs here are wonderful – as bright as if they were painted yesterday. Here are crocodiles and porcupines, and all sorts of rum fish. Come along, old man; it's quite easy getting down."

I descended too, with my candle in my hat; several more candles were to be lowered by Shoolamei afterwards, in case of accident.

I thought once I heard a groan, and Masters laughed when I said it was the ghoul.

I was by his side in a moment or two more. We left our revolvers above.

Masters shouted up:

"Take care of the rope, you duffers there; we sha'n't be long."

Still up glided the rope. Already it was beyond our reach.

"Leave the rope alone, you fools there!" shouted Masters. "Leave it, I tell you, just as it is."

Up still – quick – went the rope; it was now far beyond our reach. We could see Shoolamei grin, and the Reis show his great yellow horse-teeth, as he coiled the rope up slowly.

"Now then, English gentlemen," cried Shoolamei, kneeling on the edge of the chasm, and looking down sneeringly, "good-bye to you. No more call Arab fool Arab, ass Arab; him very good man now, if he give rope, eh? By and by, cold, hungry – then go to sleep cumf'table. Large bed there – plenty of room with King. Shoolamei take care of your money. Reis wish you good-night. Any message to Cairo? You fool, gentlemen, now – English – eh, what think?"

All became dark for a moment, then the light reappeared, and the two hideous mocking faces, illuminated with the light, were thrust over the edge of the pit.

"All rait, gentlemen?" said Shoolamei. "All very cumf'table down there? No one come here to disturb you; no traveller, no Englishman, ever come here. We go back; take boat. Say to Consul, left you mile down below Karnak, get safe to Boolak, sell boat there, take train to Alexandria, go off and spend money. O, you fool Englishmen! how you like dragoman's trick now, eh? – how you like it? Good-bye. Call Shoolamei, when you want anything, ass, thief. Dragoman you tried to drown sure to come."

There was a bellow of cruel mocking laughter – the light passed away. We were left alone there for ever – left slowly to die in that tomb, hopeless. Our death would be lingering, but it was certain. We heard a distant laugh recede; then came a deeper and more terrible silence.

O, the ineffable horrors of that moment, as the sense of the certainty of a dreadful death fell upon us like a thunderbolt, and struck us into agonising despair! I tried to speak; but my tongue clove to the roof of my mouth, and refused to utter the half-cry, half-prayer, to which I was wishing to give utterance. Then rose to my brain a rage and regret almost approaching to madness at having been the dupes of such rascals and murderers, whom with ordinary precaution we could so easily have foiled and overthrown. But was there no hope? None; no glimmer of light came to us in our utter misery. This tomb was never visited. Ramsay and Erskine were by this time probably up at the First Cataract; and the Shepherds, however soon they arrived, were not the sort of travellers who deviate much from the usual track. No; we should die of starvation; unless in some frantic moment of despair we should be tempted to kill one another. Not a moment now passed but it seemed like hours.

I clasped Masters's hand. We were silent for some minutes, then he said solemnly: "Here's a pretty go! I say, we are *in* for it."

"Villain, blackguard, treacherous villain!" I shouted in a tempest of rage, that, however, soon subsided into despair.

We knelt down together, and prayed God to deliver us. Then we began to try to cut steps in the rock with our pocket-knives, but that was hopeless. Then came hours of torpid despair.

It was night now; I thought, soon will come the gnawing pangs of starvation, the maddening agonies of despair. We should die mad with thirst. Who knew what insane and horrible impulses might not come upon us in that struggle for a few more hours of life? I could have run on the cannon or the bayonets, I could have leaped among shoals of sharks, to save a friend, or in pursuit of my duty; but death here, unpitied and alone, was too horrible. We shouted, we clasped each other's hands again, and prayed – prayed with silent tears. Our light had long since gone out.

"Hark!" cried Masters suddenly. "What was that?" He sprang to his feet.

There was indeed a sound, as of a footstep; then arose from the darkness of the staircase beneath a verse of an English hymn, sung in a deep hollow voice.

Gracious God! what could it be? A light came twinkling out of the darkness; then, slowly, a pale mournful face, bound round with white, like a corpse, came down a long avenue of tombs moving towards us. A long figure, wrapped in white, and with shrouded face, like a Lazarus emerging from the sepulchre, came nearer and nearer, holding a candle in one hand. We could hardly breathe from wonder and fear.

"I come," it said, pointing to the rows of hieroglyphic figures on the nearest wall, "to preach to you, fallen spirits, children of Hades. When the angel spoke to me in the desert, and sent me thither, did I not arise at once to bid you repent – ye who have not fallen, like Satan, for ever? Dead father, whom I knew while I was in sin, trouble me not, for I have no part or lot with you. Leave me, while I go and pronounce the prophecies of mercy and of doom to the great crowned genii in the upper chamber. Osiris, repent! Isis, seek in prayer, and thou shalt obtain mercy. Fallen dominions, great principalities of hell, ponder these things; abandon this howling darkness, this blackness of despair, and follow me to the green paradise, to the river of life, to the unfading happiness. It will be centuries, cycles of centuries, ere God again sends you another warning prophet."

We were at first astonished as by a supernatural event; but before the figure had spoken two words we had recognised those words as English. Before a whole sentence had been uttered we had recognised the speaker as our friend Erskine. In such a place, and at such a crisis, it seemed a direct miracle could alone have sent him there. Were we dreaming? Masters looked at me, and I at Masters. Then we crouched closer into the darkness lest the spectre should see us before we had formed our own conclusions as to his purpose, his humanity, and his destination.

A frantic joy now seized me, and took the place of a ghastly despair. I felt inclined to shout and dance and sing, but that a vivid sense of the imminent danger still pressed upon me. If our reason had not already gone, there was Erskine. Why he had come, we could not guess, nor could we imagine how he had found an entrance to that abyss. Perhaps he too had been decoyed there and deserted; and in that case we should but share his death. Perhaps he had gone mad, and had voluntarily descended a place from which there was no rescue. These and similar thoughts rushed in a moment through my fevered brain, over whose turbulent sea Hope once again cast its deceitful sun-gleam. I roused Masters from the torpor into which he had sunk.

As we stood there, Erskine – for it was indeed that mad enthusi-ast – sat down twenty feet off, at the entrance to a dark passage we had not before noticed, and began to sing that beautiful old hymn, "The Lord my pasture shall prepare". His fine voice rang through that great chambered tomb.

There was hope for us now Erskine had found his way there – perhaps had taken up his abode there, in some fit of temporary insanity. Perhaps he would be able to find his way out. We debated whether we should at once leap out on him, and force him to be our guide. But our only candle was burned out, and our matches were expended in our searching. If, in the struggle, Erskine's candle should also become extinguished, a fresh frenzy might come on, and he might either refuse to allow our escape, or lose his way in the darkness.

I muttered in a low voice some Arabic words. Erskine turned, and began to descend a staircase.

"Follow him," said Masters; "let's follow him. He is mad – stark mad, you see; but still he may have some means of getting out; he fancies he has been sent to convert the souls in Hades. He is living here among the tombs; he must have got some secret way out. He could not sing like that if he was starving – I defy him. Look, he does not see us yet."

"There is hope, Masters; I feel there is," said I. "See, he turns into that hall to the left; yes, he must have a way of getting out."

"Yes, God in His goodness be thanked! He must have been the ghoul, then, the people saw."

We followed, taking off our shoes to tread softly, lest he might mistake us for some of his spirit-congregation, and turn and fly, leaving us to a fate too horrible to be thought of.

We followed him down passages that seemed endless, all far lower than the level of the tombs from which we had descended. Had he, too, been left there to perish? Suddenly he turned a corner, and his candle disappeared. To our infinite horror, when we turned the corner too, in our hot but silent pursuit, we could not see the light of Erskine's candle, nor hear his voice or his footsteps.

We now gave ourselves up for lost. Erskine must have seen us, and eluded us; or he had fainted, and was dying in a fit. Suddenly my hand, moving along the wall, detected an opening broken through, and a passage beyond.

"Hurrah, Masters! cheer up, old boy!" I said. "I'm on the right track now – he certainly must have slipped through here."

In a moment we were through. We turned a corner; the light of day fell on us – blessed, glorious light of hope and life! There was a broken staircase leading into the valley. Erskine was ascending. When he saw us, he screamed insanely, and fell on his knees, with his hands raised to heaven.

"I know you," he said; "you are sent by the prince of the power of the air to tempt me back to earth; but I will not come. My mission is to preach to the dead in Hades. No, no."

We leapt on the madman, and secured him as he was about to fly from us into a neighbouring tomb.

Suddenly, at a turn of the valley, at the mouth of the famous Belzoni tomb, in the shadow of the entrance, we came upon an English party lunching, near a fire at which some Arabs were making coffee. They rose when we approached, and greeted us warmly.

"But, my boys, what in the wide world are ye doing, dragging about poor Erskine? O, I see, there's something wrong about him. Why, the Consul told us you'd gone off to Karnak. Here, let me see to Erskine."

Yes, it was that raging lion Donovan, and a friend, and the enchanting Shepherds. Donovan had started, on a sudden impulse, crocodile-shooting with a young Dublin University man.

"Well, we are charmed with everything," said Mrs Shepherd, as fussy as ever; "and so delighted to meet you and Mr Masters. And where is that dear, clever, affectionate dragoman of yours?"

I briefly related my adventure, and explained how Shoolamei and the worthy Reis had tempted us into a trap, then decamped, leaving us to what they considered certain death.

The ladies were horrified at our story, and enraptured at our escape. Poor Erskine grew gradually calmer in their society, and we gave him into the care of the Consul, who was half a doctor.

Donovan was furious at the treachery of Shoolamei and the Reis; that very night he insisted on starting off in pursuit.

"I'll track them," he said, as he wished us all good-bye, "to Alexandria; and if I miss the spalpeens there, I'll follow them to Syria, or Greece, or Abyssinia, or any blessed part of the world; and when I find them, I'll beat them to a jelly, then drag them back and get them imprisoned for life. I know the Pasha will do that for me, and they can't afford to bribe themselves off. – I say, but you two fellows had a narrow squeak for it. O, you didn't keep a tight hand enough over the dogs. I shall be sure to nab 'em – I was in the police once."

Donovan fulfilled his promise, sure enough. He caught the two rogues at Malta, and returned with them, and with our money, not much of it spent. The crew owned the plot, and came forward as witnesses. As for poor Erskine, after a brain-fever of long duration, he slowly recovered, and is now, I believe, an active missionary in Lapland. It was a fortunate day for Masters and myself, I've often thought, when his madness took the form of a wish to *dwell among the tombs*.

'MY NEW YEAR'S EVE
AMONG THE MUMMIES' (1879)

Grant Allen

Grant Allen (1848–1899) was a British-based, although Canadian-born, author of fiction who was also known for his scientific writings, such as *Physiological Aesthetics* (1877), *Evolutionist at Large* (1881), and *Flowers and Their Pedigrees* (1886). Allen wrote in several literary modes including science fiction, detective stories, and the Gothic. He also produced fiction under several aliases, including 'My New Year's Eve Among the Mummies' as J. Arbuthnot Wilson. His detective novel, *Hilda Wade* (published posthumously in 1900), was completed by his friend and neighbour, Arthur Conan Doyle, whose 'Lot No. 249' (1892) is included in this collection.

Allen's tale was published in *Belgravia* magazine in February 1879, and is notable for the jocular tone of its narrator. He gets caught up in a once-in-a-millennium New Year's Eve celebration with some revivified mummies, with whom he discusses philosophy, science and religion, and above all love, especially with the female mummy Hatasou. The tale is playful, but also contrasts the freedoms of the mummies' vivid festivities with the restrictive Victorian world from which our narrator comes.

I HAVE BEEN A WANDERER AND A VAGABOND ON THE FACE OF the earth for a good many years now, and I have certainly had some odd adventures in my time; but I can assure you, I never spent twenty-four queerer hours than those which I passed some twelve months since in the great unopened Pyramid of Abu Yilla.

The way I got there was itself a very strange one. I had come to Egypt for a winter tour with the Fitz-Simkinses, to whose daughter Editha I was at that precise moment engaged. You will probably remember that old Fitz-Simkins belonged originally to the wealthy firm of Simkinson and Stokoe, worshipful vintners; but when the senior partner retired from the business and got his knighthood, the College of Heralds opportunely discovered that his ancestors had changed their fine old Norman name for its English equivalent some time about the reign of King Richard I; and they immediately authorised the old gentleman to resume the patronymic and the armorial bearings of his distinguished forefathers. It's really quite astonishing how often these curious coincidences crop up at the College of Heralds.

Of course it was a great catch for a landless and briefless barrister like myself – dependent on a small fortune in South American securities, and my precarious earnings as a writer of burlesque – to secure such a valuable prospective property as Editha Fitz-Simkins. To be sure, the girl was undeniably plain; but I have known plainer girls than she was, whom forty thousand pounds converted into My Ladies: and if Editha hadn't really fallen over head and ears in love with me, I suppose old Fitz-Simkins would never have consented to such a match. As it was, however, we had flirted so openly and so desperately during the Scarborough season, that it would have been difficult for Sir Peter to break it off: and so I had come to Egypt on a tour of insurance to secure my prize, following in the wake of my future mother-in-law, whose lungs were supposed to require a genial climate – though in my private opinion they were really as creditable a pair of pulmonary appendages as ever drew breath.

Nevertheless, the course of our true love did not run so smoothly as might have been expected. Editha found me less ardent than a devoted squire should be; and on the very last night of the old year she got up a regulation lovers' quarrel, because I had sneaked away from the boat that afternoon, under the guidance of our dragoman, to witness the seductive performances of some fair Ghawázi, the dancing girls of a neighbouring town. How she found it out heaven only knows, for I gave that rascal Dimitri five piastres to hold his tongue: but she did find it out somehow, and chose to regard it as an offence of the first magnitude: a mortal sin only to be expiated by three days of penance and humiliation.

I went to bed that night, in my hammock on deck, with feelings far from satisfactory. We were moored against the bank at Abu Yilla, the most pestiferous hole between the cataracts and the Delta. The mosquitoes were worse than the ordinary mosquitoes of Egypt, and that is saying a great deal. The heat was oppressive even at night, and the malaria from the lotus beds rose like a palpable mist before my eyes. Above all, I was getting doubtful whether Editha Fitz-Simkins might not after all slip between my fingers. I felt wretched and feverish: and yet I had delightful interlusive recollections, in between, of that lovely little Gháziyah, who danced that exquisite, marvellous, entrancing, delicious, and awfully oriental dance that I saw in the afternoon.

By Jove, she *was* a beautiful creature. Eyes like two full moons; hair like Milton's Penseroso; movements like a poem of Swinburne's set to action. If Editha was only a faint picture of that girl now! Upon my word, I was falling in love with a Gháziyah!

Then the mosquitoes came again. Buzz – buzz – buzz. I make a lunge at the loudest and biggest, a sort of prima donna in their infernal opera. I kill the prima donna, but ten more shrill performers come in its place. The frogs croak dismally in the reedy shallows. The night grows hotter and hotter still. At last, I can stand it no longer. I rise up, dress myself lightly, and jump ashore to find some way of passing the time.

Yonder, across the flat, lies the great unopened Pyramid of Abu Yilla. We are going tomorrow to climb to the top; but I will take a turn to reconnoitre in that direction now. I walk across the moon-lit fields, my soul still divided between Editha and the Gháziyah, and approach the solemn mass of huge, antiquated granite blocks standing out so grimly against the pale horizon. I feel half awake, half asleep, and altogether feverish: but I poke about the base in an aimless sort of way, with a vague idea that I may perhaps discover by chance the secret of its sealed entrance, which has ere now baffled so many pertinacious explorers and learned Egyptologists.

As I walk along the base, I remember old Herodotus's story, like a page from the *Arabian Nights*, of how King Rhampsinitus built himself a treasury, wherein one stone turned on a pivot like a door; and how the builder availed himself of this his cunning device to steal gold from the king's storehouse. Suppose the entrance to the unopened Pyramid should be by such a door. It would be curious if I should chance to light upon the very spot.

I stood in the broad moonlight, near the north-east angle of the great pile, at the twelfth stone from the corner. A random fancy struck me, that I might turn this stone by pushing it inward on the left side. I leant against it with all my weight, and tried to move it on the imaginary pivot. Did it give way a fraction of an inch? No, it must have been mere fancy. Let me try again. Surely it is yielding! Gracious Osiris, it has moved an inch or more! My heart beats fast, either with fever or excitement, and I try a third time. The rust of centuries on the pivot wears slowly off, and the stone turns ponderously round, giving access to a low dark passage.

It must have been madness which led me to enter the forgotten corridor, alone, without torch or match, at that hour of the evening: but at any rate, I entered. The passage was tall enough for a man to walk erect, and I could feel, as I groped slowly along, that the wall was composed of smooth polished granite, while the floor sloped away downward with a slight but regular descent. I walked with trembling heart and faltering feet for some forty or fifty yards down the mysterious vestibule: and then I felt myself brought suddenly to a standstill by a block of stone placed right across the pathway. I had had nearly enough for one evening, and I was preparing to return to the boat, agog with my new discovery, when my attention was suddenly arrested by an incredible, a perfectly miraculous fact.

The block of stone which barred the passage was faintly visible as a square, by means of a struggling belt of light streaming through the seams. There must be a lamp or other flame burning within. What if this were a door like the outer one, leading into a chamber perhaps inhabited by some dangerous band of outcasts? The light was a sure evidence of human occupation: and yet the outer door swung rustily on its pivot as though it had never been opened for ages. I paused a moment in fear before I ventured to try the stone: and then, urged on once more by some insane impulse, I turned the massive block with all my might to the left. It gave way slowly like its neighbour, and finally opened into the central hall.

Never as long as I live shall I forget the ecstasy of terror, astonishment, and blank dismay which seized upon me when I stepped into that seemingly enchanted chamber. A blaze of light first burst upon my eyes, from jets of gas arranged in regular rows tier above tier, upon the columns and walls of the vast apartment. Huge pillars, richly painted with red, yellow, blue, and green decorations, stretched in endless succession down the dazzling aisles. A floor of polished syenite reflected the splendour of the lamps, and afforded a base for red granite sphinxes and dark purple images in porphyry of the cat-faced goddess Pasht, whose form I knew so well at the Louvre and the British Museum. But I had no eyes for any of these lesser marvels, being wholly absorbed in the greatest marvel of all: for there, in royal state and with mitred head, a living Egyptian king, surrounded by his coiffured court, was banqueting in the flesh upon a real throne, before a table laden with Memphian delicacies!

I stood transfixed with awe and amazement, my tongue and my feet alike forgetting their office, and my brain whirling round and round, as I remember it used to whirl when my health broke down utterly at Cambridge after the Classical Tripos. I gazed fixedly at the strange picture before me, taking in all its details in a confused way, yet quite incapable of understanding or realising any part of its true import. I saw the king in the centre of the hall, raised on a throne of granite inlaid with gold and ivory; his head crowned with the peaked cap of Rameses, and his curled hair flowing down his shoulders in a set and formal frizz. I saw priests and warriors on either side, dressed in the costumes which I had often carefully noted in our great collections; while bronze-skinned maids, with

light garments round their waists, and limbs displayed in graceful picturesqueness, waited upon them, half nude, as in the wall
paintings which we had lately examined at Karnak and Syene. I
saw the ladies, clothed from head to foot in dyed linen garments,
sitting apart in the background, banqueting by themselves at a
separate table; while dancing girls, like older representatives of my
yesternoon friends, the Ghawázi, tumbled before them in strange
attitudes, to the music of four-stringed harps and long straight
pipes. In short, I beheld as in a dream the whole drama of everyday
Egyptian royal life, playing itself out anew under my eyes, in its
real original properties and personages.

Gradually, as I looked, I became aware that my hosts were no
less surprised at the appearance of their anachronistic guest than
was the guest himself at the strange living panorama which met his
eyes. In a moment music and dancing ceased; the banquet paused
in its course, and the king and his nobles stood up in undisguised
astonishment to survey the strange intruder.

Some minutes passed before anyone moved forward on either
side. At last a young girl of royal appearance, yet strangely resembling the Gháziyah of Abu Yilla, and recalling in part the laughing
maiden in the foreground of Mr Long's great canvas at the previous
Academy, stepped out before the throng.

"May I ask you," she said in Ancient Egyptian, "who you are,
and why you come hither to disturb us?"

I was never aware before that I spoke or understood the language
of the hieroglyphics: yet I found I had not the slightest difficulty
in comprehending or answering her question. To say the truth,
Ancient Egyptian, though an extremely tough tongue to decipher
in its written form, becomes as easy as love-making when spoken
by a pair of lips like that Pharaonic princess's. It is really very much

the same as English, pronounced in a rapid and somewhat indefinite whisper, and with all the vowels left out.

"I beg ten thousand pardons for my intrusion," I answered apologetically; "but I did not know that this Pyramid was inhabited, or I should not have entered your residence so rudely. As for the points you wish to know, I am an English tourist, and you will find my name upon this card;" saying which I handed her one from the case which I had fortunately put into my pocket, with conciliatory politeness. The princess examined it closely, but evidently did not understand its import.

"In return," I continued, "may I ask you in what august presence I now find myself by accident?"

A court official stood forth from the throng, and answered in a set heraldic tone: "In the presence of the illustrious monarch, Brother of the Sun, Thothmes the Twenty-seventh, king of the Eighteenth Dynasty."

"Salute the Lord of the World," put in another official in the same regulation drone.

I bowed low to His Majesty, and stepped out into the hall. Apparently my obeisance did not come up to Egyptian standards of courtesy, for a suppressed titter broke audibly from the ranks of bronze-skinned waiting-women. But the king graciously smiled at my attempt, and turning to the nearest nobleman observed in a voice of great sweetness and self-contained majesty: "This stranger, Ombos, is certainly a very curious person. His appearance does not at all resemble that of an Ethiopian or other savage, nor does he look like the pale-faced sailors who come to us from the Achaian land beyond the sea. His features, to be sure, are not very different from theirs; but his extraordinary and singularly inartistic dress shows him to belong to some other barbaric race."

I glanced down at my waistcoat, and saw that I was wearing my tourist's check suit, of grey and mud colour, with which a Bond Street tailor had supplied me just before leaving town, as the latest thing out in fancy tweeds. Evidently these Egyptians must have a very curious standard of taste not to admire our pretty and graceful style of male attire.

"If the dust beneath Your Majesty's feet may venture upon a suggestion," put in the officer whom the king had addressed, "I would hint that this young man is probably a stray visitor from the utterly uncivilised lands of the North. The headgear which he carries in his hand obviously betrays an Arctic habitat."

I had instinctively taken off my round felt hat in the first moment of surprise, when I found myself in the midst of this strange throng, and I was standing now in a somewhat embarrassed posture, holding it awkwardly before me like a shield to protect my chest.

"Let the stranger cover himself," said the king.

"Barbarian intruder, cover yourself," cried the herald. I noticed throughout that the king never directly addressed anybody save the higher officials around him.

I put on my hat as desired. "A most uncomfortable and silly form of tiara indeed," said the great Thothmes.

"Very unlike your noble and awe-inspiring mitre, Lion of Egypt," answered Ombos.

"Ask the stranger his name," the king continued.

It was useless to offer another card, so I mentioned it in a clear voice.

"An uncouth and almost unpronounceable designation truly," commented His Majesty to the Grand Chamberlain beside him. "These savages speak strange languages, widely different from the flowing tongue of Memnon and Sesostris."

The chamberlain bowed his assent with three low genuflexions. I began to feel a little abashed at these personal remarks, and I *almost* think (though I shouldn't like it to be mentioned in the Temple) that a blush rose to my cheek.

The beautiful princess, who had been standing near me meanwhile in an attitude of statuesque repose, now appeared anxious to change the current of the conversation. "Dear father," she said with a respectful inclination, "surely the stranger, barbarian though he be, cannot relish such pointed allusions to his person and costume. We must let him feel the grace and delicacy of Egyptian refinement. Then he may perhaps carry back with him some faint echo of its cultured beauty to his northern wilds."

"Nonsense, Hatasou," replied Thothmes XXVII testily. "Savages have no feelings, and they are as incapable of appreciating Egyptian sensibility as the chattering crow is incapable of attaining the dignified reserve of the sacred crocodile."

"Your Majesty is mistaken," I said, recovering my self-possession gradually and realising my position as a free-born Englishman before the court of a foreign despot – though I must allow that I felt rather less confident than usual, owing to the fact that we were not represented in the Pyramid by a British Consul – "I am an English tourist, a visitor from a modern land whose civilisation far surpasses the rude culture of early Egypt; and I am accustomed to respectful treatment from all other nationalities, as becomes a citizen of the First Naval Power in the World."

My answer created a profound impression. "He has spoken to the Brother of the Sun," cried Ombos in evident perturbation. "He must be of the Blood Royal in his own tribe, or he would never have dared to do so!"

"Otherwise," added a person whose dress I recognised as that of a priest, "he must be offered up in expiation to Amon-Ra immediately."

As a rule I am a decently truthful person, but under these alarming circumstances I ventured to tell a slight fib with an air of nonchalant boldness. "I am a younger brother of our reigning king," I said without a moment's hesitation; for there was nobody present to gainsay me, and I tried to salve my conscience by reflecting that at any rate I was only claiming consanguinity with an imaginary personage.

"In that case," said King Thothmes, with more geniality in his tone, "there can be no impropriety in my addressing you personally. Will you take a place at our table next to myself, and we can converse together without interrupting a banquet which must be brief enough in any circumstances? Hatasou, my dear, you may seat yourself next to the barbarian prince."

I felt a visible swelling to the proper dimensions of a Royal Highness as I sat down by the king's right hand. The nobles resumed their places, the bronze-skinned waitresses left off standing like soldiers in a row and staring straight at my humble self, the goblets went round once more, and a comely maid soon brought me meat, bread, fruits, and date wine.

All this time I was naturally burning with curiosity to inquire who my strange hosts might be, and how they had preserved their existence for so many centuries in this undiscovered hall; but I was obliged to wait until I had satisfied His Majesty of my own nationality, the means by which I had entered the pyramid, the general state of affairs throughout the world at the present moment, and fifty thousand other matters of a similar sort. Thothmes utterly refused to believe my reiterated assertion that our existing civilisation was far superior to the Egyptian; "because," said he, "I see from your dress that your nation is utterly devoid of taste or invention"; but he listened with great interest to my account of modern society, the steam-engine, the Permissive Prohibitory Bill, the telegraph, the House of Commons, Home Rule, and the other blessings of our advanced era, as well as to a brief *résumé* of European history from the rise of the Greek culture to the Russo-Turkish war. At last his questions were nearly exhausted, and I got a chance of making a few counter inquiries on my own account.

"And now," I said, turning to the charming Hatasou, whom I thought a more pleasant informant than her august papa, "I should like to know who *you* are."

"What, don't you know?" she cried with unaffected surprise. "Why, we're mummies."

She made this astounding statement with just the same quiet unconsciousness as if she had said, "we're French", or "we're Americans". I glanced round the walls, and observed behind the columns, what I had not noticed till then – a large number of empty mummy-cases, with their lids placed carelessly by their sides.

"But what are you doing here?" I asked in a bewildered way.

"Is it possible," said Hatasou, "that you don't really know the object of embalming? Though your manners show you to be an agreeable and well-bred young man, you must excuse my saying that you are shockingly ignorant. We are made into mummies in order to preserve our immortality. Once in every thousand years we wake up for twenty-four hours, recover our flesh and blood, and banquet once more upon the mummied dishes and other good things laid by for us in the Pyramid. Today is the first day of a millennium, and so we have waked up for the sixth time since we were first embalmed."

"The *sixth* time?" I inquired incredulously. "Then you must have been dead six thousand years."

"Exactly so."

"But the world has not yet existed so long," I cried, in a fervour of orthodox horror.

"Excuse me, barbarian prince. This is the first day of the three hundred and twenty-seven thousandth millennium."

My orthodoxy received a severe shock. However, I had been accustomed to geological calculations, and was somewhat inclined to accept the antiquity of man; so I swallowed the statement without more ado. Besides, if such a charming girl as Hatasou had asked me at that moment to turn Mohammedan, or to worship Osiris, I believe I should incontinently have done so.

"You wake up only for a single day and night, then?" I said.

"Only for a single day and night. After that, we go to sleep for another millennium."

"Unless you are meanwhile burned as fuel on the Cairo Railway," I added mentally. "But how," I continued aloud, "do you get these lights?"

"The Pyramid is built above a spring of inflammable gas. We have a reservoir in one of the side chambers in which it collects during the thousand years. As soon as we awake, we turn it on at once from the tap, and light it with a lucifer match."

"Upon my word," I interposed, "I had no notion you Ancient Egyptians were acquainted with the use of matches."

"Very likely not. 'There are more things in heaven and earth, Cephrenes, than are dreamt of in your philosophy,' as the bard of Philoe puts it."

Further inquiries brought out all the secrets of that strange tomb-house, and kept me fully interested till the close of the banquet. Then the chief priest solemnly rose, offered a small fragment of meat to a deified crocodile, who sat in a meditative manner by the side of his deserted mummy-case, and declared the feast concluded for the night. All rose from their places, wandered away into the long corridors or side-aisles, and formed little groups of talkers under the brilliant gas-lamps.

For my part, I strolled off with Hatasou down the least illuminated of the colonnades, and took my seat beside a marble fountain, where several fish (gods of great sanctity, Hatasou assured me) were disporting themselves in a porphyry basin. How long we sat there I cannot tell, but I know that we talked a good deal about fish, and gods, and Egyptian habits, and Egyptian philosophy, and, above all, Egyptian love-making. The last-named subject we found very interesting, and when once we got fully started upon it, no diversion afterwards occurred to break the even tenor of the conversation. Hatasou was a lovely figure, tall, queenly, with smooth dark arms and neck of polished bronze: her big black eyes full of tenderness, and her long hair bound up into a bright Egyptian headdress, that harmonised to a tone with her complexion and her robe. The more we talked, the more desperately did I fall in love, and the more utterly oblivious did I become of my duty to Editha Fitz-Simkins. The mere ugly daughter of a rich and vulgar brand-new knight, forsooth, to show off her airs before me, when here was a Princess of the Blood Royal of Egypt, obviously sensible to the attentions which I was paying her, and not unwilling to receive them with a coy and modest grace.

Well, I went on saying pretty things to Hatasou, and Hatasou went on deprecating them in a pretty little way, as who should say, "I don't mean what I pretend to mean one bit"; until at last I may confess that we were both evidently as far gone in the disease of the heart called love as it is possible for two young people on first acquaintance to become. Therefore, when Hatasou pulled forth her watch – another piece of mechanism with which antiquaries used never to credit the Egyptian people – and declared that she had only three hours more to live, at least for the next thousand years, I fairly broke down, took out my handkerchief, and began to sob like a child of five years old.

Hatasou was deeply moved. Decorum forbade that she should console me with too much *empressement*; but she ventured to remove the handkerchief gently from my face, and suggested that there was yet one course open by which we might enjoy a little more of one another's society. "Suppose," she said quietly, "you were to become a mummy. You would then wake up, as we do, every thousand years; and after you have tried it once, you will find it just as natural to sleep for a millennium as for eight hours. Of course," she added with a slight blush, "during the next three or four solar cycles there would be plenty of time to conclude any other arrangements you might possibly contemplate, before the occurrence of another glacial epoch."

This mode of regarding time was certainly novel and some-what bewildering to people who ordinarily reckon its lapse by weeks and months; and I had a vague consciousness that my relations with Editha imposed upon me a moral necessity of returning to the outer world, instead of becoming a millennial mummy. Besides, there was the awkward chance of being con-verted into fuel and dissipated into space before the arrival of the next waking day. But I took one look at Hatasou, whose eyes were filling in turn with sympathetic tears, and that look decided me. I flung Editha, life, and duty to the dogs, and resolved at once to become a mummy.

There was no time to be lost. Only three hours remained to us, and the process of embalming, even in the most hasty manner, would take up fully two. We rushed off to the chief priest, who had charge of the particular department in question. He at once acceded to my wishes, and briefly explained the mode in which they usually treated the corpse.

That word suddenly aroused me. "The corpse!" I cried; "but I am alive. You can't embalm me living."

"We can," replied the priest, "under chloroform."

"Chloroform!" I echoed, growing more and more astonished: "I had no idea you Egyptians knew anything about it."

"Ignorant barbarian!" he answered with a curl of the lip; "you imagine yourself much wiser than the teachers of the world. If you were versed in all the wisdom of the Egyptians, you would know that chloroform is one of our simplest and commonest anaesthetics."

I put myself at once under the hands of the priest. He brought out the chloroform, and placed it beneath my nostrils, as I lay on a soft couch under the central court. Hatasou held my hand in hers, and watched my breathing with an anxious eye. I saw the priest leaning over me, with a clouded phial in his hand, and I experienced a vague sensation of smelling myrrh and spikenard. Next, I lost myself for a few moments, and when I again recovered my senses in a temporary break, the priest was holding a small greenstone knife, dabbled with blood, and I felt that a gash had been made across my breast. Then they applied the chloroform once more; I felt Hatasou give my hand a gentle squeeze; the whole panorama faded finally from my view; and I went to sleep for a seemingly endless time.

When I awoke again, my first impression led me to believe that the thousand years were over, and that I had come to life once more to feast with Hatasou and Thothmes in the Pyramid of Abu Yilla. But second thoughts, combined with closer observation of the surroundings, convinced me that I was really lying in a bedroom of Shepheard's Hotel at Cairo. A hospital nurse leant over me, instead of a chief priest; and I noticed no tokens of Editha Fitz-Simkins's presence. But when I endeavoured to make inquiries upon the subject of my whereabouts, I was peremptorily informed that I mustn't speak, as I was only just recovering from a severe fever, and might endanger my life by talking.

Some weeks later I learned the sequel of my night's adventure. The Fitz-Simkinses, missing me from the boat in the morning, at first imagined that I might have gone ashore for an early stroll. But after breakfast time, lunch time, and dinner time had gone past, they began to grow alarmed, and sent to look for me in all directions. One of their scouts, happening to pass the Pyramid, noticed that one of the stones near the north-east angle had been displaced, so as to give access to a dark passage, hitherto unknown. Calling several of his friends, for he was afraid to venture in alone, he passed down the corridor, and through a second gateway into the central hall. There the Fellahin found me, lying on the ground, bleeding profusely from a wound on the breast, and in an advanced stage of malarious fever. They brought me back to the boat, and the Fitz-Simkinses conveyed me at once to Cairo, for medical attendance and proper nursing.

Editha was at first convinced that I had attempted to commit suicide because I could not endure having caused her pain, and she accordingly resolved to tend me with the utmost care through my illness. But she found that my delirious remarks, besides bearing frequent reference to a princess, with whom I appeared to have been on unexpectedly intimate terms, also related very largely to our *casus belli* itself, the dancing girls of Abu Yilla. Even this trial she might have borne, setting down the moral degeneracy which led me to patronise so degrading an exhibition as a first symptom of my approaching malady: but certain unfortunate observations, containing pointed and by no means flattering allusions to her personal appearance – which I contrasted, much to her disadvantage, with that of the unknown princess – these, I say, were things which she could not forgive; and she left Cairo abruptly with her parents for the Riviera, leaving behind a stinging note, in which she denounced my perfidy and empty-heartedness with all the flowers of feminine eloquence. From that day to this I have never seen her.

When I returned to London and proposed to lay this account before the Society of Antiquaries, all my friends dissuaded me on the ground of its apparent incredibility. They declare that I must have gone to the Pyramid already in a state of delirium, discovered the entrance by accident, and sunk exhausted when I reached the inner chamber. In answer, I would point out three facts. In the first place, I undoubtedly found my way into the unknown passage – for which achievement I afterwards received the gold medal of the Société Khédiviale, and of which I retain a clear recollection, differing in no way from my recollection of the subsequent events. In the second place, I had in my pocket, when found, a ring of Hatasou's, which I drew from her finger just before I took the chloroform, and put into my pocket as a keepsake. And in the third place, I had on my breast the wound which I saw the priest inflict with a knife of greenstone, and the scar may be seen on the spot to the present day. The absurd hypothesis of my medical friends, that I was wounded by falling against a sharp edge of rock, I must at once reject as unworthy a moment's consideration.

My own theory is either that the priest had not time to complete the operation, or else that the arrival of the Fitz-Simkins's scouts frightened back the mummies to their cases an hour or so too soon. At any rate, there they all were, ranged around the walls undisturbed, the moment the Fellahin entered.

Unfortunately, the truth of my account cannot be tested for another thousand years. But as a copy of this *Belgravia Annual* will be preserved for the benefit of posterity in the British Museum, I hereby solemnly call upon Collective Humanity to try the veracity of this history by sending a deputation of archaeologists to the Pyramid of Abu Yilla, on the last day of December, Two thousand eight hundred and seventy-seven. If they do not then find Thothmes and Hatasou feasting in the central hall exactly as I have described, I shall willingly admit that the story of my New Year's Eve among the mummies is a vain hallucination, unworthy of credence at the hands of the scientific world.

'PROFESSOR PETRUS' (1884)

Justin Huntly McCarthy

Justin Huntly McCarthy (1859–1936) was an Irish nationalist politician who served as an MP between 1884 and 1892. He wrote on political matters relating to Ireland, including books such as *England Under Gladstone, 1880–1884* (1884) and *The Case for Home Rule* (1887). Like his father, also a nationalist MP (and also named Justin), he wrote popular novels, biographies, and histories. He also penned plays and short stories, many of which centre on authority figures from the past and the present, and appear to reflect his political interests.

'Professor Petrus' was published in *Belgravia* in October 1884. The tale is told by one Amber Pasha to his friend, the MP Harry Jermyn. It recounts an incident from many years previously when Pasha had encountered Professor Petrus, an eminent Egyptologist, and secretly followed Petrus back to his lodgings only to find a beautiful woman (apparently an Egyptian queen) in a room decorated with Egyptian artefacts. Images of Egypt as beguiling and seductive formed a strand in tales about ancient Egypt, in which exotic female mummies take on a semi-erotic function. It is interesting to note that this story also includes, at the end, a curse narrative – although an unusually displaced one.

A MBER PASHA HAD COME TO LONDON ON ONE OF HIS BRIEF
visits. They were always at long intervals; they were always
uncertain; they always gave pleasure to everyone who knew him,
and indeed to everyone in London who had ever heard of him.
The Pasha's strange career, his eccentric life, his long residence in
the East, and the fabulous stories that were told of his wealth and
accomplishments, made him an object of intense curiosity to the
capital, and to the Society Journals. The newspaper which was able
to be the first to chronicle the fact that Amber Pasha had made a
momentary appearance at his house in Park Lane was very proud
of its good fortune, and generally followed it up with a variety of
ingenious and inaccurate paragraphs about Amber Pasha's actions,
and with endless variations on the most marvellous versions of
his history.

It was a pleasant morning in early summer. Amber Pasha had
a friend to breakfast, a solitary friend, Harry Jermyn, Member
of Parliament, philosophical radical, and rising lawyer. Breakfast
was over, and they had come out of the Roman-like room whose
frescoed walls would have pleased the taste of Petronius without
offending the gravity of Seneca, and were sitting lazily on pleasant long chairs in the wide balcony where the great rosso antico
Caryatides eternally lifted their rounded arms to heaven. For a
time the two friends sat silently, looking down lazily through the
blue clouds of cigarette smoke at the endless pageant of London
life rolling by, and enjoying the tranquil beauty of a June midday.
The two men whom chance had brought together on that balcony

overlooking Park Lane were of curiously different types. Amber
Pasha was, in the completest sense, a citizen of the world. Before
he had settled in the East and devoted himself to the service of the
Sultan, he had passed an adventurous youth. He seemed to have
been everywhere and seen everything, to be as much at home in
an Akkhal Tekke *aoul* as in the gardens of Buen Retiro at Madrid,
or at Therapia upon the Bosphorus. Amber Pasha was an attractive character to all the world, but perhaps to no one was he more
intensely attractive than to Harry Jermyn. Jermyn was making
his way steadily, and looked forward to a seat on the ministerial
benches, should his party come into power at the next general elec-
tion. He was always going to go in for a great travel, one of these
days, but in the meantime there were so many blue-books to read,
and there were the speeches to be made to his constituents, and
there was his steadily increasing practice at the bar, and his determination to make a fortune. In long vacation and when the House
was happily up, he generally went for a long tramp in the Swiss
Alps, and sometimes even pushed into Italy, a solitary, nineteenth-
century Hannibal. He always walked as much as he could, first
because he knew it was the best thing to keep him in form for the
year's work, and next because it was the cheapest mode of travel
he knew of, and cheapness was an object with a man meaning to
make his fortune as soon as he could. So in that knowledge of the
world which A'Kempis would condemn, and which consists in
seeing a great many places, Jermyn was considerably behind the
average Cook's tourist.

The two oddly chosen companions had sat silent for some little
while. Amber Pasha had all the true Oriental capacity for that rarest
and most precious of social gifts, a companionable silence. You
might sit with him for hours if you liked without exchanging half a

dozen sentences, and yet without ever feeling that you were wasting your time, or that such grave sweet silence could possibly be dull. Amber Pasha used always to say that he was chiefly attracted to Oriental life by its capacity for keeping quiet in a too noisy world. The still serenity of a people who could sit quietly for hours and find a patient delight in interminable romance had won him at an age when life's fever was burning its highest. He used himself to say that one of the things which first lured him to an Oriental existence was an incident he witnessed during his earliest visit to Cairo. He was riding out to the Pyramids one morning. At the corner of a street some elderly Arabs were seated, gravely, silently smoking. A donkey laden with sand was trotting by, when it suddenly slipped and spilt its burden in great yellow heaps over and about the feet of the seated Arabs. They said nothing, did nothing, did not even remove the amber mouthpieces from their lips, and the Englishman rode on. He came back in the evening, and at the same spot the same Arabs still sat and smoked, and the yellow sand was still heaped about their feet. They had never moved through all those hours, had never taken the trouble to rise and shake the sand away. "There," said Amber Pasha – he was not a Pasha then, however – "there are true philosophers."

Suddenly Jermyn drew his cigarette from his lips, sent a couple of grey clouds into the air, allowed a sigh to escape after them, and said, "I often wish that I had your life, Pasha. The only romance left to us of today is the romance of travel, and though you wouldn't think it, now, I am rather of a romantic mind."

Amber Pasha smiled, for he knew of Jermyn's passion for Violet Hampden.

"There isn't much that's romantic in an ordinary London life," added Jermyn with another sigh, which he promptly silenced by resuming his cigarette. The Pasha smoked on for a few minutes before he answered.

"You're wrong, Harry, quite wrong. You say I've been every-where and done everything. Well, what would you say if I were to tell you that the most romantic, the oddest, the strangest thing that ever happened to me in my life, happened to me here in this very London you despise so much?"

Jermyn looked up at him. "How was that?" he said.

"It's a long story," said the Pasha; "some other time I'll tell you all about it."

"No, no; let me have it now," urged Jermyn, looking at his friend in eager surprise. "You may be off to Mecca or Lord knows where tomorrow, and who can say when we shall meet again?"

Amber Pasha was silent for a few minutes. "I have never told it to anyone," he said, "but with you it's different. Yet it is a painful memory."

He was silent again, and stared out into the street with a mel-ancholy wistful look on his face, unlike its wonted sweet gravity. Jermyn said nothing, but smoked and looked at him.

"It was years ago," Amber Pasha suddenly began again, "many years ago. I had just come back from my first visit to the East, when I was little more than a boy."

Jermyn nodded. "Go on," he said.

"I had not been many days in town, I had been away for a long time, and was glad to be back again. I had been ill abroad just before I came home, and was still a weakly convalescent; so I used to take a keen pleasure in simply walking about the streets and congratulating myself on being able to do so and to enjoy everything I saw; I rather steered clear of engagements for a bit, and people weren't very much in town, so I enjoyed myself in quite a primitive and pastoral fashion, lounging about all day, dining modestly at the club, and going to bed early; it was really very pleasant. Do you know, Harry, there are few pleasanter things than to be alone for a while in a place like London, and have nothing to do but lounge about and see what happens; at least I thought so then." He paused for a few seconds, and began again, in a somewhat disconnected manner.

"The first time I ever met Professor Petrus was one day when I was going into the British Museum. He was coming out as I was entering, and he held back the swinging glass door for me to pass through. I bowed my thanks for his courtesy, and as I did so I was struck with his strange face. He was not an old man, perhaps fifty, but he was curiously bent, almost to deformity, and the head which was thrust forward from between his shoulders was one of the strangest that it has ever been my fortune to look upon. Grey-black hair formed itself in short curls all over his head, and a dark beard and moustache covered the lower part of his face. There was something in his eyes that strangely fascinated me in the brief glance I had at them. They seemed to fix you through and through with their gaze, and then dropped as if they had done with you, and knew all about you, and need be troubled with you no more. Such a flashing glance he gave me, and then turned, and the door swung behind him, and we parted. But the memory of his face haunted me for some time after with a curious sense of interest. I was very glad, therefore, when it gazed upon me again one evening coming through the open doorway of the drawing-room of a friend at an evening party. The keen, sharp, deeply lined face turned on me for a moment as he stood in the doorway, before making his way to his hostess, and I felt sure that he recognised me again, though he made no sign, and in another moment he had passed me and had disappeared in the crowd. I am quick to notice peculiarities, and I observed that his evening dress was much more careful than his morning habit had been on the day I met him. I noticed also that in his shirt front three Egyptian scarabs served him for studs. The person, whoever it was, with whom I had been talking, left me, and I immediately turned to my hostess. 'Can you tell me,' I said, 'who that strange man is who spoke to you a few minutes ago, a dark man?'

"My hostess smiled and said, 'There are a good many strange people here to-night. You know I like strange people.'

"'To be more particular, the man I mean,' I said, 'is short and much stooped. He has a keen worn face, and if you want any more evidence, he wears Egyptian scarabs in his shirt front.'

"'Oh, you mean Professor Petrus,' my hostess answered.

"'Who is Professor Petrus?' I inquired.

"'Professor Petrus,' she replied, 'is the greatest Egyptologist living. I believe he knows more about the Pharaohs than any other person in the world, which I suppose is a thing to be very proud of; but he is a curious man, and a very interesting man.'

"'I should like to know him very much,' I interposed.

"'You shall, certainly,' said my hostess; 'see; there he is. He is talking just now to a young lady. You must not disturb him.'

"Professor Petrus was indeed talking in a very animated manner to a young girl who was sitting in a corner of the room near the window. There were flowers behind them, and the group was certainly strange. The girl was very lovely and very young.

"I dare say you will know her name. She was an elder sister of that pretty Miss Van Duyten, the American beauty, who disturbed London society so much some three years ago. She seemed to be listening with an air of half-dislike to what he was saying; he was speaking very rapidly, bending over her with his face quite close to hers, his whole manner informed by an almost grotesque eagerness. As my hostess spoke, some young man or other, who had met the American girl before, came out of the crowd and advanced to speak to her. She turned to him with a look of unmistakable pleasure, not indeed, as I read it, at the arrival of that particular young man, but of anybody to take her away from the observations of Professor Petrus, who himself drew back with an air of annoyance on his dark odd face.

"'You see,' I said, 'the American girl does not mind interruption, you might introduce me now.'

"My hostess took me across to where Professor Petrus was standing. He was apparently lost in reflections, for he did not seem to notice our approach, until my hostess touched him on the shoulder with her fan.

"'Professor, may I introduce to you my friend, Mr Amber?'

"Professor Petrus turned round sharply, and bowed, without, however, holding out his hand. His eyes flashed through me as before. Straight bright eyes they were, and no look of recognition came into them.

"I muttered a few words about 'pleasure at the honour', and 'anxiety to meet so distinguished a scholar'; to which the Professor listened with an unmoved countenance.

"'Do you know anything about Egyptian studies?' he asked sharply, when my hostess had moved away.

"I said I was sorry to say I knew very little about them.

"'Then why are you pleased to see me? That is my topic. I am an Egyptologist. I am nothing else. Those who speak to me do so because they wish to learn something from me which they can learn from no one else.'

"This was rather an annoying reception, and yet I felt almost inclined to laugh. There was something odd in the man's manner. I answered quietly that though I was not versed in Egyptology, I was interested in it, as in most things, and felt interested in a man whose fame for such knowledge was so great. 'Besides,' I added, 'few men really are so engrossed in any one topic that they may not find some themes in common with others of their kind.'

"Professor Petrus answered, 'You are young; I am old. You have your life before you; mine lies behind me. You have health and strength; I' – he made a curious shrugging motion of his arms and hands – 'I am what you see me.'

"I hastened to observe that a man of Professor Petrus's age need hardly speak of his life as lying behind him; but he shook his head in a deprecatory manner as if my remarks only annoyed him; so I ventured to suggest that as I had just been in Egypt, I was naturally drawn to anyone who knew much about the country.

"'You have been in Egypt?' said Professor Petrus. 'It is a wonderful country.'

"I assented.

"'We don't understand it, perhaps,' he said, 'yet, but we can try to, and with patience we may come to a fuller understanding of the great races to whom we owe so much.'

"Our talk here fell upon Egypt. He asked me many questions, as I had been there some months later than he. We found we knew one or two persons in common, and as he talked very brilliantly, and I can say that I listened with almost equal brilliancy, our conversation was singularly attractive, at least to me, and I was sorry when a fresh introduction put an end to it.

"You know that I have a peculiar method of enjoying myself in cities that are new or strange to me, and at this time London was new and strange to me; for I had been away from it for some years, and London always seems fresh to the returned traveller. In such case I love wandering by myself through the streets. Not indeed hurrying as chance directs me, for I am fond of following some one of the passers-by – the first person I happen to come across, it matters not whom, a working-man perhaps, or even a pretty woman – just to see where my brief connection with some portion of their lives may lead me; and very often it has led me into things of interest enough, but never to such strange circumstances as this trick of mine brought about one night shortly after the evening I have been speaking to you of. It was a fine evening of middle spring when the struggling sunlight tried to cheat the world into a belief that the air was warm, and when the lengthening evenings gave promise of the return of that golden age which always comes with the summer. I had nothing to do. I had been busy all day, and I strolled out after dinner and let chance take me where it would. I followed my usual plan of letting some unknown individual guide me my course, with but little result at first, for the first man I chanced to follow soon called a cab and was whirled away from me, and another speedily reached his dwelling and passed in, and a third walked too slowly, and I soon passed him and forgot him. At last I saw a working-man ahead of me with a basket of tools upon his shoulder, and I chose him to be for the moment my unconscious guide in my saunter. The evening was darkening down; lamps were being lit; the streets were dim and crowded, and I had to keep my attention carefully fixed on my self-chosen herald if I did not mean to miss him. It is almost comic the way in which the lives of others may influence without thought or intention on their part. That worthy British workman, tramping home to his late tea, never saw me, never heard of me, has not the faintest idea that he was ever an object of curiosity to any one, or that he was the cause, perhaps the ordained cause, of terrible events in the lives of three human beings with whom he had nothing whatever in common, and who, but for him – Kismet, I suppose.

"He led me into a curious part of the town, into the region of streets at the other side of Oxford Street. His destination would seem to have been somewhere in the Portland Road direction, but I never knew for certain where he was going, for as I was pursuing his steps across a way where two streets met a figure came across him from a by-street who turned my attention very speedily from my working-man.

"The figure that shot past me, and of whom I got a glimpse for a moment in the light of a lamp, was certainly that of Professor Petrus. I felt some desire to renew our talk of a few evenings before; so letting my working-man go where he would, I turned to my right and followed the quickly walking Professor. I had not gone many steps before my intention to stop and speak with him suddenly altered. I could not help thinking it vaguely curious that he should be wandering about in this odd part of London; though why I should have thought it curious I scarcely knew, and I felt somehow impelled by an unreasonable desire to find out where he was going to, and to know something more about the mysterious Professor than anyone else apparently knew. You will say, perhaps, that my curiosity was scarcely commendable, and I admit it only too willingly; but I was younger then, and thought of adventure in everything when I thought at all, and I did not reflect upon the unworthiness of seeking out any mystery in a man's life which he desired to keep to himself. I wish I had. I crossed the street and followed at a distance the bowed form which was making its way so rapidly along the busy pavement. The neighbourhood was poor, there were a great many small shops which appeared to be doing a good deal of business – it was a Saturday night – and there were stalls and wheelbarrows in the roadway lit by flaring oil lamps. People were buying and selling, bargaining and shouting; all was noise and confusion and to a stranger bewilderment. A Cairo bazaar, when a party of wealthy Franks make their appearance in its ways, could not be louder or more bustling. But Professor Petrus threaded his way through the throng with an ease and rapidity which I envied and found it hard to imitate. He glided along so quickly and so dexterously that no one seemed to notice his odd, misshapen presence. He suddenly passed out of the clamour and glare and stir into a quieter and darker street, turned sharply down another, then down a third, I still following. A third turning took him from my sight for a moment. When I got to the corner the Professor had disappeared. The turning led into a dingy crescent, composed of houses of humble appearance, girdling a space of faded grass and dismal trees. As I stood there the door of one of the dwellings at the end closed with a loud noise. For some minutes I stood wondering what I should do next, wondering too what Professor Petrus was doing there, and thinking a little that it was no business of mine to know. Then I walked quietly towards the house whose door I had heard shut. It was near one of the few lamp-posts which faintly lit the dreary place, and I could see it sufficiently distinctly, as I see it now in my memory though I have not been near the place for some years, and hope earnestly never to be near it again. It was a commonplace house in a commonplace crescent of houses. There was nothing whatever remarkable or curious in any way about it, so I decided to myself, except perhaps the fact that no gleam of light shone from any of its windows upon the street beneath, though in all the other houses faint chinks of light showed through curtains and shutters, and from garret windows, to tell the world outside that human beings dwelt there. There was really something depressing, almost uncanny, in the effect of this single lightless house that seemed as if it had gone to sleep, or indeed had been dead and buried in the midst of its living neighbours. It might have been a tomb, so still and quiet was it, so soundless and lightless in a place itself alive, a place so near to streets full of noise and brightness. I stared at it for some minutes, and then reflected that possibly Professor Petrus might be looking out of the window, and wondering what I was doing or waiting for. I turned and walked swiftly away. But I could not walk off the odd fancies that clung to me, and the curious desire I felt to know something more about Professor Petrus and his business in the gloomy silent house. There was, of course, no strong reason why Professor Petrus should not live in this crescent if he felt inclined to do so; yet it seemed a strange place for him, a scholar, and, if report told truly, a rich man, to choose for a habitation, and I had a vague impression of hearing that he lived somewhere else. Altogether the thing had something mysterious about it which set my fancy going, and made me eager to know more of the matter. That evening a friend of mine had a reception, and I felt sure that I should meet there somebody to tell me something about Professor Petrus.

"It was still early, only a little past nine. I drove home, dressed, and got to the party. Among the guests I found my hostess of the preceding week – my introducer to the Professor, who was now occupying all my thoughts. I made for her, and began a casual conversation, which I determined should lead up to the Professor, when she anticipated my intention by suddenly inquiring, 'How did you like Professor Petrus?' Somewhat surprised at a question which jumped so closely with my own thoughts, I replied that he interested me greatly, which indeed was true, if a somewhat vapid way of putting the truth. She told me much about him. He was a great scholar and unwearying student, whose word was law on the peculiar branch of knowledge he had taken for himself; he lived the lonely life of a hard-working man; he was occasionally, though not often, to be met at certain houses, and he sometimes made his appearance at the dinner-table of Lord Lancelot, who liked to gather people of name about him, and who found a great attraction in the bitter sayings and strange cynical ideas of Professor Petrus. I asked her casually where Professor Petrus lived, as I should like to call upon him; and she told me that he lodged in Great Russell Street, just opposite the British Museum.

"I was right then. He did not live in the mysterious crescent to which I had tracked him on the preceding night, and yet he certainly was not paying a visit, for there had been no knock at the door or I should have heard it. He had passed in silently and surely, as men pass into dwellings which they have a right to enter.

"The next day found me outside the mysterious dwelling. It looked still more mysterious by day than it had seemed at night, for I saw now the explanation of its absence of light on the preceding evening. Every window in the house was close-shuttered, from the windows below the area to the garrets, around which some sparrows were circulating in evident consciousness of undisturbed capacity for nest-building. It was a dingy, dirty house enough, only conspicuous in any way from the rest of its neighbours by being perhaps a shade more dusty and more dingy than they were. The paint peeled from its doors in ragged uneven patches. The railings were broken and rusty. The bell-pull hung torn and soundless from its socket. The knocker had apparently been wrenched away long ago. The house was evidently old Georgian; over the straggling ragged steps that led to the doorway an arch of iron ended in an empty square that had once supported a lamp, and below it stuck out the metal extinguishers into whose flower-like mouths the linkmen of the last century were wont to thrust their torches. It may have been a bright and splendid building enough in the days when George III was king. Fair ladies and stately gentlemen might have waited for their chairs in the crescent, and the courtly clink of swords been heard in its hallway. I thought to myself that the ghosts of eighteenth-century exquisites and wits and beauties must surely haunt that deserted shuttered dwelling, and make ghostly mirth in the abandoned rooms. But were the rooms abandoned? After all I could not tell. Behind those close-lidded eyes of windows what might not be hidden? For I felt sure, with that strange certainty which sometimes comes upon us at odd moments of our lives, – I felt certain that there was something hidden, and that Professor Petrus had a secret, and that the secret was here almost within my grasp, temptingly close yet defiantly distant in this dark and seemingly desolate dwelling-place. I had no right whatever to learn this secret, no warrant to pursue it further, but without right or warrant I pursued it to the end.

"On both the houses on each side of *the* house there were cards in the window announcing 'rooms to let'. I entered the left-hand one, and asked to be shown the rooms. There were two on the third floor, both bedrooms, poor mean-looking things enough, not too clean, and assuredly not too comfortable, and the rent they asked me was certainly not extravagant. I took both the rooms, settled all questions of reference by an immediate payment of some weeks in advance, and found myself the master of apartments next door to the mystery I was seeking after. I really felt quite excited as I surveyed my new abode, and looked at the latch-key which my landlady had put into my hand in token of part-proprietorship of her house. I felt that something strange was about to happen, and with the feeling there came that strange *exalté* mood which takes possession of us at such times, and I was indifferent to everything else but to the task I had undertaken.

"The window of my back room overlooked the garden of the house whose secret I was seeking to discover. All the gardens in the crescent were of the kind familiar in certain parts of London; long narrow strips of ground utterly abandoned in most cases to the winds and rain, or made to serve as open-air lumber rooms for the reception of rejected furniture, broken dishes, venerable meat cans, and rubbish of all sorts. Here and there, however, some citizen, more mindful of the charms of a garden, had devoted a little time and care to the improvement of his patch of earth, and had sown grass and laid down gravel, and portioned off with tiles the arid bed of pebbly earth in which dejected flowers did their best to flourish. A few houses off I saw that some occupant of more enterprising spirit than his fellows had set up a target whose painted face seemed to stare reproachfully at its uncongenial surroundings. But I never saw any one come forth equipped with bow and arrows to test his skill in the pastime sacred to the memory of Robin Hood and Roger Ascham. Of all the deserted gardens that of the mysterious house was the most deserted. There hung over it a gloom of hopeless decay which was profoundly melancholy to contemplate. All seemed barren and desolate. The trees which existed in some of the other gardens, and which lent a graciousness to the place with the fresh greenness of their spring apparel, had no fellows in this dismal spot; only a few stray tufts of grass endeavoured to put in their testimony to the fruitfulness of mother earth.

"I could not of course see the windows of the house that for the time occupied my attention, but I found an excuse for wandering into the garden of my lodging and surveying the building. All was as closely shut behind as before; no semblance of life was about the place; nothing to indicate that aught human lingered behind the sightless windows. The mystery was more strange than ever. What could Professor Petrus want in so desolate a dwelling? I became more determined than ever that I would pluck out the heart of the mystery which lurked behind the dead screen of the orbless dwelling. There come moments in the lives of most of us when we act upon a kind of instinct which seems as if it were apart from ourselves, and were practically disassociated from our own thoughts. While I was engaged upon this task I lay under the spell of a spirit of curiosity which in my wiser hours I should have regarded with contempt, and which even at the time I was able to look upon at moments with something like wonder. But I was possessed by an evil spirit of inquiry, and I was resolved to go on with the enterprise which was exercising over me its fatal fascination. It does seem sometimes as if our lives were planned out for us, and that it would hardly have been in our power to make them other than they were destined to be. I don't offer this suggestion as excuse for my conduct, which I have never since forgotten to regret.

"Though I watched the desolate garden from my back window for a whole day, no sign of life became evident in its dreary space, whose wretched earth seemed as if it had been untrodden by man for whole generations. Yet there were moments when it seemed clear to me that the house was not uninhabited, as if some human presence lurked behind the hateful mask. At one time I fancied I heard something like singing, but of this I was not sure. When evening fell I wandered out, weary of watching, to get some food and to reflect on my next course. I sat in the club smoking for some hours, trying to decide upon a plan of action, and half inclined to give up the whole business and forget the crescent and its barricaded house. But the very circles of smoke that floated about me seemed to take shape and form themselves into a gloomy building, whose shuttered windows mocked me defiantly for my inability to learn what lay hid behind them. I wandered out into the night, and of course my feet led me to my new home. I entered, went upstairs, and stationed myself at the front window staring into the street. As the room was perfectly dark behind me, I knew that I could not be observed, and I waited patiently wondering if the Professor would again make his appearance. The hour was late, and I waited so long that I began to think he must either have come already, or did not intend to appear that night, when I heard a quick tread in the deserted crescent, and in a moment I became aware that Professor Petrus was standing on the door-step of the strange house. I heard the faint scratch of his key in the lock, then the door opened and closed quietly, and the street was again given over to silence. I lingered for some few minutes at my post, my heart beating quickly with surprise and excitement; then I passed into the back room, and softly opening my window, leaned far out into the night, hoping to catch some sound in the strange place. The night was quiet as a nun, and the sky was of that deep bright blue which had always seemed to me so Eastern and therefore so lovely, long before I had ever slept beneath an Oriental heaven. There was a faint wind which lightly stirred the trees in my garden and their leafy companions all down the crescent. From the backs of neighbouring houses occasional sounds were borne, and here and there a lighted window told of a lonely student perhaps preparing to pass a white night over his books, or some belated servant working off the arrears of her day's labours. But from the place which alone interested me upon that fair spring night there came no sound. Had it been a tomb into which Professor Petrus had entered to pay his silent devotion to the silent dead, it could not have seemed more still. I waited for long, dead to the beauty of the hour, intent only on my senseless, shameless curiosity. At length, wearied out, I went into the little front room and flung myself upon its cheerless horsehair sofa. I did not go to bed, for I wished, if I could, to outwatch the night that might still hold some clue to offer me, and I did not light my lamp lest by chance it might suggest to any one inside the house who might yet go out, that there were late watchers next door. Yet, tired of thinking and watching, I had almost fallen asleep, when the faint sound as of a softly opened door aroused me to instant and painful wakefulness. I sprang to my window. A figure was passing down the street in the grey light of advancing dawn. I knew it at once to be that of Professor Petrus.

"I stood at the window long after the Professor's form had passed from sight, and the last sound of his footfall had died away from the quiet crescent. The air seemed thick with mystery, and for a moment I felt as if I should abandon my quest and forget, if I could, that I had ever penetrated so far into the hidden life of another man. With this feeling strong upon me, and all feelings are strong in the pale dawn, I got to bed, and fell into a heavy sleep. It was late when I awoke, and the bright spring morning had already long warmed with its sunlight the dingy crescent and the dilapidated gardens. At first I scarcely knew where I was. Then I recalled the new purpose I had set myself, and the strange events of the preceding night. I flung open the window, and stared out into the garden. One of the servants of my lodging house was sweeping the flagged portion by the back steps beneath me, and in a distant garden I could hear the voices of children at play, and catch glimpses of their forms as they chased each other over the patch of earth that was to them a boundless territory. But in the mysterious house all was silent. I felt that, come what might, I should somehow or other get inside that house. I did not stop to reflect that my impertinent curiosity had no justification whatever, I only felt the anxiety of a baffled purpose, and a wish to gratify a keenly roused curiosity. How was this to be accomplished? Clearly not in the daytime. No less clearly not in the night. If Professor Petrus's visits were uninterrupted, my only time then would be after Professor Petrus had gone away. I spent all that day very aimlessly. I tried to work and could hardly manage it. I wrote letters and found them drifting off into meaningless sentences. I went for a walk, but could not walk away from my curiosity. The shadow of Professor Petrus was upon me everywhere I went. How was I to kill the hours till night? I went to a play, and sat it through with difficulty. At last it came to an end, and I was free to return to my lodging. As I was walking along one of the wider streets, crowded at that hour of the night with people coming from music halls and theatres, I fancied that I saw on the other side the form of Professor Petrus moving quickly along. He was earlier than last night, and I must needs be quick if I wished to reach the crescent before him. I struck hurriedly into a by-street, and ran as quickly as I could. I got to my door breathless, opened it, and was at my window only a few minutes before the step of the Professor came round the corner. A second more and the door was opened and swallowed him up and closed again.

"How slowly the hours went by. At length, after cycles seemed to have passed away, I heard the opening of the door, and as before I saw Professor Petrus pass out. When he was out of sight and hearing, I proceeded to put into execution the plan I had formed in those hours of expectancy. I stole softly downstairs, opened the back door that led into the garden, and closed it softly behind me. All was still, and darkness yet ruled the sky, for it was but just two o'clock. I heard it strike as I stood there in the little garden, with the night wind blowing upon my hot face. The wall between the gardens was low and easy to scale. A moment and I found myself in the neighbouring garden face to face with the silent dwelling. I fancied that on the second floor a gleam of light shone through the shutters. Cautiously I advanced towards the door that opened into the garden and tried its latch. To my surprise it yielded and opened with a shrill sound of protest from its rusty hinges which set every nerve in my body tingling, and made me strain my sense of hearing to its quickest, to learn if it was answered by any other sounds than the loud and painful beating of my heart. All was quiet and profoundly dark. I advanced a step inside noiselessly, and felt as if I were stepping into a tomb, so drew back with a quick fear that was very real for its second. It was obvious that I could not go on in the dark. I had a little lantern with me, in my room that is, and to get it I should have to cross the wall again and repeat my journey. However, there was no help for it. I climbed the wall and made my way to my room, found the lantern, candle, and matches, stole downstairs again and out into the air. With the lantern held by its ring in my mouth, I crossed the wall and once more pushed the door which I had left wide open. As noiselessly as I could I lit my light and looked about me. I could hardly restrain a cry of surprise as I did so, for the narrow passage was coloured a deep dull red, and was covered with strange designs of Egyptian kings and deities. Below and around them ran the mystic inscriptions which had held from wondering centuries the secrets of the land of Nile. Doors at my right and in front of me led into rooms, kitchens apparently,

and obviously made use of, adorned also with the same strange
ornamentation. To the left a stone stairway, dark and narrow, and
similarly painted, led up to a hall lit by a swinging lamp. The walls
were painted with all the magnificence of an Egyptian temple, the
very door, so dingy outside, being adorned with the awful effigy
of Amun-Ra himself, while all around the fantastic divinities of the
Egyptian Pantheon were displayed in all the splendour and solemnity that the craftsmen of the desert land imparted to their grim
gods. Like a man in a hasheesh dream I ascended stairs covered with
Eastern carpets that completely deadened the sound of my cautious footsteps. All along the walls the weird mythology of Egypt
displayed itself in its stately repose and solemn splendour. I came
to a landing lit by a lamp that burned with a warm red flame. To
the left and in front were rooms separated from the hall by heavy
curtains of woven stuff such as might have hung in the halls of the
Pharaohs. With trembling hands I drew back one and looked in. All
was dark, but a light gleamed through curtains that shut off a room
beyond. I fancied I heard a faint sound from within, and with hands
trembling with excitement I drew back one of the heavy folds and
gazed in. The room was like the interior of an Egyptian temple.
On a pile of cushions in a corner of the room lay a woman. Even
now as I speak of her the memory of her beauty takes hold of me
and seems to burn into my very soul. I saw at once that she was an
Egyptian, one of that rare type, beautiful alike in form and face,
which is still to be met with in some of the Nilotic villages. She
must have been very young, for the Egyptian women fade early,
and this woman seemed to me, as she lay there lazily in the warm
light, to be in the very spring of youth and grace. But her dress was
such as no fellah woman, no dancing girl of Esneh, ever wore. She
was clad in the garments of an Egyptian queen, of those Egyptian

queens who still live in the tomb-paintings of the Theban Valley, and the papyrus of the scribes. As she lay there with half-closed eyes, her dark beauty enhanced by the strange richness of her attire, she seemed the very ideal of what most people imagine Cleopatra to have been like, of what Cleopatra might have been like, if she had been Egyptian and not Greek, dark of hair and skin, instead of fair as she probably was.

"I stood for some seconds gazing at her, and vaguely wondering if what I saw was truth or vision. Then I suppose I stirred, for she suddenly sprang up with a low, guttural cry, and stood erect looking at me. There was no sign of fear, or even of wonder in her eyes as she looked at me, quite still and silent for some brief interval of time. Then she asked rapidly in Arabic, 'Who are you? Are you a friend of my lord?' Even then I knew Arabic, not as I know it now, but well enough to make myself understood by fellaheen and bedaween. I hardly know what I answered, some incoherent phrases bidding her not to be alarmed; I was a friend of her lord's, and all was well. You may smile if you please, but from the moment I saw her I was completely conquered by her exquisite loveliness. I had been in love many times before, and had often pleased myself and others with a pretence of being in love, but never before had my whole being been drowned in such a flood of passion. With me then to love was to tell it, and I told her. One may make love in Arabic very delightfully, and I was terribly in earnest. You have read Théophile Gautier's wonderful *Nuit de Cléopatre*? The magic of that story was real for me once; then. You must remember that I was a young man in those days, and not the elderly individual you are familiar with. Love, too, has a stronger and quicker sway with Eastern women than with our colder Occidentals. Those beauties of the *Alf Lailah* who love so passionately at a single glance are still possible in the cities where I live my life. But Dinarizade in London – that was the marvel.

"I never knew how I got back to my own home. I must have got back to my lodgings and left them and walked to my hotel. I remember nothing. I only remember waking up one morning to find that I had been delirious for some days, that the fever which had threatened me had suddenly passed away. I suppose that the strange excitement under which I had been living had acted on a frame weakened by illness and brought on a brief fever. All that was certain was that I had been ill and was well again. Curiously, I was quite uncertain whether the Egyptian dwelling and the beautiful woman prisoned within it like Rhodope in the pyramid was actual reality or the shifting fancy of a fever-dream. Naturally, my first use of my recovered health was to walk to the crescent. There indeed was the shuttered house. Next door was the dwelling where I had taken rooms. When I rang the bell, the people of the house were not at all surprised to see me, and suffered me to go to my rooms unquestioned. So much then was true.

"As soon as it was dusk I glided into the garden, and scaled the wall again. Once again the door gave way before the pressure of my hand. Once again I found myself in the mysterious dwelling. Its mystery was not the creation of a feverous dream. On the walls the strange Egyptian gods still throned in solemn majesty; everywhere ran the bewildering hieroglyphics which held no secrets from the eyes of Professor Petrus. I crept softly up the stairs to the first floor. As I was about to pass into the hall I heard a noise at the front door. I crouched back in the shadow as I saw the door open; the effigy of Amun-Ra swung slowly inwards, and Professor Petrus himself appeared on the threshold. Noiselessly he closed the door again, and slowly ascended the stairs leading to the upper rooms. I felt as if I should choke with excitement, I may say with fear, for the place and the man were fearful enough, and strange noises seemed to beat against my ears. But I would not go back. As noiselessly as Professor Petrus himself, I crept up the thickly carpeted stairs. Cautiously I lifted the curtain of the first room, and looked in. All was silent as before, intensely dark, but a gleam of light came through the curtain that shut off the room beyond. Petrus must be in the farther room – with her. On tiptoe I crossed the room and stood for a moment breathless in front of the heavy curtain that hung down before it and separated it from its gloomy antechamber.

"There was no sound within, yet I felt sure that he was there. What could it mean? I did not dare to part the curtain, but drawing out my knife I made a quick cut in it sufficiently long to enable me to see with no danger of being seen. Oh, the agony of that moment is upon me now, as I think of it. In the centre of the room was a long low black table, and on it lay a human body swathed and enveloped in the mysterious folds that wrap the limbs of Egyptian mummies. The hands were folded on the breast in an attitude of prayer, and the head which was uncovered gazed up to heaven with the lifeless eyes of an embalmed corpse. It was she. On the swathes of linen endless processions of Egyptian figures wound themselves in fantastic convolutions. The awful effigy of the Sun was upon her breast, and the genii of Amenti bore the emblem of her soul before the eternal judge. In a corner of the room a coloured mummy case with a gilded face grinning in ghastly likeness of the dead woman, awaited its terrible freight. At the foot of the body Professor Petrus stood with folded arms. He was murmuring, almost chanting, to himself words in Arabic to which I listened eagerly; for though I thought I should fall dead, I felt the spirit of life strong within me, and I stood and looked and listened as if I were at a play.

"The Professor was motionless, all but his lips, and from his lips fell curses, such curses as only Arabs could have thought of, as only an Arab could express. He cursed the unknown foe who had stolen from him his life, and he prayed God to find him out and deliver him into his hands. If he had but known that his enemy was so within a space of him, that but one pluck at the gaudy curtains and he could have had his fingers on my throat, he would have ceased his curses and found fitter work with me. I know not why even then I did not come forward and denounce myself or him, and so give us both to death in one wild struggle together, with her embalmed body looking on in its mocking mask of death. But, as I told you, I felt like a spectator at a play, and I looked and made no sign. There was a noise below, and I heard the street door open and the tread of men. They would come perhaps into the room where I was. I drew back into the darkness, and Professor Petrus turned from the body and moved towards the curtain which hid me.

"I crouched into a corner of the darkened room, and he passed by me and called out something to those below, and passed back again, and once more I looked through the curtain. He lifted the body from the long black table and placed it in the mummy case, the lid of which seemed to move back upon a hinge, and fastened with a lock. He locked it and put the key in his pocket. With an effort of strength of which I should not have thought him capable, he lifted up the mummy case and placed it in an oblong wooden box painted of a dull red colour. This too Professor Petrus locked. Then he called out something, and I heard a tread again on the stairs. I crouched back into darkness, and a man came in from outside, a negro, tall and powerful; he passed into the inner room, and in another minute he and Petrus came out carrying the box between them. I heard them go slowly down the stairs; I heard the street door open and shut, and then I heard the sound of wheels driving away.

"I have never met Professor Petrus again; he has lived, I believe, in Egypt ever since. I heard some strange story of his building a pyramid there, and I, as you know, have been in Constantinople and in Syria since then. There is my story; it is a strange one, but a true one, and I sometimes fancy the Professor's curse has come true, when I think of that story and the pain it gives me. I am sure it is to be worked out yet. Don't think that this story I have told you darkens my life. I do not always think of it; I think of it as little as I can. But things bring their fulfilment with them, and Professor Petrus's curse has to be worked out."

'THE CURSE OF VASARTAS' (1889)

Eva M. Henry

Eva M. Henry may have been a nom de plume and little is known about her. She published seven short stories in *Belgravia* magazine from 1888 to 1892, including 'The Curse of Vasartas'.

Henry's tale appeared in the October 1889 issue. As the title suggests, it is a curse narrative in which the removal of a sarcophagus from an Egyptian tomb results in tragedy for those involved. The tale centres on the differences between figures such as Mr Blake, who was "learned in the lore of the ancients", and the rather more flippant narrator, whose "accomplishments were distinctly modern" and whose attachment to ancient Egypt is that of the tourist who desires "to 'do' the lions – the Pyramids and the Sphinx and Memphis and all that". The curse of Vasartas can only be eluded if a request she left in a parchment is granted, a request which gains urgency as it becomes the only way in which to resolve the romance plot of the story. From tomb robbing, to curses, to images of romantic love, the tale seemingly unfolds around some familiar narrative devices, but it is also about moral and social authority; the past threatens the present because of British interference.

I

"What is keeping Mr Blake?" was the question uppermost in my mind as, after dinner, I stepped out on the verandah of the sitting-room I shared with him at the Hôtel des Pyramides, Grand Cairo. He had gone out in the morning to explore among some rocks and ruins about a couple of miles down the river, but he had told me he would come back in time for *table-d'hôte* dinner at seven; so that now as the clock struck nine and he had not yet put in an appearance, I began to feel a little uneasy. Perhaps he had met with some accident, or had fallen among a marauding band of Arabs, or had tramped by mistake on a crocodile lying sleeping by the river's edge. The night was dark, for the new moon was a mere half-hooped line of silver, and, as far as I knew, Mr Blake had not taken a lantern with him.

I had come to the end of my cigar and was revolving the question as to whether it would be any use my going in the direction of the ruins in case any mischance had befallen him, when I heard his voice, from within the window behind me, exclaim excitedly: "Montague, Montague, I have found—"

Then he stopped suddenly as he remembered there might be other listeners besides myself.

"Any of those Arab devils about?" he whispered.

"No – no one," I replied, after taking a turn up and down the verandah to satisfy myself.

"Come in and shut the window: it's safer," he said; and he himself closed the door, first making sure there was no one in the passage outside to overhear his communication.

Then he came close to me, and, lowering his voice, said, "I have found a tomb!"

I was so much taken aback at the nature of the communication that I did not at first understand the full significance of the remark.

"I have found a tomb – a royal tomb," he repeated; then he sank down on a chair as if there was no more to be said.

I became interested, for I knew that Mr Blake's dearest wish was to discover something belonging to the hidden past, something of the far-away glory of Egypt lost for goodness knows how many centuries.

Mr Blake was an archaeologist, but, unlike most "ologists", he was not taken up wholly and solely with his "fad", to the exclusion of every other interest in life. He was the most agreeable companion I had ever met, and a man whom to know was to love. He was a gentleman and a real good fellow in the true sense of the word. It had been my good fortune to fall in with him on board the P. and O. steamer *Egyptian* on the voyage out to Alexandria, for which place we were both bound – I for pleasure or sight-seeing or enlarging my knowledge of men and things, and he *en route* for the interior, where he was to superintend some excavations. Why we became friends I know not, seeing that we had not many points in common. To begin with, Mr. Blake was a widower of fifty, with a daughter at a boarding-school in London. I was twenty years younger – gay, careless, without any particular object in life save that of making the best of it. Mr Blake was learned in the lore of the ancients, whereas my accomplishments were distinctly modern. I could play the banjo fairly, sing a comic song and tie an evening tie at the first trial. Whether it is that on board ship people fraternise more than under any other conditions of life I cannot say; anyhow, before the *Egyptian* was out of the English Channel, Mr Blake and I had joined the hands of friendship.

To Mr Blake Egypt was as familiar as the land of his birth, so when he offered to become my guide and philosopher until the time came for him to start on his expedition, I felt that the pleasure of my trip was assured. I agree with Tom Moore that the beauty of a place doesn't depend so much on the brightness of its waters and the green of its verdure, as on the presence of friends – the beloved of one's bosom.

Of course I went straight to work (for it *is* work, and hard work too), to "do" the lions – the Pyramids and the Sphinx and Memphis and all that – and at the end of a week I had seen all that was to be seen – "the least interesting part," as Mr. Blake remarked.

"How?" I asked, not quite understanding.

"What about all the ancient splendour?" he replied. "Where is it? Not lost. Where is all the wealth of the Egyptian kings? It was not taken out of the country or we should have traced it. It is buried, and for all we know, we may be at this moment standing on a perfect mine of wealth."

Involuntarily I glanced down as he spoke, but I saw nothing save yellow sand.

When I had "done" the place, I began to take matters more easily. After all is said and done, life is pretty much the same everywhere – we eat, we drink, we smoke and we sleep: only in hot climates variety is given to sleep by the gambols of the mosquitoes.

Mr Blake's expedition was not to start for some weeks, owing to inundations, so he spent his time in pottering about among ruins in the neighbourhood of Cairo; spent it profitably too, since the result was the finding of a royal tomb.

When, after telling me of his great good fortune, he had recovered somewhat his composure and had swallowed some refreshment, for he had eaten nothing since morning, he proceeded to relate the manner of the discovery of the tomb. He had come upon it quite by chance, by what indeed might have proved an unhappy chance for him. In descending a wall of rock, he had slipped and fallen heavily to the ground beneath. All he was conscious of at the moment was a slight clinking noise, as though one stone knocked against another. For some time he had lain senseless, stunned by the force of the fall; then, in the cool evening breeze, he recovered, and as he rose to his feet and tried to recall the circumstances of his accident, he remembered the slight clinking noise, and marvelled that a fall in the sand should have been so heavy. The particular spot where he fell was a hollow, caused by the wind having blown away the sand, and, as he glanced down he caught a glimpse of a little bit of dark surface on which the sand lay sparsely. In an instant he was on his knees, and had laid bare a slab of stone about two feet square, in one corner of which was rudely cut a dragon-fly, the sign of an ancient royal house. Unable to move the stone unaided, he had deemed it wisest to hide it from view once more by covering it with sand, and had remained in the neighbourhood until dusk, lest the Arabs should come on his treasure.

"But how do you know it is a tomb?" I asked.

"What else could it be?" he answered.

I really didn't know, so I asked him what he meant to do about it.

"I am going to sit and watch it all day tomorrow, for fear the sand should be blown off it again, and the Arabs should spy it. I will show you the spot, and when it is dusk you will bring some Englishmen, and we'll open the tomb. There is to be a *fête* tomorrow night at a village four or five miles off, to which all the Arabs will go, so we shall not be observed. Once these fellows get wind of a tomb they would murder us to get the amulets."

It is needless to relate how, in the guise of artists, in order to divert attention and to account for our presence in one spot, we watched that hollow in the sand all through the heat of the day; or how, as the shadows of evening deepened and the tall palms grew dim and indistinct, and only here and there a black glimmer showed where the Nile pursued its course between fields of rice and maize, a little band of English workmen, bearing ropes and lanterns, crossed the black waters in a track-boat, and crossed back again ere two hours had passed, carrying in their midst a long and very heavy object – the stone sarcophagus found in the tomb.

The next day, in the presence of several gentlemen interested in antiquarian research, the sarcophagus was opened. It contained the embalmed body of a woman in perfect preservation. She was apparently in the prime of life, and her thick, dark hair, drawn down on either side and confined at the ends with gold bands engraved with dragon-flies, emblematical of her royal lineage, reached almost to her feet. Her heavy gold necklace, from which depended various precious stones, was similarly engraved, and on the forefinger of the left hand she wore a gold ring, on which was the name "Vasartas", wrought in strips of agate beaten into the metal. The same name appeared also cut in the stone inside the lid of the sarcophagus. The linen wrapped round the mummy, although almost brown, was still quite good. About the left ankle there was rolled a strip of parchment, confined by a gold torque, which, however, was not so tight but that the parchment might be unrolled. Not doubting but that by this parchment the identification, so to speak, of the mummy could be effected, Mr Blake removed it carefully, but found, to his surprise, that the writing it contained was in a language totally unknown to him. A native professor, learned in Arabic and other Eastern tongues, was likewise unable to decipher it.

"It is in a peculiar dialect," he said, "and I doubt if any man can translate it save one."

"And who is that one?" asked Mr Blake.

"Ahmed Ben Anen the seer, but he lies nigh unto death at this moment."

Mr Blake showed this parchment to all the professors and experts in the neighbourhood, but they all failed to understand the hieroglyphics. Unless Ahmed Ben Anen recovered, therefore, there was no chance.

Meantime, what was to be done with the mummy? It was an awkward kind of possession, and hotel-keepers objected to it as being liable to attract robbers. Besides, Mr Blake daily expected to be sent on his expedition, so he determined to despatch Vasartas to the British Museum at once, and so get rid of his responsibility. As the period of my stay was at an end, I undertook to look after the lady on the homeward journey, though, truth to tell, I didn't half like the idea; but, as fate would have it, luckily from the mummy-escort point of view, unluckily from every other, two days before my departure I was stricken down with fever. Of course there was no knowing how long it might be until I should recover, or if ever I should recover at all, so it was decided that Vasartas should not wait for me but go by herself, protected in some measure by heavy insurance.

Mr Blake set himself to nurse me back to health and strength, and a more tender nurse never smoothed a sick man's pillow, or helped by his presence to lessen the tedium of weary hours. Fortunately, my illness was not serious, and I had turned the corner before Mr Blake got his orders to proceed up country, and, when the day of his departure came, I was strong enough to accompany him a few miles on his way. In a little grove of palm-trees we parted, and our parting was none the less manly that there were tears in the eyes of one of us – for Mr Blake had been like a father to me. This parting, too, meant more than a clasping of hands, and that sad, sad word "farewell"; for, if behind us lay the shadows of peace and friendship, and the memory of happy days spent together, in the vista of the future lay what? We knew not any more than we knew what lay a thousand miles beyond in that yellow sand stretching away before us out of sight. As I turned my face again towards Cairo, I felt the sense of having lost something – lost it past all finding; and when I traversed once more the narrow streets of the town, I thought I had never been in so dreary a place. I resolved to leave for England by the next steamer.

II

On the eve of my departure, three days after I had taken leave of Mr Blake, what was my astonishment when I received a letter from him, brought by a messenger who had ridden all night and all day in order to reach me that evening. Still more was I surprised at the contents of the letter, which ran thus:

My dear Harry [he had taken to calling me Harry when I was ill]:

You once told me that if ever you could serve me in any way you would do so gladly. Little did I think that the time was at hand when I should ask your service, not for myself, but for my child Lhora. For her sake, then, I pray of you to return to England at once (this may reach you in time for the next steamer), and bring back Vasartas. This favour I ask of you is a great one, but I ask it under a terrible necessity. Go and see my Lhora, and you will the more readily believe how fearful is the thought to me that she may be in danger, and alas! through me. At all costs bring back Vasartas, ere it may be too late, for we cannot know how Fate will reckon time, or whether we will live a day or a year. Bring back Vasartas, and if I am not [here a word was erased] in Alexandria to meet you, I will leave instructions for you, in the name of a father's love, to carry out. I have written to my bankers to place £5000 to your credit to defray expenses connected with the recovery of Vasartas.

To save Lhora's life bring back Vasartas, I implore you, and you will earn the heartfelt gratitude of your true friend,

JOHN BLAKE

P. S. Lhora is a boarder at Miss Russell's, Devonshire House, Lower Norwood. Please see her and make sure that she is well. J. B.

I read this letter over and over again, and each time I read it I became but the more perplexed as to its meaning. With what earnestness it besought me to bring back Vasartas! Four times the request was repeated and always the safety of Lhora was pleaded. In what way could the whereabouts of a mummy affect Lhora's well-being, nay, her life? It was a hopeless enigma. Once it struck me that perhaps Mr Blake was overcome by some strange hallucination.

At length I recollected that he had taken with him the mysterious strip of parchment, as Ahmed Ben Anen, who was said to be recovering, lived but a few miles off the track of his route. I inquired of the messenger who had brought me the letter if Mr Blake had visited the seer, and found that such, indeed, was the case. This letter then must, I argued, be due to something Ahmed Ben Anen had told him. I made vain conjectures as to what that "something" might be. All that was clear to me was that for some reason or other Vasartas must be brought back.

A fortnight afterward I was back in England. A letter awaited me from Mr Blake's bankers stating that £5000 had been placed to my credit. I rather wondered why he had deemed so large a sum necessary.

At once I made application to the authorities for the return of Mr Blake's gift, much to their horror and astonishment. A mummy was even more precious then than it would be now, for Rameses II, and Seti, and several other gentlemen now on view in the British Museum, had not been discovered. Besides, Vasartas was quite attractive-looking in her own way, and mummies are generally hideous. Rameses and Seti certainly are.

The charms of Vasartas had not yet been displayed; so I argued that to give her up would not be depriving the British public of its possessions, whereat the authorities hemmed and hawed, and said they would consider the matter.

Meantime I had another mission – to see Mr Blake's daughter, over whom hung apparently some mysterious doom. So I betook myself to Miss Russell's high-class establishment for young ladies, and expected to make acquaintance with the usual type of unfledged hobbledehoy with which one generally associates the idea of a schoolgirl. I was ushered into Miss Russell's own sitting-room, and I smiled at the idea of myself, a young fellow of thirty, coming to pay a sort of fatherly or brotherly visit to a girl at a boarding-school.

Miss Russell herself – a prim lady of some three score summers, in a black silk dress and a little white shawl and a violet-beribboned

cap, between which and her face on each side were three grey
curls kept in place by little combs – Miss Russell herself inspected
me before she allowed me to see the object of my visit. Was I a
relative of Miss Blake? No. An old acquaintance, perhaps? Had I
any particular message to deliver, as she did not care for the young
ladies of her select establishment to be upset by visitors. I mentally
remarked that the equilibrium preserved by the said young ladies
must be uncertain, as it was so easily upset, but I didn't dare to say
so. That cap with the violet ribbons and those three curls on either
side of the lady's face had produced something akin to awe in me.

She asked several other questions, and finally told me in so many
words that she didn't believe I had come from Mr Blake – that I was
an impostor in fact – a wolf sneaking into her fold. Then I hit on
a bold plan, and tried what a bit of real imposition would do. It's
astonishing how people mistake the real for the counterfeit and the
counterfeit for the real – just to suit their inclinations.

"By the way," I said, "will you be so very kind as to let me have a
prospectus of this splendid establishment. My aunt, Lady Belgrave,
has three daughters who—"

That was enough to have gained an audience with all the girls
in the school, had I wished it. A change came over the spirit of Miss
Russell; she became affable to me directly, and enlarged upon the
advantages which would be reaped by my aunt's three daughters
if under her charge. The aunt and daughters were fictitious, of
course, but they gained my point. Llora Blake was summoned.
Llora Blake! How shall I describe her? I cannot, and yet that first
sight of her remains an imperishable image of beauty on the negative of my memory. She was *petite* but exquisitely graceful, and a
certain *hauteur* about the carriage of her pretty head impressed one
with the idea that she was tall. Her face was perfectly oval, with

small but delicately chiselled features and finely pencilled brows, and her eyes – to what shall I compare them? I know not. Once I plucked a violet on which a drop of dew had fallen, because some-how it reminded me of Llora's eyes; yet the dew on the violet was fathomable, and her eyes were deeper than the sea. Her red-gold hair gave the idea of sun's rays that were tangible. When my eyes first met hers she was pale, but the next instant a soft rosy hue had suffused all her face and throat. I have taken a good many words to tell what perhaps any moderately far-seeing individual could sum up, and rightly too, in three words – "I loved her".

There, the truth is out! and the knowledge of that truth came to me pretty quickly, as quickly as the soft pink rushed to Llora's cheeks, and I do believe if Miss Russell had not remained in the room I should have imparted my knowledge to Llora herself then and there. As it was, we talked commonplaces, Miss Russell doing the largest share, and not forgetting to remind me every moment that my aunt had three daughters.

When I returned to town I found a reply from the authorities of the British Museum stating that on no account could they return Vasartas to the giver; that now they had her they meant to keep her. I thought of Llora, for whose sake I would have made an effort to transport St Paul's or Westminster Abbey to Egypt had it been necessary, and I determined to see if money would be of any avail. What a fool I had been not to offer it at the very first! Of course Mr Blake must have remembered that in these days money will accomplish anything, especially in England, and that was why he had placed £5000 to my credit. I do believe that if anybody offered the British public enough for it, they'd sell the Throne itself, for all their professions of loyalty. I therefore offered Mr Blake's £5000 for what he had given freely. They haggled over it, whereupon I tried the effect of another thousand, and the business was done. Vasartas was no longer a possession of the British public.

Of course I decided to start at once; but first I went to see Llora once more, on the plea that she might wish to send a message to her father. I saw Miss Russell, but alas! not Llora. She had caught a bad cold and was feverish. The doctor was not alarmed, though he could not yet say for certain if it was only a mere cold. My memory reverted to those words in the postscript of Mr Blake's letter, "Please see her and make sure that she is well." Had Mr. Blake any reason for saying this? No, assuredly not. How could he know that his daughter would catch cold nearly a month after he wrote? It was a mere coincidence, and yet he had said plainly enough that Llora's life was in danger because Vasartas was in England. The construction I had put upon this was, that perhaps some Arab, Ahmed Ben Anen himself in all probability, had vowed vengeance if the mummy was not returned to its rightful possessors. Llora's cold could not have any connection with the matter. Nevertheless, I plied Miss Russell with my fictitious aunt and cousins, and extracted from her a promise to wire me tidings of Llora to Gibraltar or Alexandria.

Next day I left England with Vasartas for Llora's sake, though for Llora's sake I would fain have remained in England.

At Gibraltar I was terribly disappointed to find no news awaiting me from Miss Russell, though I flattered myself into the belief that no news was good news. We all of us, even pessimists in spite of themselves, believe what pleases us most; without these self-deceptions, indeed, life would be unbearable. Pandora's box is the common inheritance of everybody. I told myself there was no need for anxiety on Llora's account; besides, if the presence of Vasartas had really any baneful influence on her, that influence was now at an end. Then I fell to wondering what Mr Blake meant to do with Vasartas now that I had brought her back to him.

When the mails were brought on board off Alexandria a telegram was handed to me. Hastily I tore it open and read the fatal words:

"No hope of Llora."

I sank down on a deck chair and all power of thought or action seemed to leave me. I was like a man in a dream. People with whom I had been on friendly terms during the voyage went to and fro and addressed me, but I heard not what they said. The hurry and bustle of getting into the boats passed by me unheeded. How long I might have remained thus, with senses dulled to everything save the reality of Llora's danger, I cannot tell, had not a hand been laid on my shoulder, and a voice said:

"Mr Montague."

I looked up. The man who addressed me was a Mr Frampton, who carried on business as a solicitor and general legal adviser to the English residents in Cairo and Alexandria.

"Mr Montague," he repeated, "I had instructions to deliver this into your hands so soon as you landed, and as I was afraid I might miss you on the quay I came on board."

"Mr Blake is not here?" I queried; but I did not notice that silence was his only answer.

"Thank God!" I exclaimed, "I shall not have to tell him yet."

"Mr Blake is – dead," said Mr. Frampton quietly.

"Mr Blake dead? Impossible! and Llora dying!"

"He met his death in a sad way," continued Mr. Frampton. "On the march inland with the expedition the party stopped to shoot some elephants. Mr Blake was a good shot; I've been out with him. But however it was, he fired at a great bull elephant from the open and missed, or at any rate the shot only grazed the beast's ear.

"He fired again and missed, and before he had time to get to shelter the infuriated animal was on him, and he was literally trampled to death. They buried him on the spot, poor fellow, and one of the party came back to Cairo with the sad news."

The horror of the thing took from me all power of expression, and the lawyer went on:

"About three days after the expedition started, a messenger returned and brought me this package from Mr Blake. I think the same messenger had a letter to you also. Mr Blake sent instructions that I was to deliver this into your hand immediately on your return from England, in case, through delay or accident, he might not be in Alexandria to meet you himself. How little he thought when he wrote to me that death would prevent the meeting!"

I took the packet and opened it mechanically. First I came on a letter to myself in Blake's handwriting. Trembling, I tore it open and read:

My dear Harry, – As I may not have returned from the expedition when you arrive with Vasartas, I must tell you the terrible secret which has been revealed to me by Ahmed Ben Anen the seer. Had it concerned only myself it would be of small account, as all men must die, and I have lived into middle life, and I thank God my life has been a happy one, therefore it is not for me to murmur at what must be. But it concerns also my Llora, whom by this time you have seen. She is beautiful, she is young – too young to die – and for her sake I implore you to carry out this trust if aught should occur to prevent my meeting you when you come with Vasartas. You will see in the translation of the parchment, which, with the original, I send you, that the curse on my children only lasts until Vasartas is laid once more in the tomb. This I implore you to do, first replacing the original parchment where I found it. Then shall the curse pass from Llora, and I alone shall suffer for what I did, Heaven knows unwittingly.

If it should be that I may not see you or Llora again, tell her that I thought of her always, but keep secret from her the story of Vasartas. In after years watch kindly over that young life which I ask you now to save. We may meet again, but I cannot tell, for life seems now a thing of the past to your true friend,

JOHN BLAKE

Hastily I withdrew the paper enclosing the parchment, attached to which was the translation in Mr Blake's writing. At the top of the sheet on which it was written I read: "Ahmed Ben Anen's Translation". Then came the terrible words—

Vasartas of ten kings of the Royal House of Namoth.

Cursed be the man that shall disturb the tomb of me, Vasartas. To him shall death come with violence and his bones shall be scattered with the winds. Also his children shall be cut off from life until I, Vasartas, be laid to rest and no more seen.

I, Vasartas, of mighty kings, have spoken.

The curse had fallen on Blake. And Llora? Was there yet time to save her, or was she by this cut off from life? The telegram stated that she was dying. While there is life there is hope, so I explained to Mr Frampton the necessity for haste, and he undertook to assist in the reburial of Vasartas.

It was night when we reached the site of the tomb underneath the wall of rock from which Blake had removed the sarcophagus in such triumph only a few weeks before. Unfortunately, a great pile of sand had collected where the hollow had been, and it took a dozen men about an hour to dig down to the stone slab which closed the opening to the subterranean cavern. Once more we removed it and let the sarcophagus down by means of ropes. Scarcely had we got it into position when one of our party called out:

"Here's a sand storm coming up. Quick! Get to the other side of this wall, or you're all dead men!"

Helter-skelter we clambered out of the vault, not even waiting to replace the stone, and took refuge behind the old wall that had withstood the storms of thousands of years; and not a minute too soon were we, for the great blinding sand-cloud was on us. At one moment we thought that even with the protection of the wall we were done for, as over the top of it came a great avalanche of sand, burying some of us up to our waists. Then, as the air cleared, we saw the dark-moving mass in front of us rolling away out of sight, and we knew that the danger was past.

We helped each other to scramble out of the loose sand, and having shaken out our clothing as best we could, we went round to the other side of the wall. But there was no wall to be seen – for there was a great bank of sand right up to the top of it. The tomb of Vasartas was well hidden, and, as it was open when we fled round the wall, the sand must have completely filled the cavern.

The next day I started up country with the messenger who had brought the news of poor Blake's death as guide; for I wished to remove the body from its desert resting-place and have it buried in the English cemetery at Cairo. After a six days' march we reached the sad spot, but there was no trace of the grave, although my guide told me they had raised a mound over it some six or eight feet in height, and marked it with a wooden cross. In a neighbouring village I learnt the cause of the strange disappearance. A terrific hurricane had swept over the place, and thus the curse of Vasartas was fulfilled to the letter.

When I returned to Cairo news of Llora awaited me – good news too. She was recovering, and her recovery, strangely enough, dated from the night we laid Vasartas once more in her tomb.

When I returned to England I became a pretty constant visitor at Miss Russell's high-class establishment for young ladies, and she countenanced my visits on account of my aunt and three cousins. At length, however, I was obliged to confess that those four per- sonages were myths, and that instead of bringing pupils to her, I was going to rob her of one. She forgave the deception, for she was a woman; besides, a marriage from her school was really a magnificent advertisement. The fame of the school spread amongst mothers, and she had twenty additional boarders the term after Llora and I were married.

'LOT NO. 249' (1892)

Sir Arthur Conan Doyle

Sir Arthur Conan Doyle (1859–1930) was a prolific author of novels, plays, short stories, and works of non-fiction, who holds a special place in the popular imagination because of the Sherlock Holmes tales. How the seemingly inexplicable could be rationalised by some form of putative scientific analysis is a key impulse in much of his work.

'Lot No. 249' was published in *Harper's New Monthly Magazine* in October 1892. The tale centres on the tensions between Abercrombie Smith, an Oxford medical student, and a fellow student called Edward Bellingham who has a profound knowledge of Egyptian lore and who has purchased a mummy at auction (the Lot of the title). The mummy attacks those against whom the emotionally volatile Bellingham bears a grudge. The tale reflects concerns about the place of possibly cursed Egyptian artefacts within seemingly tranquil British worlds (Bram Stoker's *The Jewel of Seven Stars* [1903, revised 1912] does something similar). The implication is that the empires of the past have not quite been defeated, and they come back and disturb confidently held ideas about science and modernity.

This story, along with 'The Ring of Thoth' (1890), represents Doyle's key contribution to the form of the mummy tale. It is a classic of the genre and is included here because of both its quality and its genuinely frightening denouement.

O F THE DEALINGS OF EDWARD BELLINGHAM WITH WILLIAM Monkhouse Lee, and of the cause of the great terror of Abercrombie Smith, it may be that no absolute and final judgement will ever be delivered. It is true that we have the full and clear narrative of Smith himself, and such corroboration as he could look for from Thomas Styles the servant, from the Reverend Plumptree Peterson, Fellow of Old's, and from such other people as chanced to gain some passing glance at this or that incident in a singular chain of events. Yet, in the main, the story must rest upon Smith alone, and the most will think that it is more likely that one brain, however outwardly sane, has some subtle warp in its texture, some strange flaw in its workings, than that the path of nature has been overstepped in open day in so famed a centre of learning and light as the University of Oxford. Yet when we think how narrow and how devious this path of nature is, how dimly we can trace it, for all our lamps of science, and how from the darkness which girds it round great and terrible possibilities loom ever shadowly upwards, it is a bold and confident man who will put a limit to the strange by-paths into which the human spirit may wander.

In a certain wing of what we will call Old College in Oxford there is a corner turret of an exceeding great age. The heavy arch which spans the open door has bent downwards in the centre under the weight of its years, and the grey, lichen-blotched blocks of stone are bound and knitted together with withes and strands of ivy, as though the old mother had set herself to brace them up against wind and weather. From the door a stone stair curves upward spirally, passing two landings, and terminating in a third one, its steps all shapeless and hollowed by the tread of so many generations of the seekers after knowledge. Life has flowed like water down this winding stair, and, waterlike, has left these smooth-worn grooves behind it. From the long-gowned, pedantic scholars of Plantagenet days down to the young bloods of a later age, how full and strong had been that tide of young English life. And what was left now of all those hopes, those strivings, those fiery energies, save here and there in some old-world churchyard a few scratches upon a stone, and perchance a handful of dust in a mouldering coffin? Yet here were the silent stair and the grey old wall, with bend and saltire and many another heraldic device still to be read upon its surface, like grotesque shadows thrown back from the days that had passed.

In the month of May, in the year 1884, three young men occupied the sets of rooms which opened on to the separate landings of the old stair. Each set consisted simply of a sitting-room and of a bed-room, while the two corresponding rooms upon the ground-floor were used, the one as a coal-cellar, and the other as the living-room of the servant, or scout, Thomas Styles, whose duty it was to wait upon the three men above him. To right and to left was a line of lecture-rooms and of offices, so that the dwellers in the old turret enjoyed a certain seclusion, which made the chambers popular among the more studious undergraduates. Such were the three who occupied them now – Abercrombie Smith above, Edward Bellingham beneath him, and William Monkhouse Lee upon the lowest storey.

It was ten o'clock on a bright spring night, and Abercrombie Smith lay back in his armchair, his feet upon the fender, and his briar-root pipe between his lips. In a similar chair, and equally at his ease, there lounged on the other side of the fireplace his old school friend Jephro Hastie. Both men were in flannels, for they had spent their evening upon the river, but apart from their dress no one could look at their hard-cut, alert faces without seeing that they were open-air men – men whose minds and tastes turned naturally to all that was manly and robust. Hastie, indeed, was stroke of his college boat, and Smith was an even better oar, but a coming examination had already cast its shadow over him and held him to his work, save for the few hours a week which health demanded. A litter of medical books upon the table, with scattered bones, models and anatomical plates, pointed to the extent as well as the nature of his studies, while a couple of single-sticks and a set of boxing-gloves above the mantelpiece hinted at the means by which, with Hastie's help, he might take his exercise in its most compressed and least distant form. They knew each other very well – so well that they could sit now in that soothing silence which is the very highest development of companionship.

"Have some whisky," said Abercrombie Smith at last between two cloudbursts. "Scotch in the jug and Irish in the bottle."

"No, thanks. I'm in for the skulls. I don't liquor when I'm training. How about you?"

"I'm reading hard. I think it best to leave it alone."

Hastie nodded, and they relapsed into a contented silence.

"By the way, Smith," asked Hastie, presently, "have you made the acquaintance of either of the fellows on your stair yet?"

"Just a nod when we pass. Nothing more."

"Hum! I should be inclined to let it stand at that. I know something of them both. Not much, but as much as I want. I don't think I should take them to my bosom if I were you. Not that there's much amiss with Monkhouse Lee."

"Meaning the thin one?"

"Precisely. He is a gentlemanly little fellow. I don't think there is any vice in him. But then you can't know him without knowing Bellingham."

"Meaning the fat one?"

"Yes, the fat one. And he's a man whom I, for one, would rather not know."

Abercrombie Smith raised his eyebrows and glanced across at his companion.

"What's up, then?" he asked. "Drink? Cards? Cad? You used not to be censorious."

"Ah! you evidently don't know the man, or you wouldn't ask. There's something damnable about him – something reptilian. My gorge always rises at him. I should put him down as a man with secret vices – an evil liver. He's no fool, though. They say that he is one of the best men in his line that they have ever had in the college."

"Medicine or classics?"

"Eastern languages. He's a demon at them. Chillingworth met him somewhere above the Second Cataract last long, and he told me that he just prattled to the Arabs as if he had been born and nursed and weaned among them. He talked Coptic to the Copts, and Hebrew to the Jews, and Arabic to the Bedouins, and they were all ready to kiss the hem of his frock-coat. There are some old hermit Johnnies up in those parts who sit on rocks and scowl and spit at the casual stranger. Well, when they saw this chap Bellingham, before he had said five words they just lay down on their bellies and wriggled. Chillingworth said that he never saw anything like it. Bellingham seemed to take it as his right, too, and strutted about among them and talked down to them like a Dutch uncle. Pretty good for an undergrad of Old's, wasn't it?"

"Why do you say you can't know Lee without knowing Bellingham?"

"Because Bellingham is engaged to his sister Eveline. Such a bright little girl, Smith! I know the whole family well. It's disgusting to see that brute with her. A toad and a dove, that's what they always remind me of."

Abercrombie Smith grinned and knocked his ashes out against the side of the grate.

"You show every card in your hand, old chap," said he. "What a prejudiced, green-eyed, evil-thinking old man it is! You have really nothing against the fellow except that."

"Well, I've known her ever since she was as long as that cherry-wood pipe, and I don't like to see her taking risks. And it is a risk. He looks beastly. And he has a beastly temper, a venomous temper. You remember his row with Long Norton?"

"No; you always forget that I am a freshman."

"Ah, it was last winter. Of course. Well, you know the tow-path along by the river. There were several fellows going along it, Bellingham in front, when they came on an old market-woman coming the other way. It had been raining – you know what those fields are like when it has rained – and the path ran between the river and a great puddle that was nearly as broad. Well, what does this swine do but keep the path, and push the old girl into the mud, where she and her marketings came to terrible grief. It was a blackguard thing to do, and Long Norton, who is as gentle a fellow as ever stepped, told him what he thought of it. One word led to another, and it ended in Norton laying his stick across the fellow's shoulders. There was the deuce of a fuss about it, and it's a treat to see the way in which Bellingham looks at Norton when they meet now. By Jove, Smith, it's nearly eleven o'clock!"

"No hurry. Light your pipe again."

"Not I. I'm supposed to be in training. Here I've been sitting gossiping when I ought to have been safely tucked up. I'll borrow your skull, if you can share it. Williams has had mine for a month. I'll take the little bones of your ear, too, if you are sure you won't need them. Thanks very much. Never mind a bag, I can carry them very well under my arm. Good-night, my son, and take my tip as to your neighbour."

When Hastie, bearing his anatomical plunder, had clattered off down the winding stair, Abercrombie Smith hurled his pipe into the waste-paper basket, and drawing his chair nearer to the lamp, plunged into a formidable green-covered volume, adorned with great coloured maps of that strange internal kingdom of which we are the hapless and helpless monarchs. Though a freshman at Oxford, the student was not so in medicine, for he had worked for four years at Glasgow and at Berlin, and this coming examination would place him finally as a member of his profession. With his firm mouth, broad forehead, and clear-cut, somewhat hard-featured face, he was a man who, if he had no brilliant talent, was yet so dogged, so patient, and so strong that he might in the end overtop a more showy genius. A man who can hold his own among Scotchmen and North Germans is not a man to be easily set back. Smith had left a name at Glasgow and at Berlin, and he was bent now upon doing as much at Oxford, if hard work and devotion could accomplish it.

He had sat reading for about an hour, and the hands of the noisy carriage clock upon the side table were rapidly closing together upon the twelve, when a sudden sound fell upon the student's ear – a sharp, rather shrill sound, like the hissing intake of a man's breath who gasps under some strong emotion. Smith laid down his book and slanted his ear to listen. There was no one on either side or above him, so that the interruption came certainly from the neighbour beneath – the same neighbour of whom Hastie had given so unsavoury an account. Smith knew him only as a flabby, pale-faced man of silent and studious habits, a man, whose lamp threw a golden bar from the old turret even after he had extinguished his own. This community in lateness had formed a certain silent bond between them. It was soothing to Smith when the hours stole on towards dawning to feel that there was another so close who set as small a value upon his sleep as he did. Even now, as his thoughts turned towards him, Smith's feelings were kindly. Hastie was a good fellow, but he was rough, strong-fibred, with no imagination or sympathy. He could not tolerate departures from what he looked upon as the model type of manliness. If a man could not be measured by a public-school standard, then he was beyond the pale with Hastie. Like so many who are themselves robust, he was apt to confuse the constitution with the character, to ascribe to want of principle what was really a want of circulation. Smith, with his stronger mind, knew his friend's habit, and made allowance for it now as his thoughts turned towards the man beneath him.

There was no return of the singular sound, and Smith was about to turn to his work once more, when suddenly there broke out in the silence of the night a hoarse cry, a positive scream – the call of a man who is moved and shaken beyond all control. Smith sprang out of his chair and dropped his book. He was a man of fairly firm fibre, but there was something in this sudden, uncontrollable shriek of horror which chilled his blood and pringled in his skin. Coming in such a place and at such an hour, it brought a thousand fantastic possibilities into his head. Should he rush down, or was it better to wait? He had all the national hatred of making a scene, and he knew so little of his neighbour that he would not lightly intrude upon his affairs. For a moment he stood in doubt and even as he balanced the matter there was a quick rattle of footsteps upon the stairs, and young Monkhouse Lee, half dressed and as white as ashes, burst into his room.

"Come down!" he gasped. "Bellingham's ill."

Abercrombie Smith followed him closely down stairs into the sitting-room which was beneath his own, and intent as he was upon the matter in hand, he could not but take an amazed glance around him as he crossed the threshold. It was such a chamber as he had never seen before – a museum rather than a study. Walls and ceiling were thickly covered with a thousand strange relics from Egypt and the East. Tall, angular figures bearing burdens or weapons stalked in an uncouth frieze round the apartments. Above were bull-headed, stork-headed, cat-headed, owl-headed statues, with viper-crowned, almond-eyed monarchs, and strange, beetle-like deities cut out of the blue Egyptian lapis lazuli. Horus and Isis and Osiris peeped down from every niche and shelf, while across the ceiling a true son of Old Nile, a great, hanging-jawed crocodile, was slung in a double noose.

In the centre of this singular chamber was a large, square table, littered with papers, bottles, and the dried leaves of some graceful, palm-like plant. These varied objects had all been heaped together in order to make room for a mummy case, which had been conveyed from the wall, as was evident from the gap there, and laid across the front of the table. The mummy itself, a horrid, black, withered thing, like a charred head on a gnarled bush, was lying half out of the case, with its clawlike hand and bony forearm resting upon the table. Propped up against the sarcophagus was an old yellow scroll of papyrus, and in front of it, in a wooden arm-chair, sat the owner of the room, his head thrown back, his widely-opened eyes directed in a horrified stare to the crocodile above him, and his blue, thick lips puffing loudly with every expiration.

"My God! he's dying!" cried Monkhouse Lee distractedly.

He was a slim, handsome young fellow, olive-skinned and dark-eyed, of a Spanish rather than of an English type, with a Celtic intensity of manner which contrasted with the Saxon phlegm of Abercrombie Smith.

"Only a faint, I think," said the medical student. "Just give me a hand with him. You take his feet. Now on to the sofa. Can you kick all those little wooden devils off? What a litter it is! Now he will be all right if we undo his collar and give him some water. What has he been up to at all?"

"I don't know. I heard him cry out. I ran up. I know him pretty well, you know. It is very good of you to come down."

"His heart is going like a pair of castanets," said Smith, laying his hand on the breast of the unconscious man. "He seems to me to be frightened all to pieces. Chuck the water over him! What a face he has got on him!"

It was indeed a strange and most repellent face, for colour and outline were equally unnatural. It was white, not with the ordinary pallor of fear, but with an absolutely bloodless white, like the underside of a sole. He was very fat, but gave the impression of having at some time been considerably fatter, for his skin hung loosely in creases and folds, and was shot with a meshwork of wrinkles. Short, stubbly brown hair bristled up from his scalp, with a pair of thick, wrinkled ears protruding on either side. His light grey eyes were still open, the pupils dilated and the balls projecting in a fixed and horrid stare. It seemed to Smith as he looked down upon him that he had never seen nature's danger signals flying so plainly upon a man's countenance, and his thoughts turned more seriously to the warning which Hastie had given him an hour before.

"What the deuce can have frightened him so?" he asked.

"It's the mummy."

"The mummy? How, then?"

"I don't know. It's beastly and morbid. I wish he would drop it. It's the second fright he has given me. It was the same last winter. I found him just like this, with that horrid thing in front of him."

"What does he want with the mummy, then?"

"Oh, he's a crank, you know. It's his hobby. He knows more about these things than any man in England. But I wish he wouldn't! Ah, he's beginning to come to."

A faint tinge of colour had begun to steal back into Bellingham's ghastly cheeks, and his eyelids shivered like a sail after a calm. He clasped and unclasped his hands, drew a long, thin breath between his teeth, and suddenly jerking up his head, threw a glance of recognition around him. As his eyes fell upon the mummy, he sprang off the sofa, seized the roll of papyrus, thrust it into a drawer, turned the key, and then staggered back on to the sofa.

"What's up?" he asked. "What do you chaps want?"

"You've been shrieking out and making no end of a fuss," said Monkhouse Lee. "If our neighbour here from above hadn't come down, I'm sure I don't know what I should have done with you."

"Ah, it's Abercrombie Smith," said Bellingham, glancing up at him. "How very good of you to come in! What a fool I am! Oh, my God, what a fool I am!"

He sunk his head on to his hands, and burst into peal after peal of hysterical laughter.

"Look here! Drop it!" cried Smith, shaking him roughly by the shoulder.

"Your nerves are all in a jangle. You must drop these little midnight games with mummies, or you'll be going off your chump. You're all on wires now."

"I wonder," said Bellingham, "whether you would be as cool as I am if you had seen—"

"What then?"

"Oh, nothing. I meant that I wonder if you could sit up at night with a mummy without trying your nerves. I have no doubt that you are quite right. I dare say that I have been taking it out of myself too much lately. But I am all right now. Please don't go, though. Just wait for a few minutes until I am quite myself."

"The room is very close," remarked Lee, throwing open the window and letting in the cool night air.

"It's balsamic resin," said Bellingham. He lifted up one of the dried palmate leaves from the table and frizzled it over the chimney of the lamp. It broke away into heavy smoke wreaths, and a pungent, biting odour filled the chamber. "It's the sacred plant – the plant of the priests," he remarked. "Do you know anything of Eastern languages, Smith?"

"Nothing at all. Not a word."

The answer seemed to lift a weight from the Egyptologist's mind.

"By the way," he continued, "how long was it from the time that you ran down, until I came to my senses?"

"Not long. Some four or five minutes."

"I thought it could not be very long," said he, drawing a long breath. "But what a strange thing unconsciousness is! There is no measurement to it. I could not tell from my own sensations if it were seconds or weeks. Now that gentleman on the table was packed up in the days of the Eleventh Dynasty, some forty centuries ago, and yet if he could find his tongue, he would tell us that this lapse of time has been but a closing of the eyes and a reopening of them. He is a singularly fine mummy, Smith."

Smith stepped over to the table and looked down with a professional eye at the black and twisted form in front of him. The features, though horribly discoloured, were perfect, and two little nut-like eyes still lurked in the depths of the black, hollow sockets. The blotched skin was drawn tightly from bone to bone, and a tangled wrap of black coarse hair fell over the ears. Two thin teeth, like those of a rat, overlay the shrivelled lower lip. In its crouching position, with bent joints and craned head, there was a suggestion of energy about the horrid thing which made Smith's gorge rise. The gaunt ribs, with their parchment-like covering, were exposed, and the sunken, leaden-hued abdomen, with the long slit where the embalmer had left his mark; but the lower limbs were wrapt round with coarse yellow bandages. A number of little clove-like pieces of myrrh and of cassia were sprinkled over the body, and lay scattered on the inside of the case.

"I don't know his name," said Bellingham, passing his hand over the shrivelled head. "You see the outer sarcophagus with the inscriptions is missing. Lot 249 is all the title he has now. You see it printed on his case. That was his number in the auction at which I picked him up."

"He has been a very pretty sort of fellow in his day," remarked Abercrombie Smith.

"He has been a giant. His mummy is six feet seven in length, and that would be a giant over there, for they were never a very robust race. Feel these great knotted bones, too. He would be a nasty fellow to tackle."

"Perhaps these very hands helped to build the stones into the pyramids," suggested Monkhouse Lee, looking down with disgust in his eyes at the crooked, unclean talons.

"No fear. This fellow has been pickled in natron, and looked after in the most approved style. They did not serve hodsmen in that fashion. Salt or bitumen was enough for them. It has been calculated that this sort of thing cost about seven hundred and thirty pounds in our money. Our friend was a noble at the least. What do you make of that small inscription near his feet, Smith?"

"I told you that I know no Eastern tongue."

"Ah, so you did. It is the name of the embalmer, I take it. A very conscientious worker he must have been. I wonder how many modern works will survive four thousand years?"

He kept on speaking lightly and rapidly, but it was evident to Abercrombie Smith that he was still palpitating with fear. His hands shook, his lower lip trembled, and look where he would, his eye always came sliding round to his gruesome companion. Through all his fear, however, there was a suspicion of triumph in his tone and manner. His eyes shone, and his footstep, as he paced the room, was brisk and jaunty. He gave the impression of a man who has gone through an ordeal, the marks of which he still bears upon him, but which has helped him to his end.

"You're not going yet?" he cried, as Smith rose from the sofa.

At the prospect of solitude, his fears seemed to crowd back upon him, and he stretched out a hand to detain him.

"Yes, I must go. I have my work to do. You are all right now. I think that with your nervous system you should take up some less morbid study."

"Oh, I am not nervous as a rule; and I have unwrapped mummies before."

"You fainted last time," observed Monkhouse Lee.

"Ah, yes, so I did. Well, I must have a nerve tonic or a course of electricity. You are not going, Lee?"

"I'll do whatever you wish, Ned."

"Then I'll come down with you and have a shake-down on your sofa. Good-night, Smith. I am so sorry to have disturbed you with my foolishness."

They shook hands, and as the medical student stumbled up the spiral and irregular stair he heard a key turn in a door, and the steps of his two new acquaintances as they descended to the lower floor.

In this strange way began the acquaintance between Edward Bellingham and Abercrombie Smith, an acquaintance which the latter, at least, had no desire to push further. Bellingham, however, appeared to have taken a fancy to his rough-spoken neighbour, and made his advances in such a way that he could hardly be repulsed without absolute brutality. Twice he called to thank Smith for his assistance, and many times afterwards he looked in with books, papers and such other civilities as two bachelor neighbours can offer each other. He was, as Smith soon found, a man of wide reading, with catholic tastes and an extraordinary memory. His manner, too, was so pleasing and suave that one came, after a time, to overlook his repellent appearance. For a jaded and wearied man he was no unpleasant companion, and Smith found himself, after a time, looking forward to his visits, and even returning them.

Clever as he undoubtedly was, however, the medical student seemed to detect a dash of insanity in the man. He broke out at times into a high, inflated style of talk which was in contrast with the simplicity of his life.

"It is a wonderful thing," he cried, "to feel that one can command powers of good and of evil – a ministering angel or a demon of vengeance." And again, of Monkhouse Lee, he said, "Lee is a good fellow, an honest fellow, but he is without strength or ambition. He would not make a fit partner for a man with a great enterprise. He would not make a fit partner for me."

At such hints and innuendoes stolid Smith, puffing solemnly at his pipe, would simply raise his eyebrows and shake his head, with little interjections of medical wisdom as to earlier hours and fresher air.

One habit Bellingham had developed of late which Smith knew to be a frequent herald of a weakening mind. He appeared to be forever talking to himself. At late hours of the night, when there could be no visitor with him, Smith could still hear his voice beneath him in a low, muffled monologue, sunk almost to a whisper, and yet very audible in the silence. This solitary babbling annoyed and distracted the student, so that he spoke more than once to his neighbour about it. Bellingham, however, flushed up at the charge, and denied curtly that he had uttered a sound; indeed, he showed more annoyance over the matter than the occasion seemed to demand.

Had Abercrombie Smith had any doubt as to his own ears he had not to go far to find corroboration. Tom Styles, the little wrinkled manservant who had attended to the wants of the lodgers in the turret for a longer time than any man's memory could carry him, was sorely put to it over the same matter.

"If you please, sir," said he, as he tidied down the top chamber one morning, "do you think Mr Bellingham is all right, sir?"

"All right, Styles?"

"Yes sir. Right in his head, sir."

"Why should he not be, then?"

"Well, I don't know, sir. His habits has changed of late. He's not the same man he used to be, though I make free to say that he was never quite one of my gentlemen, like Mr Hastie or yourself, sir. He's took to talkin' to himself something awful. I wonder it don't disturb you. I don't know what to make of him, sir."

"I don't know what business it is of yours, Styles."

"Well, I takes an interest, Mr Smith. It may be forward of me, but I can't help it. I feel sometimes as if I was mother and father to my young gentlemen. It all falls on me when things go wrong and the relations come. But Mr Bellingham, sir. I want to know what it is that walks about his room sometimes when he's out and when the door's locked on the outside."

"Eh? you're talking nonsense, Styles."

"Maybe so, sir; but I heard it more'n once with my own ears."

"Rubbish, Styles."

"Very good, sir. You'll ring the bell if you want me."

Abercrombie Smith gave little heed to the gossip of the old manservant, but a small incident occurred a few days later which left an unpleasant effect upon his mind, and brought the words of Styles forcibly to his memory.

Bellingham had come up to see him late one night, and was entertaining him with an interesting account of the rock tombs of Beni Hassan in Upper Egypt, when Smith, whose hearing was remarkably acute, distinctly heard the sound of a door opening on the landing below.

"There's some fellow gone in or out of your room," he remarked.

Bellingham sprang up and stood helpless for a moment, with the expression of a man who is half incredulous and half afraid.

"I surely locked it. I am almost positive that I locked it," he stammered. "No one could have opened it."

"Why, I hear someone coming up the steps now," said Smith.

Bellingham rushed out through the door, slammed it loudly behind him, and hurried down the stairs. About half-way down Smith heard him stop, and thought he caught the sound of whispering. A moment later the door beneath him shut, a key creaked in a lock, and Bellingham, with beads of moisture upon his pale face, ascended the stairs once more, and re-entered the room:

"It's all right," he said, throwing himself down in a chair. "It was that fool of a dog. He had pushed the door open. I don't know how I came to forget to lock it."

"I didn't know you kept a dog," said Smith, looking very thoughtfully at the disturbed face of his companion.

"Yes, I haven't had him long. I must get rid of him. He's a great nuisance."

"He must be, if you find it so hard to shut him up. I should have thought that shutting the door would have been enough, without locking it."

"I want to prevent old Styles from letting him out. He's of some value, you know, and it would be awkward to lose him."

"I am a bit of a dog-fancier myself," said Smith, still gazing hard at his companion from the corner of his eyes. "Perhaps you'll let me have a look at it."

"Certainly. But I am afraid it cannot be tonight; I have an appointment. Is that clock right? Then I am a quarter of an hour late already. You'll excuse me, I am sure."

He picked up his cap and hurried from the room. In spite of his appointment, Smith heard him re-enter his own chamber and lock his door upon the inside.

This interview left a disagreeable impression upon the medical student's mind. Bellingham had lied to him, and lied so clumsily that it looked as if he had desperate reasons for concealing the truth. Smith knew that his neighbour had no dog. He knew, also, that the step which he had heard upon the stairs was not the step of an animal. But if it were not, then what could it be? There was old Styles's statement about the something which used to pace the room at times when the owner was absent. Could it be a woman? Smith rather inclined to the view. If so, it would mean disgrace and expulsion to Bellingham if it were discovered by the authorities, so that his anxiety and falsehoods might be accounted for. And yet it was inconceivable that an undergraduate could keep a woman in his rooms without being instantly detected. Be the explanation what it might, there was something ugly about it, and Smith determined, as he turned to his books, to discourage all further attempts at intimacy on the part of his soft-spoken and ill-favoured neighbour.

But his work was destined to interruption that night. He had hardly caught up the broken threads when a firm, heavy footfall came three steps at a time from below, and Hastie, in blazer and flannels, burst into the room.

"Still at it!" said he, plumping down into his wonted arm-chair. "What a chap you are to stew! I believe an earthquake might come and knock Oxford into a cocked hat, and you would sit perfectly placid with your books among the ruins. However, I won't bore you long. Three whiffs of baccy, and I am off."

"What's the news, then?" asked Smith, cramming a plug of bird's-eye into his briar with his forefinger.

"Nothing very much. Wilson made 70 for the freshmen against the eleven. They say that they will play him instead of Buddicomb, for Buddicomb is clean off colour. He used to be able to bowl a little, but it's nothing but half-volleys and long hops now."

"Medium right," suggested Smith, with the intense gravity which comes upon a 'varsity man when he speaks of athletics.

"Inclining to fast, with a work from leg. Comes with the arm about three inches or so. He used to be nasty on a wet wicket. Oh, by-the-way, have you heard about Long Norton?"

"What's that?"

"He's been attacked."

"Attacked?"

"Yes, just as he was turning out of the High Street, and within a hundred yards of the gate of Old's."

"But who—"

"Ah, that's the rub! If you said 'what', you would be more gram-matical. Norton swears that it was not human, and, indeed, from the scratches on his throat, I should be inclined to agree with him."

"What, then? Have we come down to spooks?"

Abercrombie Smith puffed his scientific contempt.

"Well, no; I don't think that is quite the idea, either. I am inclined to think that if any showman has lost a great ape lately, and the brute is in these parts, a jury would find a true bill against it. Norton passes that way every night, you know, about the same hour. There's a tree that hangs low over the path – the big elm from Rainy's garden. Norton thinks the thing dropped on him out of the tree. Anyhow, he was nearly strangled by two arms, which, he says, were as strong and as thin as steel bands. He saw nothing; only those beastly arms that tightened and tightened on him. He yelled his head nearly off, and a couple of chaps came running, and the thing went over the wall like a cat. He never got a fair sight of it the whole time. It gave Norton a shake up, I can tell you. I tell him it has been as good as a change at the sea-side for him."

"A garrotter, most likely," said Smith.

"Very possibly. Norton says not; but we don't mind what he says. The garrotter had long nails, and was pretty smart at swinging himself over walls. By-the-way, your beautiful neighbour would be pleased if he heard about it. He had a grudge against Norton, and he's not a man, from what I know of him, to forget his little debts. But hallo, old chap, what have you got in your noddle?"

"Nothing," Smith answered curtly.

He had started in his chair, and the look had flashed over his face which comes upon a man who is struck suddenly by some unpleasant idea.

"You looked as if something I had said had taken you on the raw. By-the-way, you have made the acquaintance of Master B. since I looked in last, have you not? Young Monkhouse Lee told me something to that effect."

"Yes; I know him slightly. He has been up here once or twice."

"Well, you're big enough and ugly enough to take care of yourself. He's not what I should call exactly a healthy sort of Johnny, though, no doubt, he's very clever, and all that. But you'll soon find out for yourself. Lee is all right; he's a very decent little fellow. Well, so long, old chap! I row Mullins for the Vice-Chancellor's pot on Wednesday week, so mind you come down, in case I don't see you before."

Bovine Smith laid down his pipe and turned stolidly to his books once more. But with all the will in the world, he found it very hard to keep his mind upon his work. It would slip away to brood upon the man beneath him, and upon the little mystery which hung round his chambers. Then his thoughts turned to this singular attack of which Hastie had spoken, and to the grudge which Bellingham was said to owe the object of it. The two ideas would persist in rising together in his mind, as though there were some close and intimate connection between them. And yet the suspicion was so dim and vague that it could not be put down in words.

"Confound the chap!" cried Smith, as he shied his book on pathology across the room. "He has spoiled my night's reading, and that's reason enough, if there were no other, why I should steer clear of him in the future."

For ten days the medical student confined himself so closely to his studies that he neither saw nor heard anything of either of the men beneath him. At the hours when Bellingham had been accustomed to visit him, he took care to sport his oak, and though he more than once heard a knocking at his outer door, he resolutely refused to answer it. One afternoon, however, he was descending the stairs when, just as he was passing it, Bellingham's door flew open, and young Monkhouse Lee came out with his eyes sparkling and a dark flush of anger upon his olive cheeks. Close at his heels followed Bellingham, his fat, unhealthy face all quivering with malignant passion.

"You fool!" he hissed. "You'll be sorry."

"Very likely," cried the other. "Mind what I say. It's off! I won't hear of it!"

"You've promised, anyhow."

"Oh, I'll keep that! I won't speak. But I'd rather little Eva was in her grave. Once for all, it's off. She'll do what I say. We don't want to see you again."

So much Smith could not avoid hearing, but he hurried on, for he had no wish to be involved in their dispute. There had been a serious breach between them, that was clear enough, and Lee was going to cause the engagement with his sister to be broken off. Smith thought of Hastie's comparison of the toad and the dove, and was glad to think that the matter was at an end. Bellingham's face when he was in a passion was not pleasant to look upon. He was not a man to whom an innocent girl could be trusted for life. As he walked, Smith wondered languidly what could have caused the quarrel, and what the promise might be which Bellingham had been so anxious that Monkhouse Lee should keep.

It was the day of the sculling match between Hastie and Mullins, and a stream of men were making their way down to the banks of the Isis. A May sun was shining brightly, and the yellow path was barred with the black shadows of the tall elm-trees. On either side the grey colleges lay back from the road, the hoary old mothers of minds looking out from their high, mullioned windows at the tide of young life which swept so merrily past them. Black-clad tutors, prim officials, pale reading men, brown-faced, straw-hatted young athletes in white sweaters or many-coloured blazers, all were hurrying towards the blue winding river which curves through the Oxford meadows.

Abercrombie Smith, with the intuition of an old oarsman, chose his position at the point where he knew that the struggle, if there were a struggle, would come. Far off he heard the hum which announced the start, the gathering roar of the approach, the thunder of running feet, and the shouts of the men in the boats beneath him. A spray of half-clad, deep-breathing runners shot past him, and craning over their shoulders, he saw Hastie pulling a steady thirty-six, while his opponent, with a jerky forty, was a good boat's length behind him. Smith gave a cheer for his friend, and pulling out his watch, was starting off again for his chambers, when he felt a touch upon his shoulder, and found that young Monkhouse Lee was beside him.

"I saw you there," he said, in a timid, deprecating way. "I wanted to speak to you, if you could spare me a half-hour. This cottage is mine. I share it with Harrington of King's. Come in and have a cup of tea."

"I must be back presently," said Smith. "I am hard on the grind at present. But I'll come in for a few minutes with pleasure. I wouldn't have come out only Hastie is a friend of mine."

"So he is of mine. Hasn't he a beautiful style? Mullins wasn't in it. But come into the cottage. It's a little den of a place, but it is pleasant to work in during the summer months."

It was a small, square, white building, with green doors and shutters, and a rustic trellis-work porch, standing back some fifty yards from the river's bank. Inside, the main room was roughly fitted up as a study – deal table, unpainted shelves with books, and a few cheap oleographs upon the wall. A kettle sang upon a spirit-stove, and there were tea things upon a tray on the table.

"Try that chair and have a cigarette," said Lee. "Let me pour you out a cup of tea. It's so good of you to come in, for I know that your time is a good deal taken up. I wanted to say to you that, if I were you, I should change my rooms at once."

"Eh?"

Smith sat staring with a lighted match in one hand and his unlit cigarette in the other.

"Yes; it must seem very extraordinary, and the worst of it is that I cannot give my reasons, for I am under a solemn promise – a very solemn promise. But I may go so far as to say that I don't think Bellingham is a very safe man to live near. I intend to camp out here as much as I can for a time."

"Not safe! What do you mean?"

"Ah, that's what I mustn't say. But do take my advice, and move your rooms. We had a grand row today. You must have heard us, for you came down the stairs."

"I saw that you had fallen out."

"He's a horrible chap, Smith. That is the only word for him. I have had doubts about him ever since that night when he fainted – you remember, when you came down. I taxed him today, and he told me things that made my hair rise, and wanted me to stand in with him. I'm not strait-laced, but I am a clergyman's son, you know, and I think there are some things which are quite beyond the pale. I only thank God that I found him out before it was too late, for he was to have married into my family."

"This is all very fine, Lee," said Abercrombie Smith curtly. "But either you are saying a great deal too much or a great deal too little."

"I give you a warning."

"If there is real reason for warning, no promise can bind you. If I see a rascal about to blow a place up with dynamite no pledge will stand in my way of preventing him."

"Ah, but I cannot prevent him, and I can do nothing but warn you."

"Without saying what you warn me against."

"Against Bellingham."

"But that is childish. Why should I fear him, or any man?"

"I can't tell you. I can only entreat you to change your rooms. You are in danger where you are. I don't even say that Bellingham would wish to injure you. But it might happen, for he is a dangerous neighbour just now."

"Perhaps I know more than you think," said Smith, looking keenly at the young man's boyish, earnest face. "Suppose I tell you that someone else shares Bellingham's rooms."

Monkhouse Lee sprang from his chair in uncontrollable excitement.

"You know, then?" he gasped.

"A woman."

Lee dropped back again with a groan.

"My lips are sealed," he said. "I must not speak."

"Well, anyhow," said Smith, rising, "it is not likely that I should allow myself to be frightened out of rooms which suit me very nicely. It would be a little too feeble for me to move out all my goods and chattels because you say that Bellingham might in some unexplained way do me an injury. I think that I'll just take my chance, and stay where I am, and as I see that it's nearly five o'clock, I must ask you to excuse me."

He bade the young student adieu in a few curt words, and made his way homeward through the sweet spring evening, feeling half-ruffled, half-amused, as any other strong, unimaginative man might who has been menaced by a vague and shadowy danger.

There was one little indulgence which Abercrombie Smith always allowed himself, however closely his work might press upon him. Twice a week, on the Tuesday and the Friday, it was his invariable custom to walk over to Farlingford, the residence of Doctor Plumptree Peterson, situated about a mile and a half out of Oxford. Peterson had been a close friend of Smith's elder brother Francis, and as he was a bachelor, fairly well-to-do, with a good cellar and a better library, his house was a pleasant goal for a man who was in need of a brisk walk. Twice a week, then, the medical student would swing out there along the dark country roads, and spend a pleasant hour in Peterson's comfortable study, discussing, over a glass of old port, the gossip of the 'varsity or the latest developments of medicine or of surgery.

On the day which followed his interview with Monkhouse Lee, Smith shut up his books at a quarter past eight, the hour when he usually started for his friend's house. As he was leaving his room, however, his eyes chanced to fall upon one of the books which Bellingham had lent him, and his conscience pricked him for not having returned it. However repellent the man might be, he should not be treated with discourtesy. Taking the book, he walked downstairs and knocked at his neighbour's door. There was no answer; but on turning the handle he found that it was unlocked. Pleased at the thought of avoiding an interview, he stepped inside, and placed the book with his card upon the table.

The lamp was turned half down, but Smith could see the details of the room plainly enough. It was all much as he had seen it before – the frieze, the animal-headed gods, the hanging crocodile, and the table littered over with papers and dried leaves. The mummy case stood upright against the wall, but the mummy itself was missing. There was no sign of any second occupant of the room, and he felt as he withdrew that he had probably done Bellingham an injustice. Had he a guilty secret to preserve, he would hardly leave his door open so that all the world might enter.

The spiral stair was as black as pitch, and Smith was slowly making his way down its irregular steps, when he was suddenly conscious that something had passed him in the darkness. There was a faint sound, a whiff of air, a light brushing past his elbow, but so slight that he could scarcely be certain of it. He stopped and listened, but the wind was rustling among the ivy outside, and he could hear nothing else.

"Is that you, Styles?" he shouted.

There was no answer, and all was still behind him. It must have been a sudden gust of air, for there were crannies and cracks in the old turret. And yet he could almost have sworn that he heard a footfall by his very side. He had emerged into the quadrangle, still turning the matter over in his head, when a man came running swiftly across the smooth-cropped lawn.

"Is that you, Smith?"

"Hullo, Hastie!"

"For God's sake come at once! Young Lee is drowned! Here's Harrington of King's with the news. The doctor is out. You'll do, but come along at once. There may be life in him."

"Have you brandy?"

"No."

"I'll bring some. There's a flask on my table."

Smith bounded up the stairs, taking three at a time, seized the flask, and was rushing down with it, when, as he passed Bellingham's room, his eyes fell upon something which left him gasping and staring upon the landing.

The door, which he had closed behind him, was now open, and right in front of him, with the lamp-light shining upon it, was the mummy case. Three minutes ago it had been empty. He could swear to that. Now it framed the lank body of its horrible occupant, who stood, grim and stark, with his black shrivelled face towards the door. The form was lifeless and inert, but it seemed to Smith as he gazed that there still lingered a lurid spark of vitality, some faint sign of consciousness in the little eyes which lurked in the depths of the hollow sockets. So astounded and shaken was he that he had forgotten his errand, and was still staring at the lean, sunken figure when the voice of his friend below recalled him to himself.

"Come on, Smith!" he shouted. "It's life and death, you know. Hurry up! Now, then," he added, as the medical student reappeared, "let us do a sprint. It is well under a mile, and we should do it in five minutes. A human life is better worth running for than a pot."

Neck and neck they dashed through the darkness, and did not pull up until panting and spent, they had reached the little cottage by the river. Young Lee, limp and dripping like a broken water-plant, was stretched upon the sofa, the green scum of the river upon his black hair, and a fringe of white foam upon his leaden-hued lips. Beside him knelt his fellow-student Harrington, endeavouring to chafe some warmth back into his rigid limbs.

"I think there's life in him," said Smith, with his hand to the lad's side. "Put your watch glass to his lips. Yes, there's dimming on it. You take one arm, Hastie. Now work it as I do, and we'll soon pull him round."

For ten minutes they worked in silence, inflating and depressing the chest of the unconscious man. At the end of that time a shiver ran through his body, his lips trembled, and he opened his eyes. The three students burst out into an irrepressible cheer.

"Wake up, old chap. You've frightened us quite enough."

"Have some brandy. Take a sip from the flask."

"He's all right now," said his companion Harrington. "Heavens, what a fright I got! I was reading here, and he had gone out for a stroll as far as the river, when I heard a scream and a splash. Out I ran, and by the time I could find him and fish him out, all life seemed to have gone. Then Simpson couldn't get a doctor, for he has a game-leg, and I had to run, and I don't know what I'd have done without you fellows. That's right, old chap. Sit up."

Monkhouse Lee had raised himself on his hands, and looked wildly about him.

"What's up?" he asked. "I've been in the water. Ah, yes; I remember."

A look of fear came into his eyes, and he sank his face into his hands.

"How did you fall in?"

"I didn't fall in."

"How, then?"

"I was thrown in. I was standing by the bank, and something from behind picked me up like a feather and hurled me in. I heard nothing, and I saw nothing. But I know what it was, for all that."

"And so do I," whispered Smith.

Lee looked up with a quick glance of surprise.

"You've learned, then?" he said. "You remember the advice I gave you?"

"Yes, and I begin to think that I shall take it."

"I don't know what the deuce you fellows are talking about," said Hastie, "but I think, if I were you, Harrington, I should get Lee to bed at once. It will be time enough to discuss the why and the wherefore when he is a little stronger. I think, Smith, you and I can leave him alone now. I am walking back to college; if you are coming in that direction, we can have a chat."

But it was little chat that they had upon their homeward path. Smith's mind was too full of the incidents of the evening, the absence of the mummy from his neighbour's rooms, the step that passed him on the stair, the reappearance – the extraordinary, inexplicable reappearance of the grisly thing – and then this attack upon Lee, corresponding so closely to the previous outrage upon another man against whom Bellingham bore a grudge. All this settled in his thoughts, together with the many little incidents which had previously turned him against his neighbour, and the singular circumstances under which he was first called in to him. What had been a dim suspicion, a vague, fantastic conjecture, had suddenly taken form, and stood out in his mind as a grim fact, a thing not to be denied. And yet, how monstrous it was! how unheard of! how entirely beyond all bounds of human experience. An impartial judge, or even the friend who walked by his side, would simply tell him that his eyes had deceived him, that the mummy had been there all the time, that young Lee had tumbled into the river as any other man tumbles into a river, and that a blue pill was the best thing for a disordered liver. He felt that he would have said as much if the positions had been reversed. And yet he could swear that Bellingham was a murderer at heart, and that he wielded a weapon such as no man had ever used in all the grim history of crime.

Hastie had branched off to his rooms with a few crisp and emphatic comments upon his friend's unsociability, and Abercrombie Smith crossed the quadrangle to his corner turret with a strong feeling of repulsion for his chambers and their associations. He would take Lee's advice, and move his quarters as soon as possible, for how could a man study when his ear was ever straining for every murmur or footstep in the room below? He observed, as he crossed over the lawn, that the light was still shining in Bellingham's window, and as he passed up the staircase the door opened, and the man himself looked out at him. With his fat, evil face he was like some bloated spider fresh from the weaving of his poisonous web.

"Good-evening," said he. "Won't you come in?"

"No," cried Smith, fiercely.

"No? You are busy as ever? I wanted to ask you about Lee. I was sorry to hear that there was a rumour that something was amiss with him."

His features were grave, but there was the gleam of a hidden laugh in his eyes as he spoke. Smith saw it, and he could have knocked him down for it.

"You'll be sorrier still to hear that Monkhouse Lee is doing very well, and is out of all danger," he answered. "Your hellish tricks have not come off this time. Oh, you needn't try to brazen it out. I know all about it."

Bellingham took a step back from the angry student, and half-closed the door as if to protect himself.

"You are mad," he said. "What do you mean? Do you assert that I had anything to do with Lee's accident?"

"Yes," thundered Smith. "You and that bag of bones behind you; you worked it between you. I tell you what it is, Master B., they have given up burning folk like you, but we still keep a hangman, and, by George! if any man in this college meets his death while you are here, I'll have you up, and if you don't swing for it, it won't be my fault. You'll find that your filthy Egyptian tricks won't answer in England."

"You're a raving lunatic," said Bellingham.

"All right. You just remember what I say, for you'll find that I'll be better than my word."

The door slammed, and Smith went fuming up to his chamber, where he locked the door upon the inside, and spent half the night in smoking his old briar and brooding over the strange events of the evening.

Next morning Abercrombie Smith heard nothing of his neighbour, but Harrington called upon him in the afternoon to say that Lee was almost himself again. All day Smith stuck fast to his work, but in the evening he determined to pay the visit to his friend Doctor Peterson upon which he had started upon the night before. A good walk and a friendly chat would be welcome to his jangled nerves.

Bellingham's door was shut as he passed, but glancing back when he was some distance from the turret, he saw his neighbour's head at the window outlined against the lamp-light, his face pressed apparently against the glass as he gazed out into the darkness. It was a blessing to be away from all contact with him, if but for a few hours, and Smith stepped out briskly, and breathed the soft spring air into his lungs. The half-moon lay in the west between two Gothic pinnacles, and threw upon the silvered street a dark tracery from the stone-work above. There was a brisk breeze, and light, fleecy clouds drifted swiftly across the sky. Old's was on the very border of the town, and in five minutes Smith found himself beyond the houses and between the hedges of a May-scented Oxfordshire lane.

It was a lonely and little frequented road which led to his friend's house. Early as it was, Smith did not meet a single soul upon his way. He walked briskly along until he came to the avenue gate, which opened into the long gravel drive leading up to Farlingford. In front of him he could see the cosy red light of the windows glimmering through the foliage. He stood with his hand upon the iron latch of the swinging gate, and he glanced back at the road along which he had come. Something was coming swiftly down it.

It moved in the shadow of the hedge, silently and furtively, a dark, crouching figure, dimly visible against the black background. Even as he gazed back at it, it had lessened its distance by twenty paces, and was fast closing upon him. Out of the darkness he had a glimpse of a scraggy neck, and of two eyes that will ever haunt him in his dreams. He turned, and with a cry of terror he ran for his life up the avenue. There were the red lights, the signals of safety, almost within a stone's-throw of him. He was a famous runner, but never had he run as he ran that night.

The heavy gate had swung into place behind him, but he heard it dash open again before his pursuer. As he rushed madly and wildly through the night, he could hear a swift, dry patter behind him, and could see, as he threw back a glance, that this horror was bounding like a tiger at his heels, with blazing eyes and one stringy arm out-thrown. Thank God, the door was ajar. He could see the thin bar of light which shot from the lamp in the hall. Nearer yet sounded the clatter from behind. He heard a hoarse gurgling at his very shoulder. With a shriek he flung himself against the door, slammed and bolted it behind him, and sank half-fainting on to the hall chair.

"My goodness, Smith, what's the matter?" asked Peterson, appearing at the door of his study.

"Give me some brandy!"

Peterson disappeared, and came rushing out again with a glass and a decanter.

"You need it," he said, as his visitor drank off what he poured out for him. "Why, man, you are as white as a cheese."

Smith laid down his glass, rose up, and took a deep breath.

"I am my own man again now," said he. "I was never so unmanned before. But, with your leave, Peterson, I will sleep here tonight, for I don't think I could face that road again except by daylight. It's weak, I know, but I can't help it."

Peterson looked at his visitor with a very questioning eye.

"Of course you shall sleep here if you wish. I'll tell Mrs Burney to make up the spare bed. Where are you off to now?"

"Come up with me to the window that overlooks the door. I want you to see what I have seen."

They went up to the window of the upper hall whence they could look down upon the approach to the house. The drive and the fields on either side lay quiet and still, bathed in the peaceful moonlight.

"Well, really, Smith," remarked Peterson, "it is well that I know you to be an abstemious man. What in the world can have frightened you?"

"I'll tell you presently. But where can it have gone? Ah, now look, look! See the curve of the road just beyond your gate."

"Yes, I see; you needn't pinch my arm off. I saw someone pass. I should say a man, rather thin, apparently, and tall, very tall. But what of him? And what of yourself? You are still shaking like an aspen leaf."

"I have been within hand-grip of the devil, that's all. But come down to your study, and I shall tell you the whole story."

He did so. Under the cheery lamp-light, with a glass of wine on the table beside him, and the portly form and florid face of his friend in front, he narrated, in their order, all the events, great and small, which had formed so singular a chain, from the night on which he had found Bellingham fainting in front of the mummy case until his horrid experience of an hour ago.

"There now," he said as he concluded, "that's the whole black business. It is monstrous and incredible, but it is true."

Doctor Plumptree Peterson sat for some time in silence with a very puzzled expression upon his face.

"I never heard of such a thing in my life, never!" he said at last. "You have told me the facts. Now tell me your inferences."

"You can draw your own."

"But I should like to hear yours. You have thought over the matter, and I have not."

"Well, it must be a little vague in detail, but the main points seem to me to be clear enough. This fellow Bellingham, in his Eastern studies, has got hold of some infernal secret by which a mummy – or possibly only this particular mummy – can be temporarily brought to life. He was trying this disgusting business on the night when he fainted. No doubt the sight of the creature moving had shaken his nerve, even though he had expected it. You remember that almost the first words he said were to call out upon himself as a fool. Well, he got more hardened afterwards, and carried the matter through without fainting. The vitality which he could put into it was evidently only a passing thing, for I have seen it continually in its case as dead as this table. He has some elaborate process, I fancy, by which he brings the thing to pass. Having done it, he naturally bethought him that he might use the creature as an agent. It has intelligence and it has strength. For some purpose he took Lee into his confidence; but Lee, like a decent Christian, would have nothing to do with such a business. Then they had a row, and Lee vowed that he would tell his sister of Bellingham's true character. Bellingham's game was to prevent him, and he nearly managed it, by setting this creature of his on his track. He had already tried its powers upon another man – Norton – towards whom he had a grudge. It is the merest chance that he has not two murders upon his soul. Then, when I taxed him with the matter, he had the strongest reasons for wishing to get me out of the way before I could convey my knowledge to anyone else. He got his chance when I went out, for he knew my habits, and where I was bound for. I have had a narrow shave, Peterson, and it is mere luck you didn't find me on your doorstep in the morning. I'm not a nervous man as a rule, and I never thought to have the fear of death put upon me as it was tonight."

"My dear boy, you take the matter too seriously," said his companion. "Your nerves are out of order with your work, and you make too much of it. How could such a thing as this stride about the streets of Oxford, even at night, without being seen?"

"It has been seen. There is quite a scare in the town about an escaped ape, as they imagine the creature to be. It is the talk of the place."

"Well, it's a striking chain of events. And yet, my dear fellow, you must allow that each incident in itself is capable of a more natural explanation."

"What! even my adventure of to-night?"

"Certainly. You come out with your nerves all unstrung, and your head full of this theory of yours. Some gaunt, half-famished tramp steals after you, and seeing you run, is emboldened to pursue you. Your fears and imagination do the rest."

"It won't do, Peterson; it won't do."

"And again, in the instance of your finding the mummy case empty, and then a few moments later with an occupant, you know that it was lamp-light, that the lamp was half turned down, and that you had no special reason to look hard at the case. It is quite possible that you may have overlooked the creature in the first instance."

"No, no; it is out of the question."

"And then Lee may have fallen into the river, and Norton been garrotted. It is certainly a formidable indictment that you have against Bellingham; but if you were to place it before a police magistrate, he would simply laugh in your face."

"I know he would. That is why I mean to take the matter into my own hands."

"Eh?"

"Yes; I feel that a public duty rests upon me, and, besides, I must do it for my own safety, unless I choose to allow myself to be hunted by this beast out of the college, and that would be a little too feeble. I have quite made up my mind what I shall do. And first of all, may I use your paper and pens for an hour?"

"Most certainly. You will find all that you want upon that side table."

Abercrombie Smith sat down before a sheet of foolscap, and for an hour, and then for a second hour his pen travelled swiftly over it. Page after page was finished and tossed aside while his friend leaned back in his arm-chair, looking across at him with patient curiosity. At last, with an exclamation of satisfaction, Smith sprang to his feet, gathered his papers up into order, and laid the last one upon Peterson's desk.

"Kindly sign this as a witness," he said.

"A witness? Of what?"

"Of my signature, and of the date. The date is the most important. Why, Peterson, my life might hang upon it."

"My dear Smith, you are talking wildly. Let me beg you to go to bed."

"On the contrary, I never spoke so deliberately in my life. And I will promise to go to bed the moment you have signed it."

"But what is it?"

"It is a statement of all that I have been telling you to-night. I wish you to witness it."

"Certainly," said Peterson, signing his name under that of his companion. "There you are! But what is the idea?"

"You will kindly retain it, and produce it in case I am arrested."

"Arrested? For what?"

"For murder. It is quite on the cards. I wish to be ready for every event. There is only one course open to me, and I am determined to take it."

"For Heaven's sake, don't do anything rash!"

"Believe me, it would be far more rash to adopt any other course. I hope that we won't need to bother you, but it will ease my mind to know that you have this statement of my motives. And now I am ready to take your advice and to go to roost, for I want to be at my best in the morning."

Abercrombie Smith was not an entirely pleasant man to have as an enemy. Slow and easy-tempered, he was formidable when driven to action. He brought to every purpose in life the same deliberate resoluteness which had distinguished him as a scientific student. He had laid his studies aside for a day, but he intended that the day should not be wasted. Not a word did he say to his host as to his plans, but by nine o'clock he was well on his way to Oxford.

In the High Street he stopped at Clifford's, the gun-maker's, and bought a heavy revolver, with a box of central-fire cartridges. Six of them he slipped into the chambers, and half-cocking the weapon, placed it in the pocket of his coat. He then made his way to Hastie's rooms, where the big oarsman was lounging over his breakfast, with the *Sporting Times* propped up against the coffee-pot.

"Hullo! What's up?" he asked. "Have some coffee?"

"No, thank you. I want you to come with me, Hastie, and do what I ask you."

"Certainly, my boy."

"And bring a heavy stick with you."

"Hullo!" Hastie stared. "Here's a hunting-crop that would fell an ox."

"One other thing. You have a box of amputating knives. Give me the longest of them."

"There you are. You seem to be fairly on the war trail. Anything else?"

"No; that will do." Smith placed the knife inside his coat, and led the way to the quadrangle. "We are neither of us chickens,

Hastie," said he. "I think I can do this job alone, but I take you as a precaution. I am going to have a little talk with Bellingham. If I have only him to deal with, I won't, of course, need you. If I shout, however, up you come, and lam out with your whip as hard as you can lick. Do you understand?"

"All right. I'll come if I hear you bellow."

"Stay here, then. I may be a little time, but don't budge until I come down."

"I'm a fixture."

Smith ascended the stairs, opened Bellingham's door and stepped in. Bellingham was seated behind his table, writing. Beside him, among his litter of strange possessions, towered the mummy case, with its sale number 249 still stuck upon its front, and its hideous occupant stiff and stark within it. Smith looked very deliberately round him, closed the door, locked it, took the key from the inside, and then stepping across to the fireplace, struck a match and set the fire alight. Bellingham sat staring, with amazement and rage upon his bloated face.

"Well, really now, you make yourself at home," he gasped.

Smith sat himself deliberately down, placing his watch upon the table, drew out his pistol, cocked it, and laid it in his lap. Then he took the long amputating knife from his bosom, and threw it down in front of Bellingham.

"Now, then," said he, "just get to work and cut up that mummy."

"Oh, is that it?" said Bellingham with a sneer.

"Yes, that is it. They tell me that the law can't touch you. But I have a law that will set matters straight. If in five minutes you have not set to work, I swear by the God who made me that I will put a bullet through your brain!"

"You would murder me?"

Bellingham had half risen, and his face was the colour of putty.

"Yes."

"And for what?"

"To stop your mischief. One minute has gone."

"But what have I done?"

"I know and you know."

"This is mere bullying."

"Two minutes are gone."

"But you must give reasons. You are a madman – a dangerous madman. Why should I destroy my own property? It is a valuable mummy."

"You must cut it up, and you must burn it."

"I will do no such thing."

"Four minutes are gone."

Smith took up the pistol and he looked towards Bellingham with an inexorable face. As the second-hand stole round, he raised his hand, and the finger twitched upon the trigger.

"There! there! I'll do it!" screamed Bellingham.

In frantic haste he caught up the knife and hacked at the figure of the mummy, ever glancing round to see the eye and the weapon of his terrible visitor bent upon him. The creature crackled and snapped under every stab of the keen blade. A thick yellow dust rose up from it. Spices and dried essences rained down upon the floor. Suddenly, with a rending crack, its backbone snapped asunder, and it fell, a brown heap of sprawling limbs, upon the floor.

"Now into the fire!" said Smith.

The flames leaped and roared as the dried and tinderlike *débris* was piled upon it. The little room was like the stoke-hole of a steamer and the sweat ran down the faces of the two men; but still the one stooped and worked, while the other sat watching him with a set face. A thick, fat smoke oozed out from the fire, and a heavy smell of burned rosin and singed hair filled the air. In a quarter of an hour a few charred and brittle sticks were all that was left of Lot No. 249.

"Perhaps that will satisfy you," snarled Bellingham, with hate and fear in his little grey eyes as he glanced back at his tormentor.

"No; I must make a clean sweep of all your materials. We must have no more devil's tricks. In with all these leaves! They may have something to do with it."

"And what now?" asked Bellingham, when the leaves also had been added to the blaze.

"Now the roll of papyrus which you had on the table that night. It is in that drawer, I think."

"No, no," shouted Bellingham. "Don't burn that! Why, man, you don't know what you do. It is unique; it contains wisdom which is nowhere else to be found."

"Out with it!"

"But look here, Smith, you can't really mean it. I'll share the knowledge with you. I'll teach you all that is in it. Or, stay, let me only copy it before you burn it!"

Smith stepped forward and turned the key in the drawer. Taking out the yellow, curled roll of paper, he threw it into the fire, and pressed it down with his heel. Bellingham screamed, and grabbed at it; but Smith pushed him back, and stood over it until it was reduced to a formless grey ash.

"Now, Master B.," said he, "I think I have pretty well drawn your teeth. You'll hear from me again, if you return to your old tricks. And now good-morning, for I must go back to my studies."

★

And such is the narrative of Abercrombie Smith as to the singular events which occurred in Old College, Oxford, in the spring of '84. As Bellingham left the university immediately afterwards, and was last heard of in the Soudan, there is no one who can contradict his statement. But the wisdom of men is small, and the ways of nature are strange, and who shall put a bound to the dark things which may be found by those who seek for them?

'THE UNSEEN MAN'S STORY' (1893)

Julian Hawthorne

Julian Hawthorne (1846–1934) was the son of the American novelist Nathaniel Hawthorne and the painter Sophia Peabody Hawthorne. He worked as an engineer and travelled widely in Europe. He produced novels, short stories, essays, and two memoirs of his parents. He wrote detective tales and introduced Gothic elements into his novels and short stories. His novels included *The Professor's Sister* (1888) and *The Golden Fleece* (1892), and he also wrote a book condemning the prison system, *The Subterranean Brotherhood* (1914), after having been sentenced to a year in prison for fraud in 1913.

'The Unseen Man's Story' comes from a collection of portmanteau stories titled *Six Cent Sam's* published in 1893. The book is set in a restaurant known as Six Cent Sam's, because six cents is the price of entry. Our narrator can persuade diners to tell him their stories as long as he buys them a meal, and the collection consists of their peculiar tales. This narrative centres on the figure of Carigliano, who had discovered, some years before, a beautiful Egyptian queen in the inner recess of a tomb and now desires to find her again. The tale is a reincarnation narrative that has much in common with Henry Rider Haggard's *She* (1887), and considers whether love might be a curse.

THE FRIENDS WHOM I EXPECTED TO MEET IN ATHENS HAD been gone two days when I arrived. This was the first of October. I spent three weeks exploring the Grecian capital and its environs, and then I ran across my old college mate, Haymaker, one of the most useful men living, for he knows everyone and everything, has been everywhere, and is as full of enthusiasm and energy as on the day he entered the freshman class.

He asked me whether I had been to Egypt. I said that I had not. "Then now is your time!" was his reply; and taking out a notebook, he proceeded to jot down for me an itinerary, containing such useful details as the names of the best hotels, merchants and dragomen, the things to be seen and the order in which to see them, the number of days or weeks to be spent in various places, the fees to be paid to government officers and others, and the approximate total expenses of a six months trip.

"There you are, my dear boy," said he, handing me the paper, "and when you get home, if you don't confess that your winter on the Nile was the pleasantest experience of your travels, I'll stand a dinner for a dozen at Delmonico's, and you shall make a speech!" As we shook hands at parting, he added, "Mind and don't forget to look up old Carigliano. Charming old maniac – worth all the rest of the trip put together!"

I embarked for Alexandria a few days later, and on the fifth of November we sighted the Pharos, in a temperature of seventy-eight degrees, and in the midst of a colour, a movement, a picturesqueness, and a strangeness, such as are to be met with only in the East.

The wharves crowded with shipping, the ports, the villas and the palaces, glowed in the calm clear light of the oriental afternoon. I landed at the custom house in a perfect Babel and jostled by a crowd of dark-hued faces, bare legs, and scanty but gorgeously fine clothing. In a whirl of gesticulation, broken English, and rapacious, good-humoured excitement, I had my trunks examined and was driven (following Haymaker's advice) to the Hotel Europe. There I secured the services of Ahmed Hassan as dragoman, and my Egyptian campaign began.

Everybody has made the same campaign, or has read accounts of it, so that I will not enlarge upon my individual experiences. I stayed in Alexandria a week, and then took the train through the green antiquity of immemorial Egypt, as far as Cairo. There I remained a month – long enough to begin to feel in harmony with the oriental idea. In other words, I began to get used to turbans, to nakedness, to the union of inconceivable squalor and splendour; to streets a yard wide crammed with donkeys, camels, merchandise, and the population of a score of barbarous countries; to the awful repose of the living desert, and to the immortal simplicity of the mysterious pyramids and of the Sphinx. I became accustomed to a sky from which no rain ever fell, and to a valley whose verdure was derived from a spring which no man had ever discovered. I grew familiar with the cry of the muezzin from the minarets, and with the calm and shadowy interior of the domed and splendid mosques. Egypt is the stimulus and the despair of adjectives! I welcomed the unveiled sunshine to the marrow of my bones, and thought of Cleopatra and the Pharaohs. There is no other land so strange as this, nor any in which the stranger comes to feel himself prehistorically at home. At last I hired a *dahabeah*, and, on the fifteenth of December, I began the ascent of the Nile, not sorry to exchange the jolt and wriggle of the donkey-back for the smooth glide and musical ripple of the Egyptian sail-boat.

Now ensued three weeks of enforced but delicious inactivity, during which I had leisure to digest what I had seen, and to prepare myself for what might be to come. Though the Nile flows out of the dead past, it is itself anything but lifeless. The current runs rapidly; boats flit in all directions, impelled by oar or sail; voices are continually heard, in song, shout, and laughter; wild geese sit on the long sand strip or fly honking overhead. Cairo, with its silvery domes and minarets, sinks slowly beneath the northern horizon; on our left, beyond the desert, are the notched hills of Mokattam; on our right, the wide valley, green with abundant grain, beautiful with rows of palms, noisy with the shrill voices of dark-robed women clustered on the banks, populous with mud villages and squatting, staring Arabs. Here and there a *shadoof* laboriously irrigates the plain, or, higher up the river, the creaking *sakia* not less primitively fulfils its office. The days are a long glory of sunshine; the nights, a soft splendor of stars. We are sailing into the earliest twilight of human history; but earth and sky were never clearer or more bright. We lose all sense of time; the mere luxury of existence obliterates it; what is a lifetime compared with the immeasurable ages which gaze down upon us from the margins of this mighty stream?

It was at the close of the first week in January of the new year, that, coming on deck one morning early, I saw opening before me the great valley of Thebes. It was a splendid morning – it seemed to me even more splendid than usual. A couple of vultures, sitting on the high western bank, rose in the air and sailed away towards the Lybian hills, whose clear grey outline cut the purple sky. Were they going to seek for food in the tombs there? The plain, of vast extent, and green as the emerald, is unequally divided by the broad, swift running of the Nile; of the ancient city nothing is yet visible; though, with a good telescope, one might perhaps discern in the southern distance the forms of the twin *colossi* of the Pharaoh Amunoph, and the matchless obelisk of Hatasoo Thothmes. Nevertheless, a glow of memory and anticipation came upon me; for here was the scene of a civilisation more sumptuous and earlier than any in recorded history. For each stalk of grain that waves now in the northern breeze, there was once a living man, with ancestors before him and a posterity to follow; and the energy, power, and magnificence of their existence has dwarfed and made pallid all that came after them. As we continued to move slowly up the stream, the world-famous ruins loomed larger and more distinct; and mud villages of the present inhabitants, clustered near or upon these gigantic fragments, were like the nests of swallows under the eaves of a cathedral. It seemed as if no being of less stature and ability than Memnon himself could have hewn out and piled together such immeasurable miracles of stone.

I had made my arrangements for a prolonged stay in Thebes; and as inns are not plentiful in that region, I made a hotel, and a very comfortable one, of my *dahabeah*. We made fast near the bank, close to the temple of Luxor, and while I ate my dinner Ahmed Hassan engaged in a personal conflict with fifty or a hundred Arabs, who wanted to sell the *howadji* all the spoils of Egypt, from the time of Menes, the eternal, down to the latest Ptolemy. Presently I came on deck, and getting into our boat, Ahmed and I were rowed across to the western shore, where donkeys and more Arabs were awaiting us, and prepared to take a preliminary gallop in the direction of Karnak, a mile or two down the river.

Among the Arabs I noticed one man, who, though with them, was evidently not of them. He was tall, and of dignified bearing, and his full beard, which was nearly white, fell down over his breast. His eyes were blue, and very bright; their glance was penetrating, but restless. His complexion, though tanned by the sun, had been originally fair; his broad forehead was partly concealed by a white turban, and he wore full Turkish trousers gathered at the knee, while over his close-fitting undergarment was thrown a flowing cloak, which he gathered about him as he stood. In spite of his oriental costume, however, I was quite sure this man was not of Eastern birth; and the manner in which he had scrutinised my face and appearance seemed to indicate that his interest in me, if he had any, was of another kind than would be felt by a real son of the desert.

"Who is that?" I inquired of Ahmed, as we jogged along.

"He? Oh, he ver strange man, come here long time, tink from Europe. Five year – ten year – allays see he; he ver wise – say he crazy."

"What is his name?"

"Oh, not know right name; call he Kehr-el-Lans Effendi. He go much tomba; mebbe hunt antika; but not know."

"Does he live here?"

"Tink he live Temple Medinet Abou. We go bimeby – mebbe find he. Plenty time talk he."

There was an impression on my mind that I had heard something about this mysterious personage; but it was too vague at the moment, to enable me to analyse it; and the overpowering spectacle of Karnak effectually put the matter out of my head for the time being. But, a few days afterward, we visited Medinet Abou; and while I was endeavouring to determine, with the aid of Ahmed and a guide book, which portion of the ruins was the later work, and which that of the sister of Thothmes, the same dignified figure that I had seen on the river bank suddenly appeared from behind a neighbouring column; and after saluting me gravely, proceeded, with much courtesy, and in the French tongue, to enlighten me on the question. It was soon evident that he was profoundly versed in the lore of ancient Egypt; and I was particularly struck with his manner when mentioning Hatasoo Thothmes; or, as he called her, Queen Amunuhet. His voice, when pronouncing her name, was lowered to a reverential murmur; and he passed the palm of his hand down his face from his forehead to his chin – an oriental gesture signifying homage.

"She was a remarkable woman," I ventured to observe.

"There was none like her," he replied. "She had many subjects, many worshippers; and one at least," he added, with a sigh, and clasping his hands on his heart, "still survives, and walks the earth in the likeness of a man!"

At this moment I was visited by an inspiration of memory; the recollection of my friend Haymaker's injunction flashed over me. "Pardon me if the question is indiscreet," I said, "but have I not the honour of addressing Monsieur Carigliano?"

He bowed slightly. "I once bore that name," he replied. "But, for twenty years, since I have lived here, it has been as a mask which I have cast aside. My true name might, perhaps, be found on one of these stones; but it has never been uttered by living lips."

"So this," I thought to myself, "is Haymaker's 'charming old maniac!' His acquaintance certainly seems to be worth cultivating. To hear him talk, one would suppose he had enjoyed personal relations with a princess who died thirty-five hundred years ago! That is a form of mania that ought to be enquired into." Aloud I said, "I wish I might hope to enjoy the benefit of further intercourse with you. I am deeply interested in all that appertains to the history of the Pharaohs; and especially," I added, meeting his eyes, "in the age of the great Thothmes."

The change of expression that lightened his face showed me that I had touched a favourable chord. "It is a long time," he said, "since I have held converse with a member of what are called the civilised races; but I feel moved to speak to you: and, since you express interest in a matter nearly affecting me, it will give me pleasure to oblige you. If you will come to this spot tomorrow evening alone, I will take you to my abode, and do my best to give you satisfaction." I thanked him heartily, and promised to be on hand; he bowed, again saluted me gravely, and, retiring, was soon lost to sight behind the huge, thickly planted columns of the wondrous temple.

When I explained to Ahmed the purport of our conversation, he strongly advised me to have nothing to do with the adventure. He declared that "Kehr-el-Lans Effendi" was a powerful magician, and was quite capable of putting me under a spell and shutting me up for a thousand years in some forgotten tomb of the hills. He was often heard conversing in an unknown tongue with spectres; and was suspected of kidnapping the babies of the neighbouring poor people, and offering them up as sacrifices to the heathen deities, whom he was supposed to worship. At the very least, Ahmed added, this redoubtable wizard would in some way compel me to pay for my escape from his clutches with an immense sum of money. In spite of these warnings, however, I held to my purpose; and about sunset the next day, I presented myself, alone, at the appointed spot. In a few minutes Carigliano made his appearance; and I followed him through the ruins for a distance of perhaps fifty yards. I then saw him stoop, and push against a slab of granite, set in an apparently solid portion of the temple wall. It moved, as if upon a hidden pivot, and disclosed a flight of steps leading downward. The darkness was intense; and for a moment I hesitated. Having come so far, however, I was determined to see the end of the adventure, and I accordingly descended. I heard his footsteps preceding me; and then a light flashed up, and I found myself in a subterranean chamber which bore evidence of being used as an abode. It was of fair height, and about twenty feet in length by fifteen in width. The walls were of polished stone, engraved with pictures and hieroglyphics. It contained a mattress, and various simple but sufficient appliances of life. Everything was neat and clean, and the air was pure, though the method of ventilation was not apparent. The light proceeded from a large lamp of antique design which depended from the ceiling.

Some cushions at the head of the room served as a divan, and upon this Carigliano motioned me to be seated, while he brought forward two long-stemmed pipes, which we lighted and smoked. For some time our conversation was laconic, and on indifferent topics. But at length my entertainer took the pipe from his lips, fixed his eyes upon me, and spoke as follows:

"I have admitted you to this chamber, whither no other guest has ever penetrated, not merely for the sake of gratifying your curiosity, but because the time has come when – if ever – the history of my life must be unfolded. Tomorrow it will be twenty years since the event occurred which revealed to me my destiny; and yours are the last mortal eyes that will behold me. Before I vanish forever, I desire to leave some testimony behind me as to my past and my future.

"I came to Egypt at twenty-eight years of age, as an *attaché* of a scientific expedition sent here by the French government. My technical duties were to decipher and to take copies of the more important hieroglyphic writings and inscriptions in the tombs and temples. But I had, for a number of years previous, given my whole attention to the study of ancient Egyptian subjects, and was, even at that time, more profoundly versed than any other scholar in its problems and mysteries. I had always felt an especial and peculiar inclination toward these researches; it seemed to me far more like recalling what I had once known, than as breaking absolutely new ground in knowledge. The scenes and persons of the days of the Pharaohs were as vivid in my imagination as the memories of yesterday; I spoke their language and I comprehended their wisdom. And when, for the first time, I breathed the air of the Nile valley, and felt the sand of the desert beneath my feet, and beheld the mighty monuments of a vanished past, a voice in my heart seemed to tell me that this was no foreign country, but my home.

"It was here in Thebes that my duties chiefly lay, and it was here, also, that the mysterious home-feeling was most strong. From the first, I needed no guide; each step I took was on familiar ground; and as I gazed over the valley of ruins, some secret faculty of my mind reconstructed the scenes of four thousand years ago, and I saw once more the splendid city throbbing with life and sparkling with wealth, and witnessed the triumph of the kings, the processions and sacrifices of the priests, the glittering array of the soldiers, and the throng and tumult of the people. It was a waking dream, but it made the reality of the present seem unsubstantial. And ever and anon – especially when sauntering about the ruins of this temple – I was sensible of another feeling: a strange tremor and yearning of the heart, which I could not understand, yet which, could I have fathomed it, would, I thought, have proved the key whereby all else that was perplexing might be unlocked.

"One morning I arose early, and took my sketching materials, intending to spend the day in one or other of the great tombs that honeycomb the western hills. A foot-path leads over the ridge beyond Medinet Abou – a track of powdered limestone – and so, by a steep descent, brings one to the naked and desolate gorges beyond, where the Pharaohs were entombed. On reaching the summit of this ridge, I turned, and for a few moments gazed back on the wide valley of the Egyptian capital. The sun had just risen; its light flashed across the long curve of the Nile, and touched the lips of Memnon, as he sat eternal on his throne, his shadow falling far behind him over the green expanse of waving grain at his base. Involuntarily I bent forward, as if to catch the music of the response which, as tradition says, the colossal deity was wont to make to the salutation of the sun-god. And, in truth, a deep, melodious sound seemed to resound in the air – though whether proceeding from Memnon's lips, or from the heavens above, or from the depths of my own breast, I could not tell; a sound that resolved itself into words, saying, 'Pass on, thou favoured one, and fear not! Thy queen awaits thee!' And down I rode into the shadow and silence of the abyss of tombs.

"Threading my way among loose boulders, and down a narrow and devious track, I reached the bottom of the descent, and wound along the length of the ravine. It had been my first intention to enter one of the tombs of the kings; but I was impelled to press onward, and at length I entered another gorge, lying further toward the heart of the hills, which, as I knew, had been set apart for the interment of the queens of Egypt. Here, a sense of solitude more profound than any I had before experienced came over me; but accompanying it, and even arising out of it, was a feeling of being conducted and inspired by some intelligence or personality not my own. I fell into an abstracted mood, in which I scarcely noted the way I was going; until at length I came involuntarily to a pause, and, as it were, awoke, and gazed around me.

"I was in a region so wild and savage, so naked and desolate, that it seemed as if no human being, before me, could ever have penetrated there. Rocky walls, wholly devoid of vegetation, arose on each side, and climbed heavenward, as if they would meet in the depths of the purple sky. Loose fragments of limestone hung on the ledges of the precipices, or lay in confused masses on the narrow floor of the tortuous valley. The sun, now some hours high, flung its white luster on the western walls, yet only the upper portion of them was illuminated. No sign of life, not even an insect or a bird, disturbed the stillness; no sound was audible but the hoof-tramps of the ass that I bestrode, which were echoed in exaggerated volume from the imprisoning cliffs. On my left hand was a vertical face of rock, the base seeming to rest upon a mounded slope, composed of detached and shattered blocks. I dismounted and clambered up this ascent, and then beheld, to my surprise, the distinct outlines of a picture graven into the limestone. It covered a space about four feet in length and breadth; and from its unusual situation, as well as from its remarkable intrinsic character, it strongly fixed my attention. It represented the body of a woman, apparently of high rank, lying on a pallet; and as I judged from certain accessories, about to be prepared for embalming. But beside her stood the figure of a man in soldier's garb, who, with outstretched hand, seemed about to take the woman's heart from her bosom. Some of the details of the picture indicated that it dated back as far as the time of Thothmes – the period of the Hebrew Exodus; and yet the cutting of the lines was as sharp and undefaced as if the artist had but just given the finishing stroke of the chisel.

"I lost no time in setting up my easel, and, preparing to make a careful copy of this picture, I sat on a detached fragment of stone, with my right hand toward the face of the cliff; and in drawing I rested my hand on the mahl-stick, the end of which, for convenience, I rested against the design I was copying. As, from time to time, I had occasion to alter the position of my hand and of the mahl-stick, it happened that its point at length rested upon that part of the picture where was represented the heart of the woman upon the pallet. At the same moment I was conscious of a slight jar, causing me to make a false stroke; and the mahl-stick slipped from its place. I looked up and saw – what I had not noticed before – that the entire surface of the stone upon which the picture was engraven was sunk some distance below the surrounding surface of the rock. The depression was slight, not more than half an inch; but as I looked, it became gradually deeper and yet more deep; it was now two inches and still increasing. In the course of a few minutes, the pictured stone had receded as much as a foot, with a steady but slowly accelerating movement. Overcome with wonder, I continued to gaze at this singular phenomenon, until the stone was nearly out of sight. The direction it took was slightly inclined upward; and I perceived that the polished surfaces upon which it travelled were finely grooved, the grooves corresponding with ridges in the moving stone, which fitted into the former.

"By this time I had in some degree recovered my self-possession, and resolved to pursue the investigation of this marvel. I had brought a small lamp with me, for use in the tombs, and this I now lighted, and holding it in my hand, I crawled into the cavity left by the receding stone. This cavity was now about ten feet in depth, the sides as smooth as glass, and ascending at an angle of about twenty degrees. But after following it a little further, there was a sudden enlargement to double the former dimensions. I was now able to stand upright, and to walk on a passage beside the moving stone, instead of following in its track, as heretofore. It continued to travel upward beside me; and I now discovered that the immediate cause of its ascent was a fine but strong cable of bronze, which was fastened to its inner side, and was being drawn inward by some force beyond. The push which I had accidentally given with the mahl-stick to that particular spot in the picture which represented the woman's heart, had probably given the impetus which set the machinery in motion.

"After proceeding up the slippery incline for perhaps a hundred feet, I came to a level space, reaching to an unknown extent beyond, above, and on each hand. And here, by the dusky light of my lamp, I saw the semblance of a human figure, slowly and steadily turning the handle of a machine resembling a windlass, to the body of which the bronze cable was attached, and around which it was being wound. The figure wore the Egyptian head-dress and garb, and his face and limbs were of a brown hue; but so regular and rigid were his movements, and so imperfect was the light that I could not decide whether he was indeed a human being, or only himself a cunningly wrought part of the machine. I spoke to him but he returned no answer; and my own voice died away in a hollow whisper. As I stood there, the stone which had closed the entrance to the passage reached the summit of the ascent; and the figure, after putting a check in the cog of his wheel, sank down beside it, with his face upon his knees, and his hands clasped around his ankles, and became motionless in the attitude which, perhaps, had been undisturbed till now for more than thirty centuries.

"Shading my lamp with my hand, I moved along the walls of the chamber, which lay transversely across the ascending passage

by which I had come. It was lined with white stucco on which were
painted in brilliant colours such scenes of the daily life and habits
of the Egyptians, as are customarily found on the walls of tombs.
At length I came to an opening nearly opposite that by which
I had entered; a corridor extending further into the mountain.
After following it for awhile, I was brought to another corridor at
right angles to it, going in both directions. I chose the turn to the
left, and soon came to another turn, which descended for a long
distance, and, just as it seemed to come to an end, admitted me
into a hall much larger than the first, and more richly decorated.
Here were represented the various ceremonies of the dead, the
liturgies relating to their travels in the realm of shades, together
with astronomical designs, and figures of monsters and of deities.
In the centre of the room, moreover, stood a large sarcophagus,
richly engraved and ornamented, but empty. Here my explorations
had apparently come to an end, for there was no visible outlet from
the chamber. Accustomed as I was, however, to the concealments
of these gigantic excavations, I felt assured that the end was not
yet; and when I applied my shoulder to the upper end of the sarcophagus, it yielded to the pressure, and sliding forward, disclosed
an oblong aperture in the floor beneath it, into which I unhesitat-
ingly descended; and after wandering blindly for some minutes,
first in one direction and then in another, I discerned a gleam of
light in front of me, and, the next moment, entered an apartment
the solemn grandeur of which seemed a fitting culmination of all
that had preceded it.

"In the centre of the lofty ceiling was a representation of the
winged sun; and from it, or through it, proceeded a soft but powerful light, like that of phosphorescence in its nature, though bright
enough to fill every corner of the vast hall with a clear radiance.

The walls glowed with colour, and here were the sacred figures of Isis and Osiris, of Horus, of Athor, Anubis, Ptah, and Nofre Atmos. But these things scarcely impressed themselves on my senses, for I was arrested by a far greater marvel. The figures on the walls were but shadows; but the floor of this mighty chamber was populous with forms of concrete substance; with men and women who breathed and moved and lived. They lived, and yet it scarcely seemed like life, so slow, so almost imperceptible were their movements. It was as if the space of an ordinary lifetime had been drawn out, for them, to the measure of myriad years; that days were to them as moments, and years as hours, and centuries as years; that while the breath came and went through their nostrils, a moon might wax and wane; and that the lifting of their faces was as the turning of the earth upon its axis. It was, perhaps, the dry, unchanging atmosphere of this region, hidden deep beneath the heart of the mountain, and separated from the world without for so many hundred years, that had wrought this torpor in them; I myself had become already sensible of an alteration in the beating of my pulse and a subtle lethargy in my movements. At first, as I looked upon this strange assemblage, they seemed each one to have paused, in the accomplishment of some characteristic act. One swarthy figure was shaping a neck-let of gold brought from the deadly mines of Ethiopia; another, with mallet uplifted, was chiseling a statue; still another, held in his hand a *scarabaeus*, which he was about to polish. In another place, a man was in the act of blowing glass; near him was one with colours and a brush, making as if to add another touch to his picture; others were in the attitude of turning the potter's wheel, of breaking flax, or of playing draughts. In one corner of the room were a group of women seated on the ground, with a ball which they seemed about to toss from one to another. But, as I contemplated them, their apparent insensibility resolved itself into motion, and I saw that they were not carven images, but that the hearts which had begun to beat when Moses was an infant, still sent the blood through their veins, though in pulses as measured as the tides of ocean.

"Meanwhile, my presence was seemingly unnoticed; no eye had met mine, and I was as apparently invisible to them as if the abyss of ages that lay between us had been as wide in space as it was in time. But, as I paused near the entrance of the hall, uncertain what to do, my ears caught a faint sound of solemn music; a portal of stone at the opposite extremity of the vista was slowly unfolded and from it issued, with lingering but majestic step, a stately procession. First came boys, bearing censers in the form of a golden arm, in the hollowed hand of which burned fragrant balls of *kyphi*, diffusing a heavy perfume. Then followed an array of tall and grave-looking men in white robes, and wearing on their foreheads the sacred ostrich feather, emblem of truth, and sign of the initiated priest. Next came a bevy of attendants, men and women, brilliantly attired, some carrying vessels of Phoenician glass that sparkled in the light; and one who bore on high and shook aloft the golden sistrum, with its bars and rings, emblem of Venus. Finally, borne in a litter on the shoulders of twelve Nubian slaves, appeared a woman, at the sight of whom my heart stood still and my breath failed me. She was dusky as the Nile at evening, and beautiful with a beauty that belongs to the morning of the world. Her eyes were long, black, and brilliant; and their gaze was royal. The outline of her smooth cheeks was oval, and her features were the features of the Pharaohs, but softened with all the loveliness of a woman. Above her low, broad forehead was placed the stately head-dress of an Egyptian princess; and, from her left temple, a long black braid, plaited with golden threads, hung down to her feet, as a sign of her royal lineage. Her robe was purple, and of a tissue so delicate that the contours of her perfect form were discernible through its silky folds. Round her neck, and resting upon her bosom was a broad collar woven of pearls and precious stones; her arms were encircled by bracelets of massive gold, and in her girdle were woven turquoises from Serbal, talismans of good fortune. At her right hand crouched a monkey, sacred to Thoth, the god of her race; and on her left a white cat from Persia, in whose long silky fur the slender fingers of the princess were hidden.

"When the bearers of the litter reached the centre of the hall, beneath the illuminated semblance of the winged sun, they knelt and slowly lowered their burden to the floor. Then, with a leisurely movement, the princess arose, and stood erect to her full height, and her eyes slowly fixed themselves upon mine, for I remained opposite to her, in a vacant space alone; and a spell seemed to be upon me, so that I could move neither hand nor foot, nor remove my gaze from her transcendent countenance; yet it seemed to me a countenance that I had seen before, and had known well, and passionately loved. And it seemed to me that I was not myself, or that a truer self than I had hitherto known looked through my eyes and breathed through my nostrils.

"Then the princess spoke, in slow and measured tones, and in the clear tongue of ancient Egypt that I knew and remembered as my own.

"'Man,' she said, 'art thou he for whom I have waited?'

"And I answered her, 'I am Pantour, the son of Amosis.'

"And she said, 'Dost thou know me?'

"And I answered, 'Thou art Amunuhet the queen, the sister of Pharaoh; thou art she who didst build the temple and the obelisk, and didst perform many mighty works.'

"And she said, 'Speak on, Pantour, and tell what thou knowest.'

"And I said, 'O queen, I loved thee; and thou didst deign to return my love. And our love was hidden, that none might know it. And in the midst of our love death came to thee. And when thy body was prepared for the embalmers, I stood beside thee, and there was none to see me. And I put forth my hand and took thy heart out of thy bosom; because, I said, "My heart is hers: let me, therefore, keep her heart in the stead of it." And I kept thy heart, and none knew what I had done. But when death overtook me also, I called my friend to me and charged him, saying: "When I am dead, take thou my heart from my bosom and put in the place of it the heart of the Queen Amunuhet, whom I loved, but my heart thou shalt burn upon the altar of Osiris." And he swore to me to do as I had commanded. And in that same hour my spirit departed.'

"Then the queen answered, 'Thou hast said. Hear, now, what things have befallen me. For when I entered into Kar-Neter, Osiris appeared to me, and mine eyes were dazzled, and my limbs were as if without life; neither could I speak, or eat food, or do battle with my enemies. But I prayed to the gods, and behold, my strength returned to me; and holding the sacred beetle above my head, I entered into Hades. Then did Typhon assail me with many monsters, and I fought sore combats with them; and I had been overcome, but that Nir gave me to eat of the tree of life, and the Divine Light instructed me. So I went on, and passed through many changes, and at last I entered once more into the body from which I had gone forth; and then, undergoing many trials and tempta- tions, I sailed down the river that flows under the foundations of the world, and gained the Elysian fields. Then was I brought to the great judgment hall, where sat Osiris and the two and forty assessors, and to them I confessed both my evil and my good. But when they brought the scales of justice, with the ostrich feather of truth in the balance, and would have weighed my heart against the ostrich feather, behold the heart was gone out of my bosom. Then the judges took counsel together and said, "Thou shalt wait three thousand years, and half a thousand years, and he who took thy heart from thee shall come before thee; and if he will deliver it up to thee again, thou shalt enter into the bliss of Osiris." Now, therefore, the time is come. Deliver back to me that which thou didst take from me; and when thou hast fulfilled thy course, and conquered Typhon, and overcome temptations, thou shalt afterward be united to me in the kingdom of Osiris, and the bliss of us twain shall be unto everlasting.'

"Thus spake the Queen Amunuhet; and when she had made an end of speaking, she sat on her throne, and waved her hand to the chief of priests, that he should take me, and lay me on the altar, and pluck her heart out of my breast. But then great fear came upon me, insomuch that I turned and fled away from before her. My limbs were as though sheathed in lead, and though I strove mightily, my steps were slow, for the air of the tomb had entered into my lungs, and all power of swiftness was gone from me. But the chief of the priests, and the other priests, and the attendants, pursued me; and though their steps also were slow, yet, by reason of the air that had entered the tomb from the outer world, they gathered ever new strength and swiftness; so that it seemed as if I must be taken. Nevertheless, striving with all my might, I gained the upper platform where sat he who worked upon the windlass that lifted the stone from the entrance; and even then the hands of my pursuers were upon me. And he of the windlass arose, and loosed the check from the wheel, and the great stone slid down the incline toward its place. But I also plunged downward, and came in front of the stone as it descended, and was swept out before it, and the entrance was closed behind me; and I fell, and knew no more."

Here Carigliano paused, and bending forward as he sat, hid his face upon his knees. During several minutes there was silence; for he had spoken toward the close in a strain of exalted earnestness and passion; and the spell of his words was upon me. No doubt, the man must be mad; but his hallucination was so remarkable, and his expression of it so eloquent that, for the time being, I could not regain the equilibrium of my judgment.

"It was a narrow escape!" I said, at last.

He sat erect, passed his hand over his forehead, and sighed. "It was a dastardly escape!" he replied; "and for these twenty years past I have repented it. I was found that evening by some wandering Arab, and taken back to Luxor. For some weeks I was ill with a fever; when I recovered, I tried in vain to find again the pictured stone; I have never set eyes upon it since. But, after a year of fruitless quest, Queen Amunuhet came to me one night in a dream, and told me that if, after waiting twenty years, I was prepared to make the restitution that she had demanded of me, the place of her tomb should be once more revealed to me, and I might enter in and deliver myself up to the altar. Tomorrow the period of trial will be fulfilled, and I shall be seen of men no more. You are the last to hear my voice, and to look upon my face. Henceforth, Pantour, the son of Amosis, belongs to the dead alone."

Soon after I returned to America, my friend Haymaker and I dined at Delmonico's; but I paid for the dinner.

"By the way," he exclaimed, as we sat over our coffee, "did you ever run across that fellow Carigliano?"

"Yes," I replied.

"Charming old maniac, isn't he?" continued my friend.

"He was a remarkable person, certainly."

"I think of running over to Egypt next winter, and I will make a point of looking him up again," said Haymaker, lighting a cigar.

"You won't find him," I answered. "The day after I last saw him he disappeared, and has never been seen or heard of since. But, from certain indications, it was thought he had wandered into the ruins of the tombs of the queens; probably he found his way into one of them and never got out again. He had related some of his history to me the day before; and certain hints that he let fall have made me suspect that he had a foreshadowing of what was to befall him."

"Poor fellow," said Haymaker. "What a pity! Romantic, too! Told you his story, did he? What was it?"

"It's eleven o'clock," said I; "I'm going to bed."

"Or you might write it out," continued my friend, as we put on our hats. "You're always writing things; and I dare say you might find somebody to print it."

'THE STORY OF BAELBROW' (1898)

Kate and Hesketh Prichard

Kate Prichard (1851–1935) and Hesketh Prichard (1876–1922) were mother and son and they collaborated on a series of tales about a psychic detective named Flaxman Low, which were published in two series in *Pearson's Monthly Magazine* in 1898 and 1899 under the nom de plumes of E. and H. Heron. Hesketh Prichard would later write a popular account of his travels to and around South America (in which he was in part accompanied by his mother). His life reads a little like a boy's own adventure story. He was a big game hunter, played first-class cricket for the MCC and Hampshire, and while serving as a major in World War I helped to revolutionise strategies for snipers. During the war he was awarded the Military Cross and the Distinguished Service Order.

'The Story of Baelbrow' was published as the fourth story in 'Real Ghost Stories, featuring Flaxman Low', in *Pearson's Monthly Magazine* in April 1898. The tale is unusual as the "ghost" turns out to be a very different, but very familiar, monster who inhabits the form of a mummy. This complexly formed creature troubles the inhabitants of a 300-year-old family mansion. The extraordinary violence with which the creature is dispatched might seem excessive, but can be read as reflecting some of the aggressive British attitudes towards Egypt that are found during the period.

I T IS A MATTER FOR REGRET THAT SO MANY OF MR FLAXMAN Low's reminiscences should deal with the darker episodes of his career. Yet this is almost unavoidable, as the more purely scientific and less strongly marked cases would not, perhaps, contain the same elements of interest for the general public, however valuable and instructive they might be to the expert student. It has also been considered better to choose the completer cases, those that ended in something like satisfactory proof, rather than the many instances where the thread broke off abruptly amongst surmisings, which it was never possible to subject to convincing tests.

North of a low-lying strip of country on the East Anglian coast, the promontory of Bael Ness thrusts out a blunt nose into the sea. On the Ness, backed by pinewoods, stands a square, comfortable stone mansion, known to the countryside as Baelbrow. It has faced the east winds for close upon three hundred years, and during the whole period has been the home of the Swaffam family, who were never in any wise put out of conceit of their ancestral dwelling by the fact that it had always been haunted. Indeed, the Swaffams were proud of the Baelbrow Ghost, which enjoyed a wide notoriety, and no one dreamt of complaining of its behaviour until Professor Jungvort, of Nuremburg, laid information against it, and sent an urgent appeal for help to Mr Flaxman Low.

The Professor, who was well acquainted with Mr Low, detailed the circumstances of his tenancy of Baelbrow, and the unpleasant events that had followed thereupon.

It appeared that Mr Swaffam, senior, who spent a large portion of his time abroad, had offered to lend his house to the Professor for the summer season. When the Jungvorts arrived at Baelbrow, they were charmed with the place. The prospect, though not very varied, was at least extensive, and the air exhilarating. Also the Professor's daughter enjoyed frequent visits from her betrothed – Harold Swaffam – and the Professor was delightfully employed in overhauling the Swaffam library.

The Jungvorts had been duly told of the ghost, which lent distinction to the old house, but never in any way interfered with the comfort of the inmates. For some time they found this description to be strictly true, but with the beginning of October came a change. Up to this time and as far back as the Swaffam annals reached, the ghost had been a shadow, a rustle, a passing sigh – nothing definite or troublesome. But early in October strange things began to occur, and the terror culminated when a housemaid was found dead in a corridor three weeks later. Upon this the Professor felt that it was time to send for Flaxman Low.

Mr Low arrived upon a chilly evening when the house was already beginning to blur in the purple twilight, and the resinous scent of the pines came sweetly on the land breeze. Jungvort welcomed him in the spacious, firelit hall. He was a stout German with a quantity of white hair, round eyes emphasised by spectacles, and a kindly, dreamy face. His life-study was philology, and his two relaxations chess and the smoking of a big Bismarck-bowled meerschaum.

"Now, Professor," said Mr Low when they had settled themselves in the smoking-room, "how did it all begin?"

"I will tell you," replied Jungvort, thrusting out his chin, and tapping his broad chest, and speaking as if an unwarrantable liberty had been taken with him. "First of all, it has shown itself to me!"

Mr Flaxman Low smiled and assured him that nothing could be more satisfactory.

"But not at all satisfactory!" exclaimed the Professor. "I was sitting here alone, it might have been midnight – when I hear something come creeping like a little dog with its nails, tick-tick, upon the oak flooring of the hall. I whistle, for I think it is the little 'Rags' of my daughter, and afterwards opened the door, and I saw" – he hesitated and looked hard at Low through his spectacles, "something that was just disappearing into the passage which connects the two wings of the house. It was a figure, not unlike the human figure, but narrow and straight. I fancied I saw a bunch of black hair, and a flutter of something detached, which may have been a handkerchief. I was overcome by a feeling of repulsion. I heard a few, clicking steps, then it stopped, as I thought, at the Museum door. Come, I will show you the spot."

The Professor conducted Mr Low into the hall. The main staircase, dark and massive, yawned above them, and directly behind it ran the passage referred to by the Professor. It was over twenty feet long, and about midway led past a deep arch containing a door reached by two steps. Jungvort explained that this door formed the entrance to a large room called the Museum, in which Mr Swaffam, senior, who was something of a dilettante, stored the various curios he picked up during his excursions abroad. The Professor went on to say that he immediately followed the figure, which he believed had gone into the museum, but he found nothing there except the cases containing Swaffam's treasures.

"I mentioned my experience to no one. I concluded that I had seen the ghost. But two days after, one of the female servants coming through the passage in the dark, declared that a man leapt out at her from the embrasure of the Museum door, but she released herself and ran screaming into the servants' hall. We at once made a search but found nothing to substantiate her story.

"I took no notice of this, though it coincided pretty well with my own experience. The week after, my daughter Lena came down late one night for a book. As she was about to cross the hall, something leapt upon her from behind. Women are of little use in serious investigations – she fainted! Since then she has been ill and the doctor says 'Run down'." Here the Professor spread out his hands. "So she leaves for a change tomorrow. Since then other members of the household have been attacked in much the same manner, with always the same result, they faint and are weak and useless when they recover.

"But, last Wednesday, the affair became a tragedy. By that time the servants had refused to come through the passage except in a crowd of three or four – most of them preferring to go round by the terrace to reach this part of the house. But one maid, named Eliza Freeman, said she was not afraid of the Baelbrow Ghost, and undertook to put out the lights in the hall one night. When she had done so, and was returning through the passage past the Museum door, she appears to have been attacked, or at any rate frightened. In the grey of the morning they found her lying beside the steps dead. There was a little blood upon her sleeve but no mark upon her body except a small raised pustule under the ear. The doctor said the girl was extraordinarily anaemic, and that she probably died from fright, her heart being weak. I was surprised at this, for she had always seemed to be a particularly strong and active young woman."

"Can I see Miss Jungvort tomorrow before she goes?" asked Low, as the Professor signified he had nothing more to tell.

The Professor was rather unwilling that his daughter should be questioned, but he at last gave his permission, and next morning Low had a short talk with the girl before she left the house. He found her a very pretty girl, though listless and startlingly pale, and with a frightened stare in her light brown eyes. Mr Low asked if she could describe her assailant.

"No," she answered, "I could not see him, for he was behind me. I only saw a dark, bony hand, with shining nails, and a bandaged arm pass just under my eyes before I fainted."

"Bandaged arm? I have heard nothing of this."

"Tut – tut, mere fancy!" put in the Professor impatiently.

"I saw the bandages on the arm," repeated the girl, turning her head wearily away, "and I smelt the antiseptics it was dressed with."

"You have hurt your neck," remarked Mr Low, who noticed a small circular patch of pink under her ear.

She flushed and paled, raising her hand to her neck with a nervous jerk, as she said in a low voice:

"It has almost killed me. Before he touched me, I knew he was there! I felt it!"

When they left her the Professor apologised for the unreliability of her evidence, and pointed out the discrepancy between her statement and his own.

"She says she sees nothing but an arm, yet I tell you it had no arms! Preposterous! Conceive a wounded man entering this house to frighten the young women! I do not know what to make of it! Is it a man, or is it the Baelbrow Ghost?"

During the afternoon when Mr Low and the Professor returned from a stroll on the shore, they found a dark-browed young man with a bull neck, and strongly marked features, standing sullenly before the hall fire. The Professor presented him to Mr Low as Harold Swaffam.

Swaffam seemed to be about thirty, but was already known as a far-seeing and successful member of the Stock Exchange.

"I am pleased to meet you, Mr Low," he began, with a keen glance, "though you don't look sufficiently high-strung for one of your profession."

Mr Low merely bowed.

"Come, you don't defend your craft against my insinuations?" went on Swaffam. "And so you have come to rout out our poor old ghost from Baelbrow? You forget that he is an heirloom, a family possession! What's this about his having turned rabid, eh, Professor?" he ended, wheeling round upon Jungvort in his brusque way.

The Professor told the story over again. It was plain that he stood rather in awe of his prospective son-in-law.

"I heard much the same from Lena, whom I met at the station," said Swaffam. "It is my opinion that the women in this house are suffering from an epidemic of hysteria. You agree with me, Mr Low?"

"Possibly. Though hysteria could hardly account for Freeman's death."

"I can't say as to that until I have looked further into the particulars. I have not been idle since I arrived. I have examined the Museum. No one has entered it from the outside, and there is no other way of entrance except through the passage. The flooring is laid, I happen to know, on a thick layer of concrete. And there the case for the ghost stands at present." After a few moments of dogged reflection, he swung round on Mr Low, in a manner that seemed peculiar to him when about to address any person. "What do you say to this plan, Mr Low? I propose to drive the Professor over to Ferryvale, to stop there for a day or two at the hotel, and I will also dispose of the servants who still remain in the house for, say, forty-eight hours. Meanwhile you and I can try to go further into the secret of the ghost's new pranks?"

Flaxman Low replied that this scheme exactly met his views, but the Professor protested against being sent away. Harold Swaffam however was a man who liked to arrange things in his own fashion, and within forty-five minutes he and Jungvort departed in the dogcart.

The evening was lowering, and Baelbrow, like all houses built in exposed situations, was extremely susceptible to the changes of the weather. Therefore, before many hours were over, the place was full of creaking noises as the screaming gale battered at the shuttered windows, and the tree-branches tapped and groaned against the walls.

Harold Swaffam, on his way back, was caught in the storm and drenched to the skin. It was, therefore, settled that after he had changed his clothes he should have a couple of hours' rest on the smoking-room sofa, while Mr Low kept watch in the hall.

The early part of the night passed over uneventfully. A light burned faintly in the great wainscotted hall, but the passage was dark. There was nothing to be heard but the wild moan and whistle of the wind coming in from the sea, and the squalls of rain dashing against the windows. As the hours advanced, Mr Low lit a lantern that lay at hand, and, carrying it along the passage, tried the Museum door. It yielded, and the wind came muttering through to meet him. He looked round at the shutters and behind the big cases which held Mr Swaffam's treasures, to make sure that the room contained no living occupant but himself.

Suddenly he fancied he heard a scraping noise behind him, and turned round, but discovered nothing to account for it. Finally, he laid the lantern on a bench so that its light should fall through the door into the passage, and returned again to the hall, where he put out the lamp, and then once more took up his station by the closed door of the smoking-room.

A long hour passed, during which the wind continued to roar down the wide hall chimney, and the old boards creaked as if furtive footsteps were gathering from every corner of the house. But Flaxman Low heeded none of these; he was waiting for a certain sound.

After a while, he heard it – the cautious scraping of wood on wood. He leant forward to watch the Museum door. Click, click, came the curious dog-like tread upon the tiled floor of the Museum, till the thing, whatever it was, paused and listened behind the open door. The wind lulled at the moment, and Low listened also, but no further sound was to be heard, only slowly across the broad ray of light falling through the door grew a stealthy shadow.

Again the wind rose, and blew in heavy gusts about the house, till even the flame in the lantern flickered; but when it steadied once more, Flaxman Low saw that the silent form had passed through the door, and was now on the steps outside. He could just make out a dim shadow in the dark angle of the embrasure.

Presently, from the shapeless shadow came a sound Mr Low was not prepared to hear. The thing sniffed the air with the strong, audible inspiration of a bear, or some large animal. At the same moment, carried on the draughts of the hall, a faint, unfamiliar odour reached his nostrils. Lena Jungvort's words flashed back upon him – this, then, was the creature with the bandaged arm!

Again, as the storm shrieked and shook the windows, a darkness passed across the light. The thing had sprung out from the angle of the door, and Flaxman Low knew that it was making its way towards him through the illusive blackness of the hall. He hesitated for a second; then he opened the smoking-room door.

Harold Swaffam sat up on the sofa, dazed with sleep.

"What has happened? Has it come?"

Low told him what he had just seen. Swaffam listened half-smilingly.

"What do you make of it now?" he said.

"I must ask you to defer that question for a little," replied Low.

"Then you mean me to suppose that you have a theory to fit all these incongruous items?"

"I have a theory, which may be modified by further knowledge," said Low. "Meantime, am I right in concluding from the name of this house that it was built on a barrow or burying-place?"

"You are right, though that has nothing to do with the latest freaks of our ghost," returned Swaffam decidedly.

"I also gather that Mr Swaffam has lately sent home one of the many cases now lying in the Museum?" went on Mr Low.

"He sent one, certainly, last September."

"And you have opened it," asserted Low.

"Yes; though I flattered myself I had left no trace of my handiwork."

"I have not examined the cases," said Low. "I inferred that you had done so from other facts."

"Now, one thing more," went on Swaffam, still smiling. "Do you imagine there is any danger – I mean to men like ourselves? Hysterical women cannot be taken into serious account."

"Certainly; the gravest danger to any person who moves about this part of the house alone after dark," replied Low.

Harold Swaffam leant back and crossed his legs.

"To go back to the beginning of our conversation, Mr Low, may I remind you of the various conflicting particulars you will have to reconcile before you can present any decent theory to the world?"

"I am quite aware of that."

"First of all, our original ghost was a mere misty presence, rather guessed at from vague sounds and shadows – now we have a something that is tangible, and that can, as we have proof, kill with fright. Next Jungvort declares the thing was a narrow, long and distinctly armless object, while Miss Jungvort has not only seen the arm and hand of a human being, but saw them clearly enough to tell us that the nails were gleaming and the arm bandaged. She also felt its strength. Jungvort, on the other hand, maintained that it clicked along like a dog – you bear out this description with the additional information that it sniffs like a wild beast. Now what can this thing be? It is capable of being seen, smelt, and felt, yet it hides itself successfully in a room where there is no cavity or space sufficient to afford covert to a cat! You still tell me that you believe that you can explain?"

"Most certainly," replied Flaxman Low with conviction.

"I have not the slightest intention or desire to be rude, but as a mere matter of common sense, I must express my opinion plainly. I believe the whole thing to be the result of excited imaginations, and I am about to prove it. Do you think there is any further danger tonight?"

"Very great danger tonight," replied Low.

"Very well; as I said, I am going to prove it. I will ask you to allow me to lock you up in one of the distant rooms, where I can get no help from you, and I will pass the remainder of the night walking about the passage and hall in the dark. That should give proof one way or the other."

"You can do so if you wish, but I must at least beg to be allowed to look on. I will leave the house and watch what goes on from the window in the passage, which I saw opposite the Museum door. You cannot, in any fairness, refuse to let me be a witness."

"I cannot, of course," returned Swaffam. "Still, the night is too bad to turn a dog out into, and I warn you that I shall lock you out."

"That will not matter. Lend me a macintosh, and leave the lantern lit in the Museum, where I placed it."

Swaffam agreed to this. Mr Low gives a graphic account of what followed. He left the house and was duly locked out, and, after groping his way round the house, found himself at length outside the window of the passage, which was almost opposite to the door of the Museum. The door was still ajar and a thin band of light cut out into the gloom. Further down the hall gaped black and void. Low, sheltering himself as well as he could from the rain, waited for Swaffam's appearance. Was the terrible yellow watcher balancing itself upon its lean legs in the dim corner opposite, ready to spring out with its deadly strength upon the passer-by?

Presently Low heard a door bang inside the house, and the next moment Swaffam appeared with a candle in his hand, an isolated spread of weak rays against the vast darkness behind. He advanced steadily down the passage, his dark face grim and set, and as he came Mr Low experienced that tingling sensation, which is so often the forerunner of some strange experience. Swaffam passed on towards the other end of the passage. There was a quick vibration of the Museum door as a lean shape with a shrunken head leapt out into the passage after him. Then all together came a hoarse shout, the noise of a fall and utter darkness.

In an instant, Mr Low had broken the glass, opened the window, and swung himself into the passage. There he lit a match and as it flared he saw by its dim light a picture painted for a second upon the obscurity beyond.

Swaffam's big figure lay with outstretched arms, face downwards, and as Low looked a crouching shape extricated itself from the fallen man, raising a narrow vicious head from his shoulder.

The match spluttered feebly and went out, and Low heard a flying step click on the boards, before he could find the candle Swaffam had dropped. Lighting it, he stooped over Swaffam and turned him on his back. The man's strong colour had gone, and the wax-white face looked whiter still against the blackness of hair and brows, and upon his neck under the ear, was a little raised pustule, from which a thin line of blood was streaked up to the angle of his cheekbone.

Some instinctive feeling prompted Low to glance up at this moment. Half extended from the Museum doorway were a face and bony neck – a high-nosed, dull-eyed, malignant face, the eye-sockets hollow, and the darkened teeth showing. Low plunged his hand into his pocket, and a shot rang out in the echoing passage-way and hall. The wind sighed through the broken panes, a ribbon of stuff fluttered along the polished flooring, and that was all, as Flaxman Low half dragged, half carried Swaffam into the smoking-room.

It was some time before Swaffam recovered consciousness. He listened to Low's story of how he had found him with a red angry gleam in his sombre eyes.

"The ghost has scored off me," he said with an odd, sullen laugh, "but now I fancy it's my turn! But before we adjourn to the Museum to examine the place, I will ask you to let me hear your notion of things. You have been right in saying there was real danger. For myself I can only tell you that I felt something spring upon me, and I knew no more. Had this not happened I am afraid I should never have asked you a second time what your idea of the matter might be," he ended with a sort of sulky frankness.

"There are two main indications," replied Low. "This strip of yellow bandage, which I have just now picked up from the passage floor, and the mark on your neck."

"What's that you say?" Swaffam rose quickly and examined his neck in a small glass beside the mantelshelf.

"Connect those two, and I think I can leave you to work it out for yourself," said Low.

"Pray let us have your theory in full," requested Swaffam shortly.

"Very well," answered Low good-humouredly – he thought Swaffam's annoyance natural under the circumstances – "The long, narrow figure which seemed to the Professor to be armless is developed on the next occasion. For Miss Jungvort sees a bandaged arm and a dark hand with gleaming – which means, of course, gilded – nails. The clicking sound of the footstep coincides with these particulars, for we know that sandals made of strips of leather are not uncommon in company with gilt nails and bandages. Old and dry leather would naturally click upon your polished floors."

"Bravo, Mr Low! So you mean to say that this house is haunted by a mummy!"

"That is my idea, and all I have seen confirms me in my opinion."

"To do you justice, you held this theory before tonight – before, in fact, you had seen anything for yourself. You gathered that my father had sent home a mummy, and you went on to conclude that I had opened the case?"

"Yes. I imagine you took off most of, or rather all, the outer bandages, thus leaving the limbs free, wrapped only in the inner bandages which were swathed round each separate limb. I fancy this mummy was preserved on the Theban method with aromatic spices, which left the skin olive-coloured, dry and flexible, like tanned leather, the features remaining distinct, and the hair, teeth, and eyebrows perfect."

"So far, good," said Swaffam. "But now, how about the intermittent vitality? The pustule on the neck of those whom it attacks? And where is our old Baelbrow ghost to come in?"

Swaffam tried to speak in a rallying tone, but his excitement and lowering temper were visible enough, in spite of the attempts he made to suppress them.

"To begin at the beginning," said Flaxman Low, "everybody who, in a rational and honest manner, investigates the phenomena of spiritism will, sooner or later, meet in them some perplexing element, which is not to be explained by any of the ordinary theories. For reasons into which I need not now enter, this present case appears to me to be one of these. I am led to believe that the ghost which has for so many years given dim and vague manifestations of its existence in this house is a vampire."

Swaffam threw back his head with an incredulous gesture.

"We no longer live in the middle ages, Mr Low! And besides, how could a vampire come here?" he said scoffingly.

"It is held by some authorities on these subjects that under certain conditions a vampire may be self-created. You tell me that this house is built upon an ancient barrow, in fact, on a spot where we might naturally expect to find such an elemental psychic germ. In those dead human systems were contained all the seeds for good and evil. The power which causes these psychic seeds or germs to grow is thought, and from being long dwelt on and indulged, a thought might finally gain a mysterious vitality, which could go on increasing more and more by attracting to itself suitable and appropriate elements from its environment. For a long period this germ remained a helpless intelligence, awaiting the opportunity to assume some material form, by means of which to carry out its desires. The invisible is the real; the material only subserves its manifestation. The impalpable reality already existed, when you provided for it a physical medium for action by unwrapping the mummy's form. Now, we can only judge of the nature of the germ by its manifestation through matter. Here we have every indication of a vampire intelligence touching into life and energy the dead human frame. Hence the mark on the neck of its victims, and their bloodless and anaemic condition. For a vampire, as you know, sucks blood."

Swaffham rose, and took up the lamp.

"Now, for proof," he said bluntly. "Wait a second, Mr Low. You say you fired at this appearance?" And he took up the pistol which Low had laid down on the table.

"Yes, I aimed at a small portion of its foot which I saw on the step."

Without more words, and with the pistol still in his hand, Swaffam led the way to the Museum.

The wind howled round the house, and the darkness, which precedes the dawn, lay upon the world, when the two men looked upon one of the strangest sights it has ever been given to men to shudder at.

Half in and half out of an oblong wooden box in a corner of the great room, lay a lean shape in its rotten yellow bandages, the scraggy neck surmounted by a mop of frizzled hair. The toe strap of a sandal and a portion of the right foot had been shot away.

Swaffam, with a working face, gazed down at it, then seizing it by its tearing bandages, he flung it into the box, where it fell into a life-like posture, its wide, moist-lipped mouth gaping up at them.

For a moment Swaffam stood over the thing; then with a curse he raised the revolver and shot into the grinning face again and again with a deliberate vindictiveness. Finally he rammed the thing down into the box, and, clubbing the weapon, smashed the head into fragments with a vicious energy that coloured the whole horrible scene with a suggestion of murder done.

Then, turning to Low, he said:

"Help me to fasten the cover on it."

"Are you going to bury it?"

"No, we must rid the earth of it," he answered savagely. "I'll put it into the old canoe and burn it."

The rain had ceased when in the daybreak they carried the old canoe down to the shore. In it they placed the mummy case with its ghastly occupant, and piled faggots about it. The sail was raised and the pile lighted, and Low and Swaffam watched it creep out on the ebb-tide, at first a twinkling spark, then a flare of waving fire, until far out to sea the history of that dead thing ended 3000 years after the priests of Armen had laid it to rest in its appointed pyramid.

'THE MYSTERIOUS MUMMY' (1903)

Sax Rohmer

Sax Rohmer was the nom de plume of Arthur Henry Ward (1883–1959). Rohmer was a prolific writer whose literary output includes forty-two novels, nine collections of short stories, four plays and several works of non-fiction as well as songs and monologues for music hall stars such as George Robey. Rohmer is best known today as the author of the fifteen Fu Manchu books. He was, however, also conscious of the public's interest in Egypt and wrote many tales about mummies, as well as producing two related collections of short stories, *Tales of Secret Egypt* (1918) and *Egyptian Nights* (1944).

'The Mysterious Mummy' was Rohmer's first published story. It was printed in *Pearson's Weekly* as part of a special Christmas Extra issue on 26 November 1903. The tale is unusual, in that it toys with the reader's expectations about a possible missing mummy that might be supernaturally on the move within "Great Portland Square Museum" (modelled on the British Museum). Without giving away too many spoilers, the tale pivots on the apparent theft of a valuable vase and although it does not directly involve a mummy, it obliquely reflects narratives about tomb-raiding which were familiar from mummy tales of the period.

I T WAS ABOUT FIVE O'CLOCK ON A HOT AUGUST AFTERNOON, that a tall, thin man, wearing a weedy beard, and made conspicuous by an ill-fitting frock-coat and an almost napless silk hat, walked into the entrance hall of the Great Portland Square Museum. He carried no stick, and, looking about him, as though unfamiliar with the building, he ultimately mounted the principal staircase, walking with a pronounced stoop, and at intervals coughing with a hollow sound.

His gaunt figure attracted the attention of several people, among them the attendant in the Egyptian room. Hardened though he was to the eccentric in humanity, the man who hung so eagerly over the mummies of departed kings and coughed so frequently, nevertheless secured his instant attention. Visitors of the regulation type were rapidly thinning out, so that the gaunt man, during the whole of the time he remained in the room, was kept under close surveillance by the vigilant official. Seeing him go in the direction of the stairs, the attendant supposed the strange visitor to be about to leave the Museum. But that he did not immediately do so was shown by subsequent testimony.

The day's business being concluded, the staff of police who patrol nightly the Great Portland Square Museum duly filed into the building. A man is placed in each room, it being his duty to examine thoroughly every nook and cranny; having done which, all doors of communication are closed, the officer on guard in one room being unable to leave his post or to enter another. Every hour the inspector, a sergeant, and a fireman make a round of the entire building: from which it will be seen that a person having designs on any of the numerous treasures of the place would require more than average ingenuity to bring his plans to a successful issue.

In recording this very singular case, the only incident of the night to demand attention is that of the mummy in the Etruscan room.

Persons familiar with the Great Portland Square Museum will know that certain of the tombs in the Etruscan room are used as receptacles for Egyptian mummies that have, for various reasons, never been put upon exhibition. Anyone who has peered under the partially raised lid of a huge sarcophagus and found within the rigid form of a mummy, will appreciate the feelings of the man on night duty amid surroundings so lugubrious. The electric light, it should be mentioned, is not extinguished until the various apartments have been examined, and its extinction immediately precedes the locking of the door.

The constable in the Etruscan room glanced into the various sarcophagi and cast the rays of his bull's-eye lantern into the shadows of the great stone tombs. Satisfied that no one lurked there, he mounted the steps leading up to the Roman gallery, turning out the lights in the room below from the switch at the top. The light was still burning on the ground floor, and the sergeant had not yet arrived with the keys. It was whilst the man stood awaiting his coming that a singular thing occurred.

From somewhere within the darkened chamber beneath, there came the sound of a hollow cough!

By no means deficient in courage, the constable went down the steps in three bounds, his lantern throwing discs of light on stately statues and gloomy tombs. The sound was not repeated and having nothing to guide him to its source, he commenced a second methodical search of the sarcophagi, as offering the most likely hiding places. When all save one had been examined, the constable began to believe that the coughing had existed only in his imagination. It was upon casting the rays of his bull's-eye into the last sarcophagus that he experienced a sudden sensation of fear. It was empty; yet he distinctly remembered, from his previous examination, that a mummy had lain there!

At the moment of making this weird discovery, he realised that he would have done better, before commencing his search for the man with the cough, first to turn on the light; for it must be remembered that he had extinguished the electric lamps. Determined to do so before pursuing his investigations further, he ran up the steps – to find the Roman gallery in darkness. The bright disc of a lantern was approaching from the upper end, and the man ran forward.

"Who turned off the lights here?" came the voice of the sergeant.

"That's what I want to know! Somebody did it while I was downstairs!" said the constable, and gave a hurried account of the mysterious coughing and the missing mummy.

"How long has there been a mummy in this tomb?" asked the sergeant.

"There was one there a month back, but they took it upstairs. They may have brought it down again last week though, or it may have been a fresh one. You see, the other lot were on duty up to last night."

This was quite true, as the sergeant was aware. Three bodies of picked men share the night duties at the Great Portland Square Museum, and those on duty upon this particular occasion had not been in the place during the previous two weeks.

"Very strange!" muttered the sergeant; and a moment later his whistle was sounding.

From all over the building men came running, for none of the doors had yet been locked.

"There seems to be someone concealed in the Museum: search all the rooms again!" was the brief order.

The constables disappeared, and the sergeant, accompanied by the inspector, went down to examine the Etruscan room. Nothing was found there; nor were any of the other searchers more successful. There was no trace anywhere of a man in hiding. Beyond leaving open the door between the Roman gallery and the steps of the Etruscan room, no more could be done in the matter. The gallery communicates with the entrance hall, where the inspector, together with the sergeant and fireman, spends the night, and the idea of the former was to keep in touch with the scene of these singular happenings. His action was perfectly natural; but these precautions were subsequently proved to be absolutely useless.

The night passed without any disturbing event, and the mystery of the vanishing mummy and the ghostly cough seemed likely to remain a mystery. The night-police filed out in the early morning, and the inspector, with the sergeant, returned, as soon as possible, to the Museum, to make further inquiries concerning the missing occupant of the sarcophagus.

"A mummy in the end tomb!" exclaimed the curator of Etruscan antiquities; "my dear sir, there has been no mummy there for nearly a month!"

"But my man states that he saw one there last night!" declared the inspector.

The curator looked puzzled. Turning to an attendant, he said: "Who was in charge of the Etruscan room immediately before six last night?"

"I was, sir!"

"Were there any visitors?"

"No one came in between five-forty and six."

"And before that?"

"I was away at tea, sir!"

"Who was in charge then?"

"Mr Robins."

"Call Robins."

The commissionaire in question arrived.

"How long were you in the Etruscan room last night?"

"About half-an-hour, sir."

"Are you sure that no one concealed himself?"

The man looked startled. "Well, sir," he said hesitatingly, "I'm sorry I didn't report it before; but when Mr Barton called me, at about twenty-five minutes to six, there was someone there, a gent in a seedy frock-coat and a high hat, and I don't remember seeing him come out."

"Did you search the room?"

"Yes, sir; but there was no one to be seen!"

"You should have reported the matter at once. I must see Barton."

Barton, the head attendant, remembered speaking to Robins at the top of the steps leading to the Etruscan room. He saw no one come out, but it was just possible for a person to have done so and yet be seen by neither himself nor Robins.

"Let three of you thoroughly overhaul the room for any sign of a man having hidden there," directed the curator briskly.

He turned to the sergeant and inspector with a smile, "I rather fancy it will prove to be a mare's nest!" he said. "We have had these mysteries before."

The words had but just left his lips when a Museum official, a well-known antiquarian expert, ran up in a perfect frenzy of excitement. "Good heavens, Peters!" he gasped. "The Rienzi Vase has gone!"

"What!" came an incredulous chorus.

"The circular top of the case has been completely cut out and ingeniously replaced, and a plausible imitation of the vase substituted!"

They waited for no more, but hurried upstairs to the Vase room, which, in the Great Portland Square Museum, is really only a part of the Egyptian room. The Rienzi Vase, though no larger than an ordinary breakfast-cup, all the world knows to be of fabulous value. It seemed inconceivable that anyone could have stolen it. Yet there, in the midst of a knot of excited officials, stood the empty case, whilst the imitation antique was being passed from hand to hand.

Never before nor since has such a scene been witnessed in the Museum. The staff, to a man, had lost their wits. What is to be done? was the general inquiry. In less than half an hour the doors would have to be opened to the public, and the absence of the famous vase would inevitably be noticed. It was at this juncture, and whilst everyone was speaking at once, that one of the party, standing close to a wall-cabinet, suddenly held up a warning finger. "Hush!" he said; "listen!"

A sudden silence fell upon the room so that people running about in other apartments could be plainly heard. And presently, from somewhere behind the glass doors surrounding the place, came a low moan, electrifying the already excited listeners. The keys were promptly forthcoming and then was made the second astounding discovery of the eventful morning.

A man, gagged and bound, was imprisoned behind a great mummy case!

Eager hands set to work to release him, and restoratives were applied, as he seemed to be in a very weak condition. He was but partially dressed, and breathed heavily through his nose, like a man in a drunken slumber. All waited breathlessly for his return to consciousness; for certainly he, if anyone, should be in a position to furnish some clue to the deep mystery. On regaining his senses, he had disappointingly little to tell. He was Constable Smith, who had been on night-duty in the Egyptian room. Sometime during the first hour, and not long after the alarm in the basement, he had been mysteriously pinioned as he paraded the apartment. He caught no glimpse of his opponent, who held him from behind in such a manner that he was totally unable to defend himself. Some sweet-smelling drug had been applied to his nostrils, and he remembered no more until regaining consciousness in the mummy case! That was the whole of his testimony. In setting out the particulars of this remarkable affair, a third and final discovery must be noted. The three men who had been directed to examine the Etruscan room brought to light a bundle of old garments, containing an ancient opera-hat, a faded frock-coat, a pair of shiny trousers, and a pair of elastic-sided boots. They were wedged high up at the back of a tall statue, where they had evidently escaped the eyes of all previous searchers. That constituted the entire data on which investigations had to be based. The Egyptian room was closed indefinitely, "for repairs". No further useful evidence could be obtained from anyone. Several witnesses furnished consistent descriptions of the shabby stranger with the hollow cough; but it may here be mentioned that no one of them ever set eyes upon him again. The inspector, the sergeant, and the fireman solemnly swore to having visited the Egyptian room at the end of each hour throughout the night, and to having found the constable on duty as usual! Smith swore, with equal solemnity, that he had been drugged during the first hour and subsequently confined in the mummy case.

The matter was carefully kept out of the papers, although the Museum, throughout many following days, positively bristled with detectives. As the second week drew to a close and the Egyptian room still remained locked, well-informed persons began to whisper that a scandal could no longer be avoided. There can be no doubt that, in many quarters, Constable Smith's share in the proceedings was regarded with grave suspicion. It was at this critical juncture, when it seemed inevitable that the loss of the world-famous Rienzi Vase must be made known to an unsympathetic public, that certain high authorities gave out that the vase had been removed, and that none of the night staff were in any way implicated in its disappearance!

On this announcement being made, several strange theories were mooted. Some stated that the vase had never left the Museum! Others averred that it had been pawned to a foreign government!

Whatever the real explanation, and the secret was jealously guarded by the highly placed officials who alone knew the truth, suffice it that the Egyptian room was again thrown open and the Rienzi Vase shown to be reposing in its usual position.

Now that it again stands in its place for all to see, there can be no objection to my relating how I once held the famous Rienzi Vase in my possession for twelve days. If there be any objection…

I am sorry. You must understand that I am no common thief – no footpad: I am a person of keenly observant character, and my business is to detect vital weaknesses in great institutions and to charge a moderately high fee for my services. Thus I discovered that a certain famous tiara in a French museum was inadequately protected, and accordingly removed it, replacing it by a substitute.

The authorities refused me my fee, and all the world knows that my clever forgery was detected by the experts. That brought them to their senses; it is the genuine tiara that reposes in their cabinet now!

In the same way I removed a world-renowned, historical mummy from its resting place in Cairo, and two days later they grew suspicious of my imitation – it was the handiwork of a clever Birmingham artist – and the department was closed. The bulky character of the mummy nearly brought about my downfall, and it was only by abandoning it that I succeeded in leaving Cairo. I am not proud of that case; I was clumsy. But of the case of the Rienzi Vase I have every reason to be highly proud. That you may judge of the neatness and dispatch with which I acted, I will relate how the whole business was conducted.

You must know, then, that the first flaw I discovered in the arrangements at the Great Portland Square Museum was this: the wall-cases were badly guarded. I learnt this interesting fact one afternoon as I strolled about the Egyptian room. A certain gentle-man – I will not name him – was showing a party of ladies round the apartment. He had unlocked a wall-case, and was standing with a handsome bead-necklet in his hand, explaining where and when it was found. He was only a few yards away, but with his back toward the case. Enough! The key, with others attached, was in the glass door. You will admit that this was exceedingly careless; but the presence of four charming American ladies… one can excuse him!

I regret to have to confess that I was somewhat awkward – the keys rattled. The whole party looked in my direction. But the immaculate man-about-town, with his cultivated manner and his very considerable knowledge of Egyptology – how should they suspect? I apologised; I had brushed against them in passing; I made myself agreeable, and the uncomfortable incident was forgotten, by them – not by me. I had a beautiful wax impression to keep my memory fresh!

The scheme formed then. I knew that a body of picked police promenaded the Museum at night, and that each of the rooms was usually in charge of the same man. I learnt, later, that there were three bodies of men, so that the same police were in the Museum but one week in every three. I made the acquaintance of seven constables and frequented eight different public-houses before I met the man of whom I was in search.

The first policeman I found, who paraded the Egyptian room at night, was short and thick-set, and I gave him up as a bad job. I learnt from him, however, who was to occupy the post during the coming week, and presently I unearthed the private bar which this latter officer, his name was Smith, used. Eureka! He was tall and thin. Incidentally, he was also surly. But the winning ways of the jovial master-plumber, who was so free with his money, ultimately thawed him.

Every night throughout the rest of the week I spent in this constable's company, studying his somewhat colourless personality. Then, one afternoon, I entered the Museum. My weedy beard, my gaunt expression, and my hollow cough – they were all in the part! I went up to the Egyptian room to assure myself that a certain mummy case had not been removed, and having found it to occupy its usual place, I descended to the Etruscan basement.

For half-an-hour I occupied myself there, but the commissionaire never budged from his seat. I knew that this particular man was only in temporary charge whilst another was at tea, for I was well posted, and wondered if his companion were ever coming back. Luckily, an incident occurred to serve my purpose. The chief attendant appeared at the head of the steps. "Robins!" he called.

Robins ran briskly upstairs at his command, and then – in fifteen seconds my transformation was complete. Gone were the weedy grey beard and moustache – gone the seedy, black garments and the elastic-sided boots – gone the old opera-hat – and, behold, I was Constable Smith, attired in mummy wrappings!

An acrobatic spring, and the bundle of aged garments was wedged behind a tall statue, where nothing but a most minute search could reveal it. Down again, not a second to spare! Into the empty sarcophagus at the further end of the room; and, lastly, a hideous rubber mask slipped over the ruddy features of Constable Smith and attached behind the ears, my arms stiffened and my hands concealed in the wrappings, and I was a long-dead mummy – with a neat leather case hidden beneath my arched back! Brisk work, I assure you; but one grows accustomed to it in time. The commissionaire entered the room very shortly afterwards. He had not seen me go out, but, as I expected, neither was he absolutely sure that I had not done so. He peered about suspiciously, but I did not mind. The real ordeal came a couple of hours later, when a police officer flashed his lantern into all the tombs.

For a moment my heart seemed to cease beating as the light shone on my rubber countenance.

But he was satisfied, this stupid policeman, and I heard his footsteps retreating to the door. I allowed him time to get to the top, and extinguished the light in the Etruscan room, and then… I was out of my tomb and hidden in the little niche immediately beside the foot of the stairs. I coughed loudly. Heavens! He came back down the steps with such velocity that he was carried halfway along the room. He began to flash his lantern into the tombs again; but, before he had examined the first of them, I was upstairs in the Roman gallery!

Without the electric light it was quite dark in the Etruscan room, which is in the basement; but, being a bright night, I knew I could find what I required in the Roman gallery without the aid of artificial light; besides, I had not to act in the open – someone might arrive too soon. So, thoroughly well posted as to the situation of the switches, I extinguished the lamps, and dodged in among the Roman stonework to the foot of a great pillar, towering almost to the lofty roof and surmounted by an ornate capital.

I had planned all this beforehand, you see; but I must confess it was an awful scramble to the top. I had only just curled up on the summit, the handle of my invaluable leather-case held fast in my teeth, when a sergeant came running down the gallery, almost into the arms of the constable who was running up the steps from the Etruscan room.

A moment's hurried conversation, and then the lights turned on and the sound of a whistle. It was foolish, of course; but I had expected it. From all over the building the police arrived, and, fatigued as I was with my climb, yet another acrobatic feat was before me.

The top of my pillar was no great distance from the stone balustrade of the first-floor landing, on which the Egyptian room opens, and a narrow ledge, perhaps of eleven inches, runs all round the wall of the Roman gallery some four feet below the ceiling. I cautiously stepped from the pillar to the ledge – I was invisible from the other end of the place – and, pressing my body close against the wall, reached the balustrade. Before Constable Smith – who had left his post and descended to the lower gallery on hearing the sergeant's whistle – re-entered the Egyptian room, my bright, new key had found the lock of a certain cabinet, and I was secure behind a mummy case – whilst a little steel pin prevented the spring of the lock from shutting me in.

Poor Constable Smith! I was sorry to have to act so: but, ten minutes after the closing of the doors of communication, I came on him from behind, having silently crept from the case as he passed me, and followed him down the darkened room, the thin linen wrappings that covered my feet making no sound upon the wooden floor. I had a pad ready in my hand, saturated with the contents of a small phial that had reposed in my mummy garments.

I thrust my knee in his spine and seized his hands by a trick which you may learn for a peseta any day in the purlieus of Tangier. A muscular man, he tried hard to cope with his unseen opponent; but the pad never left his mouth and nostrils, and the few muffled cries that escaped him were luckily unheard. He soon became unconscious, and I had to work hard lest the inspector should make his round before I was ready for him. The mummy case had to be lowered on to the floor, and the heavy body tightly bound and lifted into it, then stood up again and securely locked behind the glass doors. It was hot work, and I had but just accomplished the task and climbed into the constable's uniform, when the inspector's key sounded in the door. Ah! it is an exciting profession! The rest was easy. Wrapped up in my yellow mummy linen were the various appliances I required, and in the leather box was the imitation Rienzi Vase. The circular glass top of the case gave some trouble. So hard and thick was it that I had to desist five times and conceal my tools, owing to the hourly visits of the inspector. Poor Constable Smith began to groan toward six o'clock, and a second dose of medicine was necessary to keep him quiet for another hour or so.

I filed out with the other police in the morning, the Rienzi Vase inside my helmet. As to the sequel, it is brief. Of course the detectives tried their hands at the affair; but, pooh! I am too old a bird to leave "clues"! It is only amateurs that do that!

My fee, and the conditions to be observed in paying it, I conveyed to the authorities privately.

They thought they had a "clue" then, and delayed another week. They actually detained my unhappy agent, a most guileless and upright person, who knew positively nothing. Oh! it was too funny! But, realising that only by the vase being returned to its place could a scandal be avoided – they met me in the matter.

'THE DEAD HAND' (1904)

Hester White

Little is known about Hester White, who is not referenced in the *Oxford Dictionary of National Biography* and does not appear on databases of women writers. Hester White wrote novels such as *Fleming of Brierwood* (1891), *Mountains of Necessity* (1901; now back in print), *Uncle Jem* (1907), and a children's novel *On the Sea of Life* (1893). The early novels were published by the Society for Promoting Christian Knowledge and could, conceivably, have been written by a different Hester White from the later novels. The tale included here certainly does not have an overt Christian message, although arguably it does contain an implicit one.

'The Dead Hand' appeared in *The Gentleman's Magazine* in December 1904. The dead hand of the title brings bad luck to our narrator until it is restored to its rightful owner. The tale centres on the British military presence in Egypt, with the focus on officer-class leisure-time activities such as horse riding and parties – activities which become disturbed by a strange figure with "piercing dark eyes". The idea of a cursed hand was central to W.W. Jacob's 'The Monkey's Paw' (1902) and White may well have had Jacob's story in mind.

HENRY PERKINS JOINED THE REGIMENT WHEN WE WERE IN Egypt, quartered at Assouan, a place which, for monotony and heat, beats any other spot on the globe known to me; my friends, however, when I venture on this remark, tell me that I am a lucky beggar, and vaguely mention the unintelligible names of various localities in India, West Africa, or Burmah, which so far have not been honoured by my presence.

But to return to Henry Perkins; there was some irregularity about his papers, his age appeared to have been incorrectly entered on his attestation paper, and I, being adjutant at the time, decided to write to the parson of the village in which he was born for the missing information, which he assured me would be found in the church register.

I am a bit of a scribe when in the vein, and I felt that evening rather as if I were writing an article for a magazine, therefore indited what I considered a very suitable epistle to the reverend gentleman. No doubt it raised a picture in his mind of a conscientious scholarly individual, the outcome of competitive examination, who combined soldiering with an interest in Egyptian lore, for he answered somewhat effusively, said he envied me my sojourn in so wonderful a country, confessed to a great partiality for curios of all sorts, and finally mentioned that, instead of the fee of a few shillings due to him for the enclosed document, he would much prefer a small Egyptian antiquity, which would no doubt be procurable up the Nile, where the regiment was quartered.

I sent for Henry Perkins and read him the portion of the letter which concerned himself; he was a square-faced ordinary specimen of Thomas Atkins, small eyes, black lock over the forehead, and a snub nose.

"Have you got anything of the sort?" I asked, alluding to the clergyman's request. He reflected, rubbing his jaw thoughtfully, then answered.

"Well, sir, now you come to mention it, I 'ave one hobject of the kind – a dead 'and."

"A dead hand!"

"The 'and of a dead party, sir."

I stared, but then remembered Bob Jenkins, a Rugby pal of mine, who had turned up at Assouan unexpectedly, and spent his time grubbing amongst departed Egyptians.

"Bring it to me," I commanded briefly. And sure enough it proved to be nothing more nor less than the shrivelled hand of a mummy. A queer brown thing, which fascinated me somehow; its long bony fingers and flattened leather-like palm possessed the attraction of the unusual. It seemed to have been broken off from the arm at the wrist, for one of the little bones was missing and another emerged irregularly from the dry skin. I began to wonder, as I gazed at it meditatively, what those fingers had done, whether they had been fingers of note, whether they had carved some of the wonderful hieroglyphics Bob was continually poring over, handled the ribbons at a chariot race, dismissed courtiers with a haughty gesture, smoothed a lady's brow, or perhaps strangled – I pulled up; my flights of fancy were becoming slightly unpleasant.

"All right, that'll do, Perkins," I said. "By the way, where did you get it?"

"Bought it yesterday from Corporal Jones, of the 10th, for five piastres, sir."

"Cremation for me," I thought, as he left the room without any regret for his treasure, which remained on my writing-table.

And now I must confess to the only fraud I have, to my own knowledge, ever been guilty of. When I sat down to my table the next morning my eyes fell on the mummy hand. Simonds, my soldier servant, being of a decorative turn of mind, had stuck it up in a pipe-rack which adorned the opposite wall, beneath a photograph of Edna May in *Three Little Maids*, and amongst several briar pipes, more or less dilapidated. There it was, with its uncomfortable stiff brown fingers and shattered wrist, and again I felt its weird fascination. I distinctly did not wish to send it to the reverend doctor; I would keep it for a bit; he should have his five shillings and Perkins his five piastres. I was busy at that time, and hot, which is synonymous with worried, and the journalistic phase had passed; therefore I cannot deny that my new acquisition remained in its place and the Rector of Mudton-in-the-Marsh did not get his money nor his Egyptian curio. Perhaps I shall meet him one day and explain the matter – I'm sure he will forgive me.

And now comes the strange part of the story. I don't ask anyone to believe it, or to attach a meaning to it, which might offend their common sense; I can only say that the facts are absolutely true, although my interpretation of them may be due to a disordered liver after a spell of Egypt in hot weather, imaginative folly, or whatever the sceptics choose to call it.

I have mentioned Bob Jenkins, but not that he had taken up his quarters, at the time I am speaking of, in no less a place than a tomb, where he thoroughly enjoyed himself, hard at it all day, scantily attired in the most disreputable undress, and, when engaged in exterior work, with an enormous khaki helmet planted on his head at an angle of 45°, beneath which appeared his keen intelligent face, now dark with sunburn.

I sometimes rode out to look him up in the evening, and did so a few days after I came into possession of the mummy hand; we smoked our pipes together beneath the shadow of two grim figures which were Bob's admiration just then, but which I must confess did not fill me with the same enthusiasm. He was a good chap, although slightly egotistical; he used a lot of Arabic words and expected me to like it, but did not seem to care as much for listening to what I had to say about polo and the small society of Assouan, as to tell me of his own doings.

He had apparently unearthed goodness knows how many kings, queens, potentates, to say nothing of minor personages: in fact had struck a mine of dignitaries; slim princesses with the lotos flower still upon their bosoms, and warriors with classical features and stalwart limbs. I never professed to be an Egyptologist, therefore such fossils don't interest me particularly, but for his sake I was glad he was in for a good thing which would bring him kudos, and so sympathised as best I could, though I listened carelessly, wondering when I should get a chance of producing a little bit of gossip, which was exciting us all, viz. that Brown of "ours" had just got engaged to Miss Julia Moss of Alexandria, whose mother had been trying to catch him for many months. My efforts to communicate this piece of information made me entirely forget to tell him of Henry Perkins and the "dead 'and" (which, by the way, had been missing that morning from the pipe-rack): a matter, after all, rather more in his line.

It was when I was returning home on Sparrow, my favourite polo pony, that a curious, not to say disastrous, thing happened to me. It was a clear bright night, such as is possible only in the East, where the shadows are black and clean-edged as if cut out of paper with a sharp pair of scissors, and the moonlight whiter and more vivid than anything we know at home. The weird expanse of sand stretched to the horizon like a dim yellow sea, and the air, still too hot to please me, was heavy with the odours of the past day, grain, smoke, and others less endurable, which at times increased in volume and pungency.

The Egyptians are rum fellows; some of them certainly show that they come of a fine race despite a backsheesh-seeking spirit raised by the ubiquitous tourist.

"They walk and carry themselves like the sons of kings," I thought, as my eyes followed a figure in long white draperies who was stalking silently in front of me. I had not noticed the first moment of his appearance, but this was scarcely wonderful, for I must confess I was in rather a sentimental mood that night, and my thoughts were occupied with a certain P. & O. steamer, which just then was ploughing her way along the Mediterranean and bringing nearer our late colonel and his daughter. He was travelling to Australia, to visit a sheep-farmer son, accompanied by Eva, who – well I'll speak more of her later, I only mention her at present to explain possible abstraction on my part, for at the time I had no suspicion of anything unusual in connection with the slim stately Egyptian, nor did I consider subsequent events peculiar, merely regarding them as disagreeably accidental.

What happened was this. I had no sooner begun to watch the silent figure ahead of me with a certain interest, for there was a curious distinction about him that irresistibly attracted me, than we reached a small collection of mud houses, and he vanished into the shadows just as mysteriously as he had risen out of them.

Anyone who knows these villages will recall the broad and sandy track between the houses, not worthy of the name of a street, where the great Eastern smell-fiend puffs himself out with relish, ready and able to knock down and overcome a man of ordinary sensibilities, where miserable pariah dogs wallow in dirt and offal, and still forms lurk in corners. Sparrow was sure-footed, and we made our way as quickly as was feasible across the black shadows and bright moon-patches.

In riding out I had chosen the main thoroughfare, but now a strange thing occurred, and for the life of me I cannot to this day explain why I acted as I did.

In turning the corner of one of the square low white houses I again saw the Egyptian I have spoken of; he was leaning against the wall in the full moonlight and facing me; there was no mistaking him, and even more than before was I struck with the air of distinction that especially marked him. His white drapery was over his head, but I could see his prominent well-formed features and his piercing dark eyes, which were fixed on me with an expression almost uncanny; I might have imagined that he meditated evil, but the near vicinity of various other inhabitants of the village made this seem improbable. Indeed, the opposite appeared to be the case, for as I looked at him he drew a long skinny brown hand from the folds of his white garments, and, with a gleam of teeth that did duty for a smile, pointed down a side-path, waving me, as it were, away from the road by which I had come in the morning. No doubt I was a fool, but although he did not speak I felt, the Lord only knows why, that he intended to show me an easier and more convenient route. Without a moment's thought, and quite at a loss to account for the peculiar fascination his keen gaze exercised over me, and for the dominant power of his will, I followed his direction, and in less than three minutes found myself turning a somersault in the air, as Sparrow came violently to the ground. In

the dark confusion of the inky shadows, both he and I had omitted
to notice a deep unfinished trench, cut half across the road, which
omission was our undoing.

Well, I won't say much about this part of the story; it contains
some of the most miserable moments of my life. If only I had
broken my own leg it wouldn't have mattered, but Sparrow was
my favourite pony, I loved him dearly (a clean-bred chestnut, 13.3,
the best "back" I have ever ridden), and he broke his instead. I shall
never quite forget the sound of the shot that put the poor beast out
of his pain. As for that damned Gippy, I did my best to find him,
but I never came across the smallest trace of him; that he didn't
belong to the village I proved without a doubt.

The following morning when I sat down to my writing-table
feeling a bit off colour, my eyes fell on the mummy's hand, which
was once more in its place in the pipe-rack. Upon my soul, the sight
of the beastly thing gave me quite a turn; it recalled for a moment
the hand that had lured poor Sparrow to destruction.

"Where did you find that hand, Simonds?" I asked.

"It had fallen down behind the sofa, sir, though who touched it
I can't think. I've stuck it up pretty firm this time, sir. It's a mercy
Pat didn't get at it, sir." (Pat is my terrier.)

"I wish he had," I said, under my breath.

The P. & O. steamship *Mercia* arrived at Port Said in due course,
and certainly my lucky star was in the ascendant, for just as I was
preparing to run down from Cairo (where I had gone in advance)
for a brief interview with Colonel Colleton and his daughter, during
the operation of coaling, I received a telegram telling me that a large
French vessel had gone aground in the canal, and consequently they
would be delayed in her wake for two days at least.

Those two days were very blissful ones to me, and, but for an unfortunate incident that happened the last evening, would have ended as happily as they had begun. I must now mention that I had known Eva Colleton from childhood, and we were what is called "rather more than friends", although her good old dad was entirely ignorant of the fact, and I was anxious he should remain so (after all there was no definite "understanding" between us). A man does not consider an impecunious captain in a line regiment a particularly desirable husband for his beautiful, only daughter. And Eva was beautiful, more so than ever, I thought, when having reached that vile iniquitous hole, Port Said, by the earliest train possible, I stepped on board the ship and saw her eyes light up with pleasure as they met mine. She had not forgotten me, that was certain, and happily the colonel's hearty exclamation, "Hullo, Travers, my boy, that is capital. Upon my soul I am very glad to see you. How's the old regiment?" covered our confusion and the significance of our silent greeting.

"Awful bore, being delayed like this," he continued, to which remark I could scarcely respond.

"We are going to have great fun," broke in Eva; "a concert to-night, a fancy ball tomorrow night, and the people are coming from the other ships."

Then up strolled one or two objectionable young bounders, and a bevy of shrill-voiced Australian girls, who seemed to consider Eva their especial property, and talked about a great many things connected with the voyage, unknown to me, and therefore entirely without interest.

But my time came, when we sat alone together beneath the awning on deck, watching the lazy life on the sandy shore: donkeys with bright-coloured trappings, little brown boys who cried for

backsheesh, and the quivering mirage, so real and so utterly un-
poetical. How I loathed it all! Yet her interest and excitement over
what was novel to her almost made me change my mind, even as
regards the horrible wriggling urchins, who dived, and spluttered,
and shrieked for unmerited reward.

We were both happy, and I suppose that is enough for anybody.
She was not one of those girls who like to play with a chap, make
him miserable one moment and blissful the next. She always preferred plain sailing, as I do; and although it was understood that
nothing could be put into words, her sweet candid eyes told me all
I wanted to know, and I don't fancy she found mine less expressive.
She listened, with the patience exercised often by unselfish woman
towards selfish man, to a long catalogue of my woes, beginning
with flies and heat, and ending with the story of Sparrow's untimely
death; then I ingeniously made her talk of her home, and, to my
own intense satisfaction, managed to elicit the fact that no one as yet
stood higher in her favour than myself. "Some day" was the refrain
of all we said to each other, yet the magic word was never spoken;
it was written in our hearts and read only by means of that strange
telepathy which exists between those who love each other truly.

Ted Knox and Harry Barton, two of our fellows, came down
next day from Cairo, and the fancy ball on board the *Mercia* was a
fruitful topic of conversation. Ted and Barty determined to aston-
ish the assembled company by especially original and startling
costumes, and therefore chose to represent Romulus and Remus,
in reference to their regimental nickname "the twins", which
had been given owing to a remote likeness between them. They
brought their dresses from Cairo, and I can't say that I considered
them particularly successful. In the first place the joke which had
inspired them was unknown to the "Mercians", and I'm bound to

say that wigs of corkscrew ringlets, combined with classical white calico tunics and short frilly trousers, made two rather good-looking chaps look uncommonly ugly.

However, I was not in the most cheerful of moods, for across my happiness came lurid gleams of consciousness that the boundary of my heaven was limited, and that in the early morning I should hold Eva's hand in mine for the last time, and watch the *Mercia* steam away into a world of uncertainty.

It being still permitted in those days, I wore my uniform, for "tomfoolery", as I mentally called it, didn't appeal to me just then. Simonds had sent it down, and I read his letter quickly, in which he apologised for certain omissions. It was only later that I recalled his postscript. "Did you happen, sir, to take the skeleton with you? It's gone again this morning, and I can't find it nowhere." I did not understand this allusion at the moment, and had no leisure to consider its meaning; I prepared to make the most of my time in paradise, and I did so, I think. Afterwards, when all had passed as a watch in the night, and I was down with a bout of fever, those hours came back to me as a strange jumble of music and laughter, visions of fair Bacchantes in white, wound about with garlands of vine-leaves cut out of green paper, Ophelia in a pair of sheets, the inevitable baby of six feet with coral and blue bows, shepherd-esses, Turks, red and black demons, and the tramp of many feet; then through all, the quiet moonlight, a distant corner beneath a sheltering boat, Eva's clear eyes, and a farewell kiss which was not denied me.

But my story is not with that; I must go back to the moment when the ball came to an end, and I left her at the foot of the companion ladder, saying that we should meet in the morning. I won't describe my feelings, they would not interest anyone particularly;

for the strange part of the tender passion is, that however deeply we have sunned ourselves in its boundless glory, and listened to its subtle music, we fail signally in sympathising when we hear of others equally affected.

I confess I was in somewhat of a maze, yet I shall declare to the end of my life that I felt sane enough when I saw what I did, and when the thing happened which I am going to describe. As I passed through the motley crowd with an involuntary feeling of astonishment that people could make such fools of themselves, and anxious to get back to the hotel and be alone with my thoughts, a man stepped from amongst them and walked in front of me. He was thin, of middle height, and dressed in long white classical draperies, a popular dress, for the obvious reason that it was easily obtainable and easily adjusted. It became evident that he was also leaving the ship, and I, not being quite sure of the way, followed him. The rest happened in a few minutes. He strode slowly along with a sedateness that made me think he must be a middle-aged man, and then suddenly, at a corner, turned and looked me straight in the face. I swear it was none other than the Egyptian who had made me change my course so unluckily that night when poor Sparrow came to grief. They may say what they like about flickering lights and deceptive moon-rays, but although my astonishment was great (for what was he doing there at all?), I knew him at once, recognised the strange magnetic gaze, the clear-cut features. I started forward with an exclamation, determined that my reckoning with him should at last be settled. He had reached the top of the gangway and now proceeded to walk down it. How shall I explain what occurred? Eager that he should not escape me, I stepped after him, then suddenly seemed to be treading on air; there was no longer a plank beneath my feet. I fell, clove the water with a blow and splash, hit my head violently against something hard, struggled, spluttered, choked, sank, rose again; choked again, sank again, and then remembered nothing, until I awoke in my hotel bedroom.

Someone was rubbing me, a doctor, I discovered afterwards; I then became aware that Ted Knox, our major, was also standing near. He was still in his Romulus dress and he looked so inexpressibly funny – for his face, surrounded by auburn ringlets, was very grave and solemn – that I burst out laughing.

"What's the matter?" I asked, and then he smiled.

"That's all right, old chap," he said cheerfully; "you are yourself again, but you pretty nearly snuffed out, and we've had the devil of a time trying to bring you round."

"I remember now—"

"The champagne was good, I must say, and there was plenty of it," interrupted another voice, and Remus stepped forward, "but if you will walk over the side of the ship, instead of down the gangway—"

"What time is it? When does the *Mercia* go?" I asked quickly; memory was returning.

"In an hour; lie still, old man."

"I must get up, I have an appointment—"

"You can't possibly, I tell you. I'm not humbugging; you were as nearly drowned as you could be."

"I will, I tell you."

Here the doctor intervened.

Well, the long and short of it was, he wouldn't let me go and I had to give in. The *Mercia* sailed and I didn't see Eva again; at midday I received a little note, which had been left for me and was given me with the best intentions by Barty, as a possible "pick-me-up". Its results were rather unfortunate as it happened; it contained very few words, but meant much to me:

> Oh, Tom, I am sorry, so sorry, but so thankful you are alive. I don't want to be hard, because we were so happy and I know you felt miserable; it is difficult then, and the temptation is great. But I am sorry, and I wish it hadn't happened on your last night. Goodbye, dear, and try not to for my sake.
>
> Yours,
>
> EVA

What had people told her? The fools! I could imagine their rotten chaff, which would vex her tender soul. It was an incoherent little letter; the mingled love and reproach went to my heart, for the reproach was unmerited, and I could not tell her so.

It was after this that fever overtook me, and for many days I lay and tossed and talked nonsense. When I was myself again, I wrote to her and also made inquiries about my enemy, but with no result; indeed, my remarks were met with such irritating scepticism, bordering on ridicule, that I soon found it best to drop the subject.

There is not much more to tell. For some time I was free from the strange overshadowing that had proved so baneful. I thought very seriously about it, and whether political enmity could have anything to do with the matter. As far as I remembered, I had never personally done a wrong to any native or given cause for private spite. Yet again, I was too unimportant an individual surely to fall a victim to political vengeance; had hatred of the dominant race formed the motive, another than myself would have been chosen for purposes of revenge.

The only person I might have taken into my confidence was Bob Jenkins. He would have listened without scoffing to the weird fancies that at times crept through my brain, for they were after his own heart, and I have heard him talk by the half-hour about sensory automatism, telaesthesia, and goodness knows what. But Bob had gone home to England, accompanied by a retinue of mummies, destined for the British Museum; he was no end of a swell now, it seemed, with a lot of letters after his name, for the ancient Egyptians can apparently confer benefits indirectly, thousands of years after their decease.

As for the "dead hand", I was relieved to see that it no longer adorned my pipe-rack, and asked no questions. It was only when Simonds left me that I realised it was still in my possession.

"That there skeleton is at the back of the table drawer, sir," he said; "I put it there for safety. I can't get clear about it somehow, sir—" but I cut him short and changed the subject.

I had never been quite fit since that spell of fever at Port Said, so early the following year I got six months' leave and went home, before Eva and her father returned from Australia. One can't always arrange these things satisfactorily, but I had received a dear letter from her apologising for her "heartless note and odious suspicion". A woman's faith in the man she loves is very wonderful, and ought to make him jolly careful how he behaves himself. She believed my fantastic story, bless her, though no one else did.

They were not long in following me, and I will pass over our meeting and the hopes raised in my mind by a piece of good luck that befell me just then in the shape of a few hundreds a year, which I inherited through the unexpected death of a distant relation.

Time went very quickly. I put up at my old lodgings in Jermyn Street, and, having plenty of pals at Woolwich, went down constantly from London, enjoying more than one good day with the "drag" hounds.

Merriton, of the Remount Department, lent me a horse, a grand old grey, under 15.3, steady as time over his fences, as knowing as they make 'em, and as spry and ready as a two-year-old.

By some curious chance, connected, I fancy, with certain letters between Eva and a cousin who had married a gunner then quartered at Woolwich, it came about that, to my intense delight, I unexpectedly met her one afternoon at some sports in Charlton Park, and learnt that she was staying on the Common with the Evanses.

"I heard you were here," she said quietly, with her usual straightness, instead of pretending surprise at seeing me.

On the following day there was a meet of the "drag" and I went down by an early train, full of excitement. Curiously enough I had a note from Bob Jenkins that morning, asking me to look him up.

"When I do I'll take him that infernal hand," I thought, glancing viciously at the chest of drawers on which I believed I had thrown it the night before in my disgust at discovering that it had been packed amongst some books in a box I had newly opened (it was not there, however).

It was a ripping day. Mrs Evans was driving her smart little dog-cart, and Eva sat by her side. They took up their position at a good point of vantage, in view of some pretty big fences and a rather awkward water-jump. Eva has often told me since that, in spite of her sporting tendencies, she would have preferred another position, but did not dare give herself away by such a faint-hearted confession. Yet I think she had plenty of trust in me all the same (for one thing, Surprise was at his best, as fresh as paint), and a look in her eyes, as I rode up and spoke to her for a few moments before we started, made me say to myself, "I'll be hanged if I don't get her to settle it all today, and have done with uncertainty."

We had a splendid run. It was one of the best "lines" in the country; a few nasty jumps, which Surprise tackled in a manner worthy of his reputation; now and then a long sweep of turf which gave the chance of a glorious gallop, then a drop into a lane, broken ground, corners where riders and horses scrambled for first chance, and more than one came down, as it was a bit slippery.

The good grey held on his way; nothing disturbed him, not even the shouting yokels at the water-jump; he never made a mistake. It was one of the crowning moments of my life when, having cleared the brook by two good feet, we rushed the hill towards the hedge and post and rails that divided us from the road, and I saw Eva stand up in the cart and wave her handkerchief.

But now comes the most extraordinary part of my extraordinary story, the climax of all that has gone before. I don't expect anyone will ever understand it; Eva and I only speak of it to each other, and that not often. I can merely say that I tell it as it befell, without exaggeration.

The point at which I intended to take the jump was near a corner, and another hedge ran at right angles to it, skirting a field. I'll swear I saw no one as we approached, but suddenly a figure moved out from a clump of thorn. He looked to me like a country-man or tramp with a sack or coat over his head, but as he appeared I suddenly caught sight of his face. Was I mad? By all that's holy, it was the face of that cursed Egyptian.

Surprise saw him too. He, who had been given his name because nothing astonished him, swerved, checked, then rose awkwardly to the jump and muddled it. I don't know what happened; the last I remember was a bewildering journey through the air, both of us wrong side up, it seemed; then a fall, two hoofs near my eyes, a heavy weight crushing me, stars, something snapping, and keen pain like the stab of a knife, all passed in a few seconds.

Surprise was none the worse, strange to say, not hurt a bit beyond a scratch on the off hind-quarter; but I broke several ribs, my jaw and collar bone, and very nearly my neck.

Well, all's well that ends well, and my dear girl played up like the angel she is; so did her dad and the rest of them, the Evanses especially, for I was ill in their house for close on two months.

At first I was unconscious and delirious, they told me, and talked "a lot of rot" about Egyptians and mummies and skeleton hands, the last things a spill out hunting would reasonably call from the recesses of the brain; about Eva too, I am afraid; but most of all I asked for Bob, and at last Eva guessed something and found out his address.

One day when I was better, but very weak and not quite my normal self, he came down, looking just the same except that a sallow, somewhat pasty complexion had replaced the Egyptian sunburn.

"Well, you've had a narrow shave," he said, grinning rather unnaturally.

"Yes," I answered, with some wildness, I fear, "but it will be all right now. You will take it, it won't hurt you, and you'll find it there at my diggings; it was missing, but it's certain to turn up again."

He interrupted, the grin giving way to a pitying expression, and remarked evasively:

"You seem to be in very comfortable quarters here, you lucky dog."

However, I insisted on telling my tale, and when once he heard it he no longer thought I was off my head, but listened with the keenest attention and interest, using, as was his wont, a great many long words which I can't remember, and which would do me no good if I could.

I suppose all people with hobbies are more or less selfish. "I'll take it, I'll have it with pleasure," he said, and I'm quite sure he left by an earlier train in order to secure the treasure without delay.

The following morning I received a short note from him, written in the writing room of the British Museum:

You've conferred the greatest favour on me, old chap, and I can't thank you enough. Bless'd if the mummified hand which I found knocking about on the floor in your bedroom in Jermyn Street doesn't belong, as I half suspected, to Nephah, chief magician to Sethi II, a great man in his time. I have wasted hours in searching for it. The smallest of the carpal bones is missing, I regret to say, but even that may be remedied some day, perhaps.

(I hope that bone is buried fathoms deep in the sands of the desert.)

I have just had the infinite pleasure of fitting it into its place, and it will soon take up its original position permanently. Mind you come and see it when you are all right, and in town again.

But neither I nor my wife have visited Sethi II's chief magician, nor do we intend to do so.

And I have never seen the lean Egyptian again, thank God.

'A PROFESSOR OF EGYPTOLOGY' (1904)

Guy Boothby

Guy Boothby (1867–1905) was a British-based Australian writer of detective tales, including the very popular series of Dr Nikola novels, two collections of ghost stories, and other Gothic tales which often focused on ancient Egypt. Boothby's novel, *Pharos the Egyptian* (1899), centres on the magical powers of a mummy and its sinister activities as it attempts to take revenge against the West. This type of revenge narrative constituted a popular strand in tales about Egypt at the time.

'A Professor of Egyptology' was printed in *The Graphic* in December 1904. Like *Pharos the Egyptian*, it suggests that the past is not quite a dead letter. In a story of reincarnation the emphasis is placed on ancient images of perceived betrayal and a need for forgiveness. The tale is set within the social context of British high society at leisure in Edwardian Cairo, which provides a cultural and historical counterpoint to the narrative of ancient Egypt. The focus on how to make atonement for historical misdeeds and how to resolve the problems of the past reflects the often ambivalent attitude that many in Britain held towards the occupation of Egypt, even if here it is a representative of ancient Egyptian authority who seeks pardon but also, tellingly, peace.

F ROM SEVEN O'CLOCK IN THE EVENING UNTIL HALF PAST, THAT is to say for the half-hour preceding dinner, the Grand Hall of the Hôtel Occidental, throughout the season, is practically a lounge, and is crowded with the most fashionable folk wintering in Cairo. The evening I am anxious to describe was certainly no exception to the rule. At the foot of the fine marble staircase – the pride of its owner – a well-known member of the French Ministry was chatting with an English Duchess whose pretty, but somewhat delicate, daughter was flirting mildly with one of the Sirdar's Bimbashis, on leave from the Soudan. On the right-hand lounge of the Hall an Italian Countess, whose antecedents were as doubtful as her diamonds, was apparently listening to a story a handsome Greek *attaché* was telling her; in reality, however, she was endeavouring to catch scraps of a conversation being carried on, a few feet away, between a witty Russian and an equally clever daughter of the United States. Almost every nationality was represented there, but, fortunately for our prestige, the majority were English. The scene was a brilliant one, and the sprinkling of military and diplomatic uniforms (there was a Reception at the Khedivial Palace later) lent an additional touch of colour to the picture. Taken altogether, and regarded from a political point of view, the gathering had a significance of its own.

At the end of the Hall, near the large glass doors, a handsome, elderly lady, with grey hair, was conversing with one of the leading English doctors of the place – a grey-haired, clever-looking man, who possessed the happy faculty of being able to impress everyone

with whom he talked with the idea that he infinitely preferred his or
her society to that of any other member of the world's population.
They were discussing the question of the most suitable clothing
for a Nile voyage, and as the lady's daughter, who was seated next
her, had been conversant with her mother's ideas on the subject
ever since their first visit to Egypt (as indeed had been the Doctor),
she preferred to lie back on the divan and watch the people about
her. She had large, dark, contemplative eyes. Like her mother she
took life seriously, but in a somewhat different fashion. One who
has been bracketed third in the Mathematical Tripos can scarcely be
expected to bestow very much thought on the comparative merits
of Jaeger, as opposed to dresses of the Common or Garden flannel.
From this, however, it must not be inferred that she was in any way
a blue stocking, that is, of course, in the vulgar acceptation of the
word. She was thorough in all she undertook, and for the reason
that mathematics interested her very much the same way that
Wagner, chess, and, shall we say, croquet, interest other people, she
made it her hobby, and it must be confessed she certainly succeeded
in it. At other times she rode, drove, played tennis and hockey, and
looked upon her world with calm, observant eyes that were more
disposed to find good than evil in it. Contradictions that we are,
even to ourselves, it was only those who knew her intimately, and
they were few and far between, who realised that, under that apparently sober, matter-of-fact personality, there existed a strong leaning
towards the mysterious, or, more properly speaking, the occult.
Possibly she herself would have been the first to deny this – but that
I am right in my surmise this story will surely be sufficient proof.

Mrs Westmoreland and her daughter had left their comfortable
Yorkshire home in September, and, after a little dawdling on the
Continent, had reached Cairo in November – the best month to

arrive, in my opinion, for then the rush has not set in, the hotel servants have not had sufficient time to become weary of their duties, and what is better still, all the best rooms have not been bespoken. It was now the middle of December, and the fashionable caravanserai, upon which they had for many years bestowed their patronage, was crowded from roof to cellar. Every day people were being turned away, and the manager's continual lament was that he had not another hundred rooms wherein to place more guests. He was a Swiss, and for that reason regarded hotel-keeping in the light of a profession.

On this particular evening Mrs Westmoreland and her daughter Cecilia had arranged to dine with Dr Forsyth – that is to say, they were to eat their meal at his table in order that they might meet a man of whom they had heard much, but whose acquaintance they had not as yet made. The individual in question was a certain Professor Constanides – reputed one of the most advanced Egyptologists, and the author of several well-known works. Mrs Westmoreland was not of an exacting nature, and so long as she dined in agreeable company did not trouble herself very much whether it was with an English earl or a distinguished foreign *savant*.

"It really does not matter, my dear," she was wont to observe to her daughter. "So long as the cooking is good and the wine above reproach, there is absolutely nothing to choose between them. A Prime Minister and a country vicar are, after all, only men. Feed them well and they'll lie down and purr like tame cats. They don't want conversation." From this it will be seen that Mrs Westmoreland was well acquainted with her world. Whether Miss Cecilia shared her opinions is another matter. At any rate, she had been looking forward for nearly a fortnight to meeting Constanides, who was popularly supposed to possess an extraordinary intuitive knowledge – instinct, perhaps, it should be called – concerning the localities of tombs of the Pharaohs of the Eleventh, Twelfth and Thirteenth Dynasties.

"I am afraid Constanides is going to be late," said the Doctor, who had consulted his watch more than once. "I hope, in that case, as his friend and your host, you will permit me to offer you my apologies."

The Doctor at no time objected to the sound of his own voice, and on this occasion he was even less inclined to do so. Mrs Westmoreland was a widow with an ample income, and Cecilia, he felt sure, would marry ere long.

"He has still three minutes in which to put in an appearance," observed that young lady, quietly. And then she added in the same tone, "Perhaps we ought to be thankful if he comes at all."

Both Mrs Westmoreland and her friend the Doctor regarded her with mildly reproachful eyes. The former could not understand anyone refusing a dinner such as she felt sure the Doctor had arranged for them; while the latter found it impossible to imagine a man who would dare to disappoint the famous Dr Forsyth, who, having failed in Harley Street, was nevertheless coining a fortune in the Land of the Pharaohs.

"My good friend Constanides will not disappoint us, I feel sure," he said, consulting his watch for the fourth time. "Possibly I am a little fast, at any rate I have never known him to be unpunctual. A remarkable – a very remarkable man is Constanides. I cannot remember ever to have met another like him. And such a scholar!"

Having thus bestowed his approval upon him the worthy Doctor pulled down his cuffs, straightened his tie, adjusted his *pince-nez* in his best professional manner, and looked round the hall as if searching for someone bold enough to contradict the assertion he had just made.

"You have, of course, read his *Mythological Egypt*," observed Miss Cecilia, demurely, speaking as if the matter were beyond doubt.

The Doctor looked a little confused.

"Ahem! Well, let me see," he stammered, trying to find a way out of the difficulty. "Well, to tell the truth, my dear young lady, I'm not quite sure that I have studied that particular work. As a matter of fact, you see, I have so little leisure at my disposal for any reading that is not intimately connected with my profession. That, of course, must necessarily come before everything else."

Miss Cecilia's mouth twitched as if she were endeavouring to keep back a smile. At the same moment the glass doors of the vestibule opened and a man entered. So remarkable was he that everyone turned to look at him – a fact which did not appear to disconcert him in the least.

He was tall, well shaped, and carried himself with the air of one accustomed to command. His face was oval, his eyes large and set somewhat wide apart. It was only when they were directed fairly at one that one became aware of the power they possessed. The cheek bones were a trifle high, and the forehead possibly retreated towards the jet-black hair more than is customary in Greeks. He wore neither beard nor moustache, thus enabling one to see the wide, firm mouth, the compression of the lips of which spoke for the determination of their possessor. Those who had an eye for such things noted the fact that he was faultlessly dressed, while Miss Cecilia, who had the precious gift of observation largely developed, noted that, with the exception of a single ring and a magnificent pearl stud, the latter strangely set, he wore no jewellery of any sort.

He looked about him for Dr Forsyth, and, when he had located him, hastened forward.

"My dear friend," he said in English, which he spoke with scarcely a trace of foreign accent, "I must crave your pardon a thousand times if I have kept you waiting."

"On the contrary," replied the Doctor, effusively, "you are punctuality itself. Permit me to have the pleasure – the very great pleasure – of introducing you to my friends, Mrs Westmoreland and her daughter, Miss Cecilia, of whom you have often heard me speak."

Professor Constanides bowed and expressed the pleasure he experienced in making their acquaintance. Though she could not have told you why, Miss Cecilia found herself undergoing very much the same sensation as she had done when she had passed up the Throne Room at her presentation. A moment later the gong sounded, and, with much rustling of skirts and fluttering of fans, a general movement was made towards the dining-room.

As host, Dr Forsyth gave his arm to Mrs Westmoreland, Constanides following with Miss Cecilia. The latter was conscious of a vague feeling of irritation; she admired the man and his work, but she wished his name had been anything rather than what it was.

(It should be here remarked that the last Constanides she had encountered had swindled her abominably in the matter of a turquoise brooch, and in consequence the name had been an offence to her ever since.)

Dr Forsyth's table was situated at the further end, in the window, and from it a good view of the room could be obtained. The scene was an animated one, and one of the party, at least, I fancy, will never forget it – try how she may.

During the first two or three courses the conversation was practically limited to Cecilia and Constanides; the Doctor and Mrs

Westmoreland being too busy to waste time on idle chatter. Later, they became more amenable to the discipline of the table – or, in other words, they found time to pay attention to their neighbours.

Since then I have often wondered with what feelings Cecilia looks back upon that evening. In order, perhaps, to punish me for my curiosity, she has admitted to me since that she had never known, up to that time, what it was to converse with a really clever man. I submitted to the humiliation for the reason that we are, if not lovers, at least old friends, and, after all, Mrs Westmoreland's cook is one in a thousand.

From that evening forward, scarcely a day passed in which Constanides did not enjoy some portion of Miss Westmoreland's society. They met at the polo ground, drove in the Gezîreh, shopped in the Muski, or listened to the band, over afternoon tea, on the balcony of Shepheard's Hotel. Constanides was always unobtrusive, always picturesque and invariably interesting. What was more to the point, he never failed to command attention whenever or wherever he might appear. In the Native Quarter he was apparently better known than in the European. Cecilia noticed that there he was treated with a deference such as one would only expect to be shown to a king. She marvelled, but said nothing. Personally, I can only wonder that her mother did not caution her before it was too late. Surely she must have seen how dangerous the intimacy was likely to become. It was old Colonel Bettenham who sounded the first note of warning. In some fashion or another he was connected with the Westmorelands, and therefore had more or less right to speak his mind.

"Who the man is, I am not in a position to say," he remarked to the mother; "but if I were in your place I should be very careful. Cairo at this time of the year is full of adventurers."

"But, my dear Colonel," answered Mrs Westmoreland, "you surely do not mean to insinuate that the Professor is an adventurer. He was introduced to us by Dr Forsyth, and he has written so many clever books."

"Books, my dear madam, are not everything," the other replied judicially, and with that fine impartiality which marks a man who does not read. "As a matter of fact I am bound to confess that Phipps – one of my captains – wrote a novel some years ago, but only one. The mess pointed out to him that it wasn't good form, don't you know, so he never tried the experiment again. But as for this man, Constanides, as they call him, I should certainly be more than careful."

I have been told since that this conversation worried poor Mrs Westmoreland more than she cared to admit, even to herself. To a very large extent she, like her daughter, had fallen under the spell of the Professor's fascination. Had she been asked, point blank, she would doubtless have declared that she preferred the Greek to the Englishman – though, of course, it would have seemed flat heresy to say so. And yet – well, doubtless you can understand what I mean without my explaining further.

I am inclined to believe that I was the first to notice that there was serious trouble brewing. I could see a strained look in the girl's eyes for which I found it difficult to account. Then the truth dawned upon me, and I am ashamed to say that I began to watch her systematically. We have few secrets from each other now, and she has told me a good deal of what happened during that extraordinary time – for extraordinary it certainly was. Perhaps none of us realised what a unique drama we were watching – one of the strangest, I am tempted to believe, that this world of ours has ever seen.

Christmas was just past and the New Year was fairly under way when the beginning of the end came. I think by that time even Mrs Westmoreland had arrived at some sort of knowledge of the case. But it was then too late to interfere. I am as sure that Cecilia was not in love with Constanides as I am of anything. She was merely fascinated by him, and to a degree that, happily for the peace of the world, is as rare as the reason for it is perplexing.

To be precise, it was on Tuesday, January the 3rd, that the crisis came. On the evening of that day, accompanied by her daughter and escorted by Dr Forsyth, Mrs Westmoreland attended a reception at the palace of a certain Pasha, whose name I am obviously compelled to keep to myself. For the purposes of my story it is sufficient, however, that he is a man who prides himself on being up-to-date in most things, and for that and other reasons invitations to his receptions are eagerly sought after. In his drawing-room one may meet some of the most distinguished men in Europe, and on occasion it is even possible to obtain an insight into certain political intrigues that, to put it mildly, afford one an opportunity of reflecting on the instability of mundane affairs and of politics in particular.

The evening was well advanced before Constanides made his appearance. When he did, it was observed that he was more than usually quiet. Later, Cecilia permitted him to conduct her into the balcony, whence, since it was a perfect moonlight night, a fine view of the Nile could be obtained. Exactly what he said to her I have never been able to discover; I have, however, her mother's assurance that she was visibly agitated when she rejoined her. As a matter of fact, they returned to the hotel almost immediately, when Cecilia, pleading weariness, retired to her room.

And now this is the part of the story you will find as difficult to believe as I did. Yet I have indisputable evidence that it is true.

It was nearly midnight and the large hotel was enjoying the only quiet it knows in the twenty-four hours. I have just said that Cecilia had retired, but in making that assertion I am not telling the exact truth, for though she had bade her mother "Goodnight" and had gone to her room, it was not to rest. Regardless of the cold night air she had thrown open the window, and was standing looking out into the moonlit street. Of what she was thinking I do not know, nor can she remember. For my own part, however, I incline to the belief that she was in a semi-hypnotic condition and that for the time being her mind was a blank.

From this point I will let Cecilia tell the story herself.

How long I stood at the window I cannot say; it may have been only five minutes, it might have been an hour. Then, suddenly, an extraordinary thing happened. I knew that it was imprudent, I was aware that it was even wrong, but an overwhelming craving to go out seized me. I felt as if the house were stifling me and that if I did not get out into the cool night air, and within a few minutes, I should die. Stranger still, I felt no desire to battle with the temptation. It was as if a will infinitely stronger than my own was dominating me and that I was powerless to resist. Scarcely conscious of what I was doing I changed my dress, and then, throwing on a cloak, switched off the electric light and stepped out into the corridor. The white-robed Arab servants were lying about on the floor as is their custom; they were all asleep. On the thick carpet of the great staircase my steps made no sound. The hall was in semi-darkness and the watchman must have been absent on his rounds, for there was no one there to spy upon me. Passing through the vestibule I turned the key of the front door. Still success attended me, for the lock shot back with scarcely a sound and

I found myself in the street. Even then I had no thought of the folly of this escapade. I was merely conscious of the mysterious power that was dragging me on. Without hesitation I turned to the right and hastened along the pavement, faster I think than I had ever walked in my life. Under the trees it was comparatively dark, but out in the roadway it was well-nigh as bright as day. Once a carriage passed me and I could hear its occupants, who were French, conversing merrily – otherwise I seemed to have the city to myself. Later I heard a *muezzin* chanting his call to prayer from the minaret of some mosque in the neighbourhood, the cry being taken up and repeated from other mosques. Then at the corner of a street I stopped as if in obedience to a command. I can recall the fact that I was trembling, but for what reason I could not tell. I say this to show that while I was incapable of returning to the hotel, or of exercising my normal will power, I still possessed the faculty of observation.

I had scarcely reached the corner referred to, which, as a matter of fact, I believe I should recognise if I saw it again, when the door of a house opened and a man emerged. It was Professor Constanides, but his appearance at such a place and at such an hour, like everything else that happened that night, did not strike me as being in any way extraordinary.

"You have obeyed me," he said by way of greeting. "That is well. Now let us be going – the hour is late."

As he said it there came the rattle of wheels and a carriage drove swiftly round the corner and pulled up before us. My companion helped me into it and took his place beside me. Even then, unheard-of as my action was, I had no thought of resisting.

"What does it mean?" I asked. "Oh, tell me what it means? Why am I here?"

"You will soon know," was his reply, and his voice took a tone I had never noticed in it before.

We had driven some considerable distance, in fact, I believe we had crossed the river, before either of us spoke again.

"Think," said my companion, "and tell me whether you can remember ever having driven with me before?"

"We have driven together many times lately," I replied. "Yesterday to the polo, and the day before to the Pyramids."

"Think again," he said, and as he did so he placed his hand on mine. It was as cold as ice. However, I only shook my head.

"I cannot remember," I answered, and yet I seemed to be dimly conscious of something that was too intangible to be a recollection. He uttered a little sigh and once more we were silent. The horses must have been good ones for they whirled us along at a fast pace. I did not take much interest in the route we followed, but at last something attracted my attention and I knew that we were on the road to Gizeh. A few moments later the famous Museum, once the palace of the ex-Khedive Ismail, came into view. Almost immediately the carriage pulled up in the shadow of the *Lebbek* trees and my companion begged me to alight. I did so, whereupon he said something, in what I can only suppose was Arabic, to his coachman, who whipped up his horses and drove swiftly away.

"Come," he said, in the same tone of command as before, and then led the way towards the gates of the old palace. Dominated as my will was by his I could still notice how beautiful the building looked in the moonlight. In the daytime it presents a faded and unsubstantial appearance, but now, with its Oriental tracery, it was almost fairylike. The Professor halted at the gates and unlocked them. How he had obtained the key, and by what right he admitted us, I cannot say. It suffices that, almost before I was aware of it, we had passed through the garden and were ascending the steps to the main entrance. The doors behind us, we entered the first room. It is only another point in this extraordinary adventure when I declare that even now I was not afraid; and yet to find oneself in such a place and at such an hour at any other time would probably have driven me beside myself with terror. The moonlight streamed in upon us, revealing the ancient monuments and the other indescribable memorials of those long-dead ages. Once more my conductor uttered his command and we went on through the second room, passed the Shekh-El-Beled and the Seated Scribe. Room after room we traversed, and to do so it seemed to me that we ascended stairs innumerable. At last we came to one in which Constanides paused. It contained numerous mummy cases and was lighted by a skylight through which the rays of the moon streamed in. We were standing before one which I remembered to have remarked on the occasion of our last visit. I could distinguish the paintings upon it distinctly. Professor Constanides, with a deftness which showed his familiarity with the work, removed the lid and revealed to me the swathed-up figure within. The face was uncovered and was strangely well-preserved. I gazed down on it, and as I did so a sensation that I had never known before passed over me. My body seemed to be shrinking, my blood to be turning to ice. For the first time I endeavoured to exert myself, to tear myself from the bonds that were holding me. But it was in vain. I was sinking – sinking – sinking – into I knew not what. Then the voice of the man who had brought me to the place sounded in my ears as if he were speaking from a long way off. After that a great light burst upon me, and it was as if I were walking in a dream; yet I knew it was too real, too true to life to be a mere creation of my fancy.

It was night and the heavens were studded with stars. In the distance a great army was encamped and at intervals the calls of the sentries reached me. Somehow I seemed to feel no wonderment at my position. Even my dress caused me no surprise. To my left, as I looked towards the river, was a large tent, before which armed men paced continually. I looked about me as if I expected to see someone, but there was no one to greet me.

"It is for the last time," I told myself. "Come what may, it shall be the last time!"

Still I waited, and as I did so I could hear the night wind sighing through the rushes on the river's bank. From the tent near me – for Usirtasen, son of Amenemhait – was then fighting against the Libyans and was commanding his army in person – came the sound of revelry. The air blew cold from the desert and I shivered, for I was but thinly clad. Then I hid myself in the shadow of a great rock that was near at hand. Presently I caught the sound of a footstep, and there came into view a tall man, walking carefully, as though he had no desire that the sentries on guard before the Royal tent should become aware of his presence in the neighbourhood. As I saw him I moved from where I was standing to meet him. He was none other than Sinûhît – younger son of Amenemhait and brother of Usirtasen – who was at that moment conferring with his generals in the tent.

I can see him now as he came towards me, tall, handsome, and defiant in his bearing as a man should be. He walked with the assured step of one who has been a soldier and trained to warlike exercises from his youth up. For a moment I regretted the news I had to tell him – but only for a moment. I could hear the voice of Usirtasen in the tent, and after that I had no thought for anyone else.

"Is it thou, Nofrît?" he asked as soon as he saw me.

"It is I!" I replied. "You are late, Sinûhît. You tarry too long over the wine cups."

"You wrong me, Nofrît," he answered, with all the fierceness for which he was celebrated. "I have drunk no wine this night. Had I not been kept by the Captain of the Guard I should have been here sooner. Thou art not angry with me, Nofrît?"

"Nay, that were presumption on my part, my lord," I answered. "Art thou not the King's son, Sinûhît?"

"And by the Holy Ones I swear that it were better for me if I were not," he replied. "Usirtasen, my brother, takes all and I am but the jackal that gathers up the scraps wheresoever he may find them." He paused for a moment. "However, all goes well with our plot. Let me but have time and I will yet be ruler of this land and of all the Land of Khem beside." He drew himself up to his full height and looked towards the sleeping camp. It was well known that between the brothers there was but little love, and still less trust.

"Peace, peace," I whispered, fearing lest his words might be overheard. "You must not talk so, my lord. Should you by chance be heard you know what the punishment would be!"

He laughed a short and bitter laugh. He was well aware that Usirtasen would show him no mercy. It was not the first time he had been suspected, and he was playing a desperate game. He came a step closer to me and took my hand in his. I would have withdrawn it – but he gave me no opportunity. Never was a man more in earnest than he was then.

"Nofrît," he said, and I could feel his breath upon my cheek, "what is my answer to be? The time for talking is past; now we must act. As thou knowest, I prefer deeds to words, and tomorrow my brother Usirtasen shall learn that I am as powerful as he."

Knowing what I knew I could have laughed him to scorn for this boastful speech. The time, however, was not yet ripe, so I held my peace. He was plotting against his brother, whom I loved, and it was his desire that I should help him. That, however, I would not do.

"Listen," he said, drawing even closer to me, and speaking in a voice that showed me plainly how much in earnest he was, "thou knowest how much I love thee. Thou knowest that there is nought I would not do for thee or for thy sake. Be but faithful to me now and there is nothing thou shalt ask in vain of me hereafter. All is prepared, and ere the moon is gone I shall be Pharaoh and reign beside Amenemhait, my father."

"Are you so sure that your plans will not miscarry?" I asked, with what was almost a sneer at his recklessness – for recklessness it surely was to think that he could induce an army that had been admittedly successful to swerve in its allegiance to the general who had won its battles for it, and to desert in the face of the enemy. Moreover, I knew that he was wrong in believing that his father cared more for him than for Usirtasen, who had done so much for the kingdom, and who was beloved by high and low alike. But it was not in Sinûhît's nature to look upon the dark side of things. He had complete confidence in himself and in his power to bring his conspiracy against his father and brother to a successful issue. He revealed to me his plans, and, bold though they were, I could see that it was impossible that they could succeed. And in the event of his failing, what mercy could he hope to receive? I knew Usirtasen too well to think that he would show any. With all the eloquence I could command I implored him to abandon the attempt, or at least to delay it for a time. He seized my wrist and pulled me to him, peering fiercely into my face.

"Art playing me false?" he asked. "If it is so it were better that you should drown yourself in yonder river. Betray me and nothing shall save you – not even Pharaoh himself."

That he meant what he said I felt convinced. The man was desperate; he was staking all he had in the world upon the issue of his venture. I can say with truth that it was not my fault that we had been drawn together, and yet on this night of all others it seemed as if there were nothing left for me but to side with him or to bring about his downfall.

"Nofrît," he said, after a short pause, "is it nothing, thinkest thou, to be the wife of a Pharaoh? Is it not worth striving for, particularly when it can be so easily accomplished?"

I knew, however, that he was deluding himself with false hopes. What he had in his mind could never come to pass. I was like dry grass between two fires. All that was required was one small spark to bring about a conflagration in which I should be consumed.

"Harken to me, Nofrît," he continued. "You have means of learning Usirtasen's plans. Send me word tomorrow as to what is in his mind and the rest will be easy. Your reward shall be greater than you dream of."

Though I had no intention of doing what he asked, I knew that in his present humour it would be little short of madness to thwart him. I therefore temporised with him, and allowed him to suppose that I would do as he wished, and then, bidding him good-night, I sped away towards the hut where I was lodged. I had not been there many minutes when a messenger came to me from Usirtasen, summoning me to his presence. Though I could not understand what it meant I hastened to obey.

On arrival there I found him surrounded by the chief officers of his army. One glance at his face was sufficient to tell me that he was violently angry with someone, and I had the best of reasons for believing that that someone was myself. Alas! it was as I had expected. Sinûhît's plot had been discovered; he had been followed and watched, and my meeting with him that evening was known. I protested my innocence in vain. The evidence was too strong against me.

"Speak, girl, and tell what thou knowest," said Usirtasen, in a voice I had never heard him use before. "It is the only way by which thou canst save thyself. Look to it that thy story tallies with the tales of others!"

I trembled in every limb as I answered the questions he put to me. It was plain that he no longer trusted me, and that the favour I had once found in his eyes was gone, never to return.

"It is well," he said when I had finished my story. "And now we will see thy partner – the man who would have put me – the Pharaoh who is to be – to the sword had I not been warned in time."

He made a sign to one of the officers who stood by, whereupon the latter left the tent, to return a few moments later with Sinûhît.

"Hail, brother!" said Usirtasen, mockingly, as he leaned back in his chair and looked at him through half-shut eyes. "You tarried but a short time over the wine cup this night. I fear it pleased thee but little. Forgive me; on another occasion better shall be found for thee lest thou shouldst deem us lacking in our hospitality."

"There were matters that needed my attention and I could not stay," Sinûhît replied, looking his brother in the face. "Thou wouldst not have me neglect my duties."

"Nay! nay! Maybe they were matters that concerned our personal safety?" Usirtasen continued, still with the same gentleness. "Maybe you heard that there were those in our army who were not well disposed towards us? Give me their names, my brother, that due punishment may be meted out to them."

Before Sinûhît could reply, Usirtasen had sprung to his feet.

"Dog!" he cried, "darest thou prate to me of matters of impor-tance when thou knowest thou hast been plotting against me and my father's throne. I have doubted thee these many months and now all is made clear. By the Gods, the Holy Ones, I swear that thou shalt die for this ere cock-crow."

It was at this moment that Sinûhît became aware of my pres-ence. A little cry escaped him, and his face told me as plainly as any words could speak that he believed that I had betrayed him. He was about to speak, probably to denounce me, when the sound of voices reached us from outside. Usirtasen bade the guards ascertain what it meant, and presently a messenger entered the tent. He was travel-stained and weary. Advancing towards where Usirtasen was seated, he knelt before him.

"Hail, Pharaoh," he said. "I come to thee from the Palace of Titoui."

An anxious expression came over Usirtasen's face as he heard this. I also detected beads of perspiration on the brow of Sinûhît. A moment later it was known to us that Amenemhait was dead, and, therefore, Usirtasen reigned in his stead. The news was so sudden, and the consequences so vast, that it was impossible to realise quite what it meant. I looked across at Sinûhît and his eyes met mine. He seemed to be making up his mind about something. Then with lightning speed he sprang upon me; a dagger gleamed in the air; I felt as if a hot iron had been thrust into my breast, and after that I remember no more.

As I felt myself falling I seemed to wake from my dream – if dream it were – to find myself standing in the Museum by the mummy case, and with Professor Constanides by my side.

"You have seen," he said. "You have looked back across the

centuries to that day when, as Nofrît, I believed you had betrayed me, and killed you. After that I escaped from the camp and fled into Kaduma. There I died; but it was decreed that my soul should never know peace till we had met again and you had forgiven me. I have waited all these years, and see – we meet at last."

Strange to say, even then the situation did not strike me as being in any way improbable. Yet now, when I see it set down in black and white, I find myself wondering that I dare to ask anyone in their sober senses to believe it to be true. Was I in truth that same Nofrît who, four thousand years before, had been killed by Sinûhît, son of Amenemhait, because he believed that I had betrayed him? It seemed incredible, and yet, if it were a creation of my imagination, what did the dream mean? I fear it is a riddle of which I shall probably never know the answer.

My failure to reply to his question seemed to cause him pain.

"Nofrît," he said, and his voice shook with emotion, "think what your forgiveness means to me. Without it I am lost, both here and hereafter."

His voice was low and pleading and his face in the moonlight was like that of a man who knew the uttermost depths of despair.

"Forgive – forgive," he cried again, holding out his hands to me. "If you do not, I must go back to the sufferings which have been my portion since I did the deed which wrought my ruin."

I felt myself trembling like a leaf.

"If it is as you say, though I cannot believe it, I forgive you freely," I answered, in a voice that I scarcely recognised as my own.

For some moments he was silent, then he knelt before me and took my hand, which he raised to his lips. After that, rising, he laid his hand upon the breast of the mummy before which we were standing. Looking down at it he addressed it thus,—

"*Rest, Sinûhît, son of Amenemhait* – for that which was foretold for thee is now accomplished, and the punishment which was decreed is at an end. Henceforth thou mayest sleep in peace."

After that he replaced the lid of the coffin, and when this was done he turned to me.

"Let us be going," he said, and we went together through the rooms by the way we had come.

Together we left the building and passed through the gardens out into the road beyond. There we found the carriage waiting for us, and we took our places in it. Once more the horses sped along the silent road, carrying us swiftly back to Cairo. During the drive not a word was spoken by either of us. The only desire I had left was to get back to the hotel and lay my aching head upon my pillow. We crossed the bridge and entered the city. What the time was I had no idea, but I was conscious that the wind blew chill as if in anticipation of the dawn. At the same corner whence we had started, the coachman stopped his horses and I alighted, after which he drove away as if he had received his orders beforehand.

"Will you permit me to walk with you as far as your hotel?" said Constanides, with his customary politeness.

I tried to say something in reply, but my voice failed me. I would much rather have been alone, but as he would not allow this we set off together. At the corner of the street in which the hotel is situated we stopped.

"Here we must part," he said. Then, after a pause, he added, "And for ever. From this moment I shall never see your face again."

"You are leaving Cairo?" was the only thing I could say.

"Yes, I am leaving Cairo," he replied with peculiar emphasis. "My errand here is accomplished. You need have no fear that I shall ever trouble you again."

"I have no fear," I answered, though I am afraid it was only a half truth.

He looked earnestly into my face.

"Nofrît," he said, "for, say what you will, you are the Nofrît I would have made my Queen and have loved beyond all other women, never again will it be permitted you to look into the past as you did to-night. Had things been ordained otherwise we might have done great things together, but the gods willed that it should not be. Let it rest therefore. And now – farewell! Tonight I go to the rest for which I have so long been seeking."

Without another word he turned and left me. Then I went on to the hotel. How it came about I cannot say, but the door was open and I passed quickly in. Once more, to my joy, I found that the watchman was absent from the hall.

Trembling lest anyone might see me, I sped up the stairs and along the corridor, where the servants lay sleeping just as I had left them, and so to my room. Everything was exactly as I had left it, and there was nothing to show that my absence had been suspected. Again I went to the window, and, in a feeling of extraor-dinary agitation, looked out. Already there were signs of dawn in the sky. I sat down and tried to think over all that had happened to me that evening, endeavouring to convince myself, in the face of indisputable evidence, that it was not real and that I had only dreamt it. Yet it would not do! At last, worn out, I retired to rest. As a rule I sleep soundly; it is scarcely, however, a matter for won-derment that I did not do so on this occasion. Hour after hour I tumbled and tossed – thinking – thinking – thinking. When I rose and looked into the glass I scarcely recognised myself. Indeed, my mother commented on my fagged appearance when we met at the breakfast table.

"My dear child, you look as if you had been up all night," she said, and little did she guess, as she nibbled her toast, that there was a considerable amount of truth in her remark.

Later she went shopping with a lady staying in the hotel, while I went to my room to lie down. When we met again at lunch it was easy to see that she had some news of importance to communicate.

"My dear Cecilia," she said, "I have just seen Dr Forsyth, and he has given me a terrible shock. I don't want to frighten you, my girl, but have you heard that *Professor Constanides was found dead in bed this morning?* It is a most terrible affair! He must have died during the night!"

I am not going to pretend that I had any reply ready to offer her at that moment.

'THE NECKLACE OF DREAMS' (1910)

W. G. Peasgood

W. G. Peasgood may have been a nom de plume, but little is known about this author other than that he or she also wrote a tale, 'The Shaft of Silence', which was published in the *Pall Mall Magazine* in 1911.

'The Necklace of Dreams' appeared in the *Pall Mall Magazine* in April 1910. The tale centres on a necklace which had once belonged to an Egyptian magician, Taia, who had employed it to influence and kill her enemies. Those that wear it are subject to dream-like visions which will ultimately lead to their death. The tale is an account of one such dream endured by an Egyptologist, Professor Keston, who – believing himself "safe and sound in Kensington" – puts on the necklace with near-fatal consequences. Keston's vision recounts Taia's attempt to bring the figure of Nitocris under her influence. Nitocris was an Egyptian queen (and according to Herodotus's *Histories* a possible murderer) who appears in several tales and novels including George Griffith's *The Mummy and Miss Nitocris: A Phantasy of the Fourth Dimension* (1906), and H. P. Lovecraft's 'Imprisoned with the Pharaohs' (1924) and 'The Outsider' (1926). The sixteen-year-old Tennessee Williams's first tale 'The Vengeance of Nitocris' was published in *Weird Tales* in 1928.

I

Professor Keston, the eminent Egyptologist, held a belt buckle in red jasper close to the shaded electric lamp on the study table, and scrutinised it carefully. "Now, this belt buckle," he said, reflectively, "may possibly have belonged to some fair Egyptian maid, who laughed and flirted with the amorous youths of her circle when this old world of ours was some thousands of years younger. What a tremendous gulf of time between then and now! And the buckle remains!"

The study table was crowded with similar evidences of a bygone civilisation – scarabs in enamels, cone-shaped perfume vases of alabaster, glazed ware from Thebes, queerly shaped spoons with curved duck's-neck handles, amphorae of various colours, hinged bracelets worked in enamels on a groundwork of gold, amulets in green feldspar and lapis lazuli, poniards of black bronze, even a doll with movable limbs!

"Now, this doll," said the Professor, taking it up carefully, "if it could only speak and tell me all it saw when, say, Sneferû, the Smiter—" He stopped. His little daughter Doris had opened the door of the study, and was looking at him inquiringly.

"Let's play bears," she suggested, coaxingly.

He glanced at the oak clock on the mantelpiece. It was ten minutes to seven. "At half-past seven, my dear," he said gravely, "I will so far forget my professorial dignity as to become a rampant specimen of the ursine family for your edification."

"But I want to play bears!"

"At half-past seven, Doris."

"Oh, bother!"

"Doris!" But his small daughter had gone.

"This is a queer-looking thing," said the Professor, picking up a necklace of coloured spindle-shaped stone beads. He referred to his notebook. "Obtained from Hassan, who says that it was taken seven months ago from a tomb in the neighbourhood of Memphis. Have visited tomb, but found practically everything of archaeological interest missing." "The Vandals!" he ejaculated, looking up from the notebook. "And yet I suppose I am a Vandal, too, of a kind." He looked at the notebook again. "According to Hassan, the necklace exerts some sinister influence. Seeing I am interested, Hassan draws on his imagination. Evidence for Hassan's theory: 1st, the Arab who found it died same day, cause unknown; 2nd, his wife took necklace – ditto, but necklace not suspected; 3rd, wife of another tribesman took it – ditto; 4th, daughter of same – ditto.

"Obviously there was a kind of epidemic in the tribe, which these superstitious folk attributed to a sinister influence.

"I urge Hassan on to fresh efforts. Arabs, now suspicious, give the thing to a wandering holy man, who tells tribesmen they are wrong in attributing a malign influence to a few trifling stone beads of no value. Similar necklaces, he said, and he spoke truly, could be frequently picked up in certain places in the sands. Result – one prophet the less in the land! Evidence against Hassan's theory: he admits he has had it some six months, yet he is still living, and romances more artistically than ever. Name of mummy – Taia."

"There!" said the Professor. "And I have had it in my possession a full year or more, and here I am safe and sound in Kensington, with a policeman on point duty at the corner of the Square." He examined the necklace with the microscopical eye of the born antiquary. "Wonderful pigments! The colours have slightly faded, of course, and yet," taking up a penknife, "if I scrape one of the beads, so, the pigment looks as fresh as ever. I wonder how it feels to wear a necklace worn by an Egyptian woman thousands of years ago!" He clasped it around his neck as he spoke, and, leaning back in his chair, proceeded to arrange mentally his forthcoming book.

"Now, that little fairy tale of friend Hassan's," he said, after a while, "foolish in itself, may yet serve to brighten my monograph on Egyptian ornaments. A profusely illustrated book. In colours. Strange how my thoughts go back to that land of mystery yonder that is not as yet half explored. Now, at the present moment, sitting here with closed eyes, I can see the yellow desert, and some tents dotted about an oasis. Also wells and date-palms. And now I am in one of the tents. This, I should think, is the result of some slight degree of overwork on a somewhat free imagination. Everything is so marvellously clear!

"It is evening here, and, yes, certainly I am in one of the tents, and the gay romancer Hassan is bending over one of those poor fanatics of the desert who make so much mischief in the land and disturb our research work. Now what is Hassan doing to the sleeper? Ah, the good enchanter, whoever he is, has waved his magic wand, I suppose, for the scene is changed! I am imagining things rather quickly. I am in another tent, apparently. It is rather misty here, something like the beginning of a minor London fog, but I can just see a child stretched out on a heap of rugs. An Arab woman is taking something – an amulet of some kind – from the neck of the child. That confounded romance of Hassan's!

"My unknown friend has apparently waved his wand again. The child has gone, and a woman is lying, asleep apparently, in the place of the child. It is the same tent, and it is the same woman. The plot is improving. There is somebody with her – another woman!

"Now I am in yet another tent, but still at the oasis. I can see the date-palms through the opening in the tent but now the place looks cool and restful even in the glorious sunshine. Far away in the distance a long line of camels is approaching. Here, in the tent, a group of people are gathered around somebody. If some of them would only step aside—

"And now the whole scene has gone – oasis, tents, Arabs, camels, sunshine – gone as quickly as the flame of a candle when the extinguisher is dropped on it. This is a weird experience for an Egyptologist with a blameless past!

"I am standing," murmured the Professor, dreamily, "in the tomb where Hassan said the necklace was found, and which I examined. There is a man – an Arab – sitting on the ground with his back to the wall, asleep or dead, I can't see which, on account of the mistiness dancing about the place. Ah, now the mist has gone and everything is clear. The Arab is dead, and the necklace is around his neck. And the mummy – the mummy of Taia – is here. Extraordinary!" The Professor's remarks here became slightly confused.

"This semi-dream of mine is far better than – the reality," he murmured, after a short silence. "There was nothing in the tomb – in the tomb of – Taia—"

At this point the Professor fell asleep. Then he experienced the sensation of being carried swiftly towards a spot far away on the horizon; as if his unfettered spirit, breaking loose from the fragile bonds that held it in an inglorious subjection, had obeyed the call of some far-distant voice ringing down the centuries, and was speeding through space and time.

II

The red sun was setting, and magnificent Memphis, the ancient capital of Egypt, the city of departed Menes, first monarch of the first Egyptian dynasty, and first to wear the double crown of the two Egypts, lay in all its early glory, bathed in the dying light. The fortifications, the massive buildings of the interior, and the lofty watch towers that looked over the surrounding country, showed here and there an edge, sharply cut, against the cloudless sky. Slowly the radiance softened as the fiery sun sank into the western desert. Under the bright stars, and the yellow moon travelling slowly in the jewelled sky, the glittering city became shadowy and unreal, until at length it resembled nothing more substantial than the swiftly moulded fabric of a poet's dream.

At the end of one of the principal streets of the city, in a part from which even the moonlight was excluded owing to the narrowing of the street, two men were walking slowly backwards and forwards, engaged in low-toned but angry conversation. The younger of the two was a man of the true Egyptian type, active and sinewy in build, with an alert, intellectual face, denoting both energy and self-reliance. The other was darker-skinned and more strongly built, with a heavy-featured face, closely approaching the negroid type, and restless, beady eyes. He wore a massive gold chain around his short, thick neck, indicating a man of considerable wealth and standing in the city. He was listening sullenly to the eager voice of his companion. At last he motioned him to be silent.

"Tomorrow," he said, slowly, "I must tell how Setos slew a sacred ibis with a throwing-stick, on the bank of the river yonder. I, Mosû, saw the deed. Was not the ibis struck while wading in that shallow pool to the left of the great bed of reeds?"

"It was an accident!" said Setos, hotly. "I was hunting the waterfowl."

Mosû laughed mockingly. "What is that to those who sit in judgement? The sacred bird is dead, and woe awaits the slayer! Can you deny it? Shall not the people tear to pieces the man who did this thing?"

"Take all I possess, Mosû, but swear by the gods to be silent! Why should the gods be angry with their servant when the deed was not intended? I have brought no dishonour on the mighty gods of Egypt, and in their wisdom they acquit me of all wrong."

"The ibis is dead, Setos. If the gods will forgive, the people will not. And yet there is a way of safety for the slayer, an easy way that will permit him to escape the fate of those who kill the sacred animals." Mosû glanced at his companion, and then looked up at an unpretentious one-storeyed building on his right.

The heart of Setos sank as he divined the other's meaning. "Speak!" he said, hoarsely.

"In this building," said Mosû, softly, "lives Nitocris, the adopted daughter of the good Ameni, the architect. Foolishly she favours, or appears to favour, Setos, the landless and unknown; but on Mosû, the rich and the powerful, who could give her all that the heart of woman could desire, she turns the eye of scorn. Surrender Nitocris to me, and I will forget what happened yonder. I swear it by Osiris!"

"These are hard terms," said Setos, after a pause, during which the other had watched him keenly. "Nitocris is mine."

"By right of requited love, doubtless," replied Mosû, sneeringly. "Setos has but to stretch out his hand and he may pluck the fairest flower of Egypt."

"I cannot do this hard thing, even although I suffer the last penalty."

"Fool! I offer you fair terms. If you agree to forfeit the fair Nitocris, you live; if you do not agree, you die – and not easily, for in Egypt there are many ways in which a man may die. Impalement is an interesting ceremony – for those who look on! Cannot you see that in either case you lose her? Therefore it only remains for you to choose between life and death. Who but a fool would hesitate!"

Setos was silent. His usually active brain could not grapple with the situation.

The other made an impatient gesture as he turned away. "Tomorrow," he said, mockingly, "I will meet you where the four date-palms stand together. Then Setos shall tell me whether he chooses a long and happy life with some other fair maid of Egypt or – the death that lingers! I will be there soon after the dawn. If Setos, who believes himself the chosen of Nitocris, is not there at the appointed time, I shall know that he chooses – the death that lingers!" And with a sardonic smile the speaker turned into one of the many alleys leading out of the main street and disappeared in the darkness, leaving Setos standing in front of the house of Ameni, the architect.

Entering the dimly lighted entrance hall of the house, Setos passed quickly into a small court with rooms on either side. In one of the rooms on the right he found Nitocris sitting alone, embroidering a gala robe of fine linen. She rallied him on his gloomy looks, until he had made her acquainted with the trend of events, when, woman-like, she became tearful.

"I will escape to one of the ports of the Nile on the Mediterranean," said Setos. "There are many exiles there, and I have friends among them. I cannot surrender you to Mosû, Nitocris."

"I will not be surrendered to anyone but you, Setos!" she exclaimed, indignantly. "Something will happen shortly to this wretch Mosû, for it has long been rumoured in secret that he belongs to the Society of Thieves, they who rob the tombs of the dead and grow rich on the spoil. Then, when he is taken, my father Ameni, who stands high in the King's favour, will whisper to the King that the word of a fallen robber like Mosû should not be allowed to keep a true-hearted Egyptian in exile, and he may hearken unto Ameni, and relent. None is mightier than the King, the Son of the Sun."

Setos smiled at the girl's earnestness. "But Mosû may not be taken," he said gently.

"I will watch him myself!" the girl exclaimed her dark eyes flashing. "I will watch him everywhere. The vulture of the desert, seeking his lawful prey, shall not be keener-sighted than I! I will be very cunning for your sake, Setos! And my friends shall watch him also. They shall follow him every evening, until the robber is caught."

"It is said that some of the priests of the temple are members of this society of night-prowlers. Such priests are cunning and dangerous foes."

"Since I seek Mosû only I shall not incur the anger of the priests."

"But if Mosû be taken all may be taken."

"Then the dead will lie in peace, for there will be no robbers to disturb their tombs."

"And if, after all, it prove only a rumour?" he said, smiling at her ready answers.

"For a whole year I will wait and watch. If by that time Mosû is not proved to be a robber, I will ask my good father's consent to come to you wherever you may be on the Mediterranean." She looked at him quickly. "That is, of course, if you want me," she added, shyly.

He pressed her to him.

"And you will do all this, Nitocris, for the poor exile?"

"Indeed, I will! But stay, the gods have given me a bright thought. I will go to Taia, that old, old woman who is so deeply skilled in all magic, she who can read the stars in their courses, and foretell the destinies of men. Did she not prophesy that last year there would be misery in the land of Egypt, and did it not come true? I will go and ask her help."

"It may be that Taia has had her will in the framing of the lives of many men – and in the ending of them. I have heard that she is not over-scrupulous in her dealings, although she loves the gods. Still, it is a good thought, Nitocris, even although Taia may read the stars in the way she deems politic. But make her promise first to say nothing of the killing of the sacred ibis, or she may prove as pitiless a foe as Mosû."

"And now I go to Taia," said Nitocris.

"And I to the desert, for I dare not stay longer in the city. I shall not go to meet Mosû at the four date-palms."

"Listen then, Setos. Two miles to the south of the city, on the bank of the river, lies a broken column of red granite that came from the quarries of the south. As soon as it is light I will send a trusty messenger to the spot. If he gives you the leaf of an acacia you will know that Taia has given me hope, and you will not go far from the city, but be very watchful always. If he gives you the leaf of a sycamore go with all speed to the north, but even then we shall meet again, Setos, in a year from now. My good father Ameni will never see me unhappy."

And with a last embrace they parted.

The dwelling of Taia, the far-famed magician – respected and feared for her knowledge of supernatural matters and the ancient history of the land of Egypt, and also for the diabolical cunning with which she contrived to bring confusion on the heads of her enemies – was situated at not more than a hundred yards from the house of Ameni. Two well-worn steps led into the entrance hall, which in turn admitted the visitor to a small paved court. At the far end of this court a narrow stone stairway gave access to the rooms above the ground floor.

After entering this court, into which a lamp from one of the upper rooms cast a dim, uncertain light, half afraid to advance further into the house of Taia, the magician, and yet driven forward by her determination to save Setos from the fate that threatened him, Nitocris was conducted by a swarthy slave-girl up the stone stairway into the presence of a shrivelled old woman. She was sitting on a small chest of sycamore wood. This chest was quaintly and beautifully carved in a barbaric style, foreign to the art of the time, and was studded with large ivory bosses. In front of Taia, for this shrivelled old woman was the renowned wise woman of Memphis, some small pieces of scented wood were burning in a kind of brazier, diffusing an aromatic odour about the room. The floor was carpeted with the skins of lions and other animals of the chase. Drawings of the sacred animals covered the walls.

Taia looked up as Nitocris entered, and motioned to the slave-girl to withdraw.

"Taia is honoured by the visit of Nitocris, adopted daughter of Ameni, and the fairest lotus-flower of the city," she said, speaking with wonderful distinctness for so old a woman. "Has the youthful Setos proved faithless that you come to me, or is the ugly, dark-skinned Mosû too attentive?"

"You know much, Taia," said the girl, timidly, seating herself, in obedience to Taia's pointing finger, on a low stool near the brazier.

"The things that are great and the things that are small are alike known to you. It is said that you gain your great knowledge of the past, the present, and the future from the gleaming world-stars above us, and that the old history of the Egyptian people is known to you alone."

Taia looked into the girl's face with her small, glittering eyes. "You speak truly, Nitocris. Whence came this chest of sycamore wood? It was not made in Egypt, but it was fashioned by a cunning craftsman, and the blood that ran in that craftsman's veins was akin to that which runs in the veins of the King of Egypt today! Can you read that riddle? Or whence came that bronze-legged stool on which you sit? Perhaps it was a Queen's favourite stool a thousand years ago! Perhaps she has sat there, as you sit now, while a lover-king played with her dark tresses, and called her the pretty names that lovers love! Yet who can tell, save Taia?"

"It is a pity that the records of our ancient history have been lost. I should like to know more about that lover-king. Perhaps you could find them if you invoked the aid of the supernatural beings with whom you converse."

"Perhaps!" said the old woman, with a cunning look.

The girl looked at her curiously. "You can read the past, Taia. Read me now the future from the bright stars that instruct you. Tell me, what is the destiny of Mosû?"

"I see a dead body on the sands," said Taia, after a few moments of silence. She closed her eyes and rocked herself gently backwards and forwards. "On the body there is no wound, nor any hurt that can be seen by mortal eye. Neither lion nor man has slain him, yet Mosû lies dead!"

"How then did he die?" the girl asked breathlessly.

"By the gods' decree. And now a man approaches, a man who fears the eyes of other men, for he looks furtively around him. And now he looks into the face of Mosû. The man is Setos!" Taia stopped suddenly and looked keenly at her visitor. "Was it to learn the fate of Mosû that you came to me, Nitocris?"

"I want your help, Taia, but promise first by Osiris that you will keep secret the things that I may tell you."

"Does the fire of love burn so strongly even now?" said Taia, half-mockingly; "as strongly as when the lover-king played with his sweetheart's raven hair? Still, I promise." And she listened with an expressionless face as Nitocris related the incidents of the evening, rocking herself gently until her visitor had finished.

"Can you help me, Taia, and make Mosû forget the killing of the ibis? I do not ask his death, only his forgetfulness of that one thing."

"Listen!" said the old woman. "Because Mosû derided me before the people, you shall have your wish, and Mosû *shall* forget!" She laughed merrily, as if the thought of Mosû's forgetfulness was pleasing to her. "Did I not prophesy, two years ago, that in the following year the Nile would not rise to its usual height, and that therefore many starving people would wander in the land? This Mosû jeered at me, but he did not jeer when the prophecy came true. Perhaps he had drunk too deeply from the wine-cup. Yet Taia does not forget such insults, although they be uttered by fools like Mosû!" With a sudden fierce movement she stretched out her thin, wiry arms, as if to grasp and rend the doubter. "He insulted me, Taia, she who is favoured by the gods and endowed by them with some trifle of their infinite wisdom. In deriding me he derided *them*. The anger of the gods must be appeased, even although Mosû die!" She paused. "I hear them calling to me to avenge them!" she whispered. Then she let her arms fall and looked wildly at the trembling girl opposite. "Perhaps you are the messenger of death, Nitocris!"

"I only ask his forgetfulness of that one thing," the girl repeated.

"Take this necklace, then!" She touched a spring in the lid of the chest, took from a cavity a necklace of coloured beads made of some soft stone, and gave it to the girl. "Do not hold it in your hands too long, Nitocris, for it is a magic necklace! It is the necklace of forgetfulness! It is the necklace of dreams!"

"And if I do hold it too long?"

"You would forget Setos!"

The girl cast a terrified glance at the necklace, and then hid it quickly in her robe. "What must I do with it?" she asked.

"You must ask Mosû to wear it for at least one hour. Then he will forget, and never again will he remember! Never again!" She laughed gleefully. "Tell the miserly fool that if he wears it for at least one full hour he will obtain whatever he desires most in this world, save only the double crown of the two Egypts. That will arouse his greediness, and he will wear it. Or he may wish for Nitocris, the daughter of Ameni!" she added, slily. "Who knows?"

The girl shivered at the thought.

"Still, he may not come to me before he tells what he saw, and then I cannot give him the necklace."

"When he does not find Setos at the four date-palms he will come to you to try and make terms."

"And how am I to repay you, Taia?"

"First, promise by all the gods of Egypt, by your hope of a favourable judgement in the World of Souls, that you will not wear the necklace yourself—"

"And forget Setos! Never!"

"Nor allow anyone else to wear it."

"I promise, Taia."

"Secondly, you shall give me, as a token of your visit, that pretty necklace I see shining on your slender neck."

"Willingly."

Nitocris unclasped the necklace of bluish-white chalcedonies, with one small emerald hanging from the centre in a setting of gold, and gave it to the old woman.

"A pretty thing!" said Taia, taking it in her thin brown fingers and admiring the waxy lustre of the translucent stones. "Chalcedonies from the eastern desert, and an emerald from the mines on the borders of the Red Sea, where the slaves and the condemned labour hardly until they die! Truly, these pretty stones are tears of the desert!"

For a long time after Nitocris had left her Taia sat silently watching the light smoke curling up from the brazier. When at last she spoke her withered face wore a look of exultation.

"The poor tool!" she muttered. "She has gone away happy with the necklace of dreams, the necklace of death! How carefully I mixed that rare essence with the pigments before I painted the beads! The subtle essence that has broken the power of kings and priests before one stone of this mighty city was laid! And what did they become? Less than the humblest of their cringing servants, who still had life left to them to fawn and flatter. They who wear it after Mosû shall dream of the things that went before! Is it not endowed with the magic art of Taia? The art that shall pass away with Taia! How easily and deeply the sweet-scented essence sank into the soft stones, there to remain until the warmth of Mosû's body should awaken its hidden power. Stealthily it shall creep through the pores of his skin until at last it reaches his false heart. A painless sleep, Mosû! So quiet, so gentle – yet so sure!"

She flung herself on her face on the floor.

"Osiris!" she cried, "judge of the dead in the World of Souls, I send you the soul of Mosû! O Shû, Lord of Light, slay this soul before the gates of heaven, for he has insulted the gods of Egypt – the gods whose mighty reign shall be shown to the sons of men, although they will no longer believe, when nothing remains of this proud city save a few half-buried fragments, when the splendour of great Egypt shall have passed away, and there are strangers in the land!" She paused. "And for his crime, let Setos die also!"

Alone with the throbbing silence of the night, in which there seemed to breathe the spirit of loneliness – a silence only broken at rare intervals by the deep, sullen roar of a wandering lion, or the crashing sound made by some heavy animal pushing its way through the thick beds of reeds – Setos waited for the dawn. The red granite pillar, broken in two, lay close at hand, and so near the river that the water washed against the end.

Hour after hour passed slowly and wearily. Still the delicate hues of the dawn remained hidden in the east, as if hesitating to bring with their glory a new day to the man who, in a few hours, might be hunted for his life by the infuriated population of the great city that lay, massively, two miles away to the north.

To pass the time, and to keep his thoughts from dwelling too much on the loneliness of the place, he talked to the river at intervals as it went sweeping by his feet. It even seemed to him to understand and to answer him. The Nile, coming from the unknown lands beyond Syêné, the southernmost limit of Egypt, was regarded by all his countrymen with awe and reverence.

"O Hapi!" he cried, "the Hidden One, river of deep mystery, what secrets lie in your bosom? Mighty Hapi! When your waters are ruddy you give a three-fold harvest! Your waters have made Egypt the granary of the world! Without you the land would be a barren waste! There would be no treading of the grapes in the winepress, no driving of the lowing oxen through the heaps of golden grain!"

The cool northerly breeze from the distant Mediterranean fanned his face as he waited and watched for the dawn.

At last the day came, and with it the promised messenger. "From Nitocris, the daughter of Ameni," he said, and he gave Setos – the leaf of an acacia!

The four date-palms grew close together a long stone's-throw from the walls of the city. Here the impatient Mosû, who met the messenger of Nitocris returning, waited a full hour for his unfortunate rival. Then he determined to see Nitocris, as Taia had expected.

Realising that, if he did denounce Setos, even secretly, he might still fail to dazzle Nitocris with his wealth, he decided to make her promise to be his wife the price of his silence. "It will be easy," he meditated, as he returned slowly to the city, "if she does consent, to rid myself of Setos after the wedding on some other charge, otherwise her thoughts may revert to him while he is in the flesh. If she does not consent, then by Osiris and all the gods I will give information!"

He made his way after a time to the house of Ameni. Nitocris, outwardly calm, was sitting in the court, still embroidering the linen robe. In her lap lay Taia's necklace. He fancied that she greeted him with unusual friendliness.

"I have a question to ask you, Nitocris," he said, and hesitated as he saw her startled look. His glance fell on the necklace. "Do you wear such trifles as that?" he asked, contemptuously.

"Do not treat my poor necklace with scorn!" said the girl, laughing merrily. "That is a magic necklace, given to me only yesterday by a friend, and therefore it has a double value."

His eyes sparkled. Like all Egyptians, he had a strong belief in the magical arts.

"And its powers?" he asked.

"It is a strange story, and one that can scarcely be believed, but some day, when I have the courage, I shall test its truth. It is said that whoever wears it for one full hour obtains whatever he or she desires most in this world. Yet no one may wish for the double crown of the two Egypts. That wish is excepted, for it is a crime to aspire to the glory of the Son of the Sun. I am afraid that I shall never have the courage to wear it."

"Did your friend obtain her wish?"

"She also is afraid. And it is said that after one wish the charm is broken. No one has yet dared to invoke the aid of its power. Would you like to wear it?"

She held the necklace out to him with fingers that trembled slightly, fearing that he would refuse.

But Mosû saw in the necklace an easy way out of the difficulty. He took it eagerly.

"Won't you tell me your wish?" asked Nitocris, looking at him with smiling eyes. She felt that she could well be friendly now that he was so soon to forget the killing of the ibis.

He laughed and shook his head.

"In two hours I will come and tell you."

"You were going to ask me a question."

"That also I will ask when I return," said Mosû.

Half-an-hour later he had returned to the date-palms for the sake of the solitude. He sat down, with his back resting against one of the trees. He held the necklace out in the full sunshine and looked at it doubtfully.

"Well," he said, "I will prove now the power or uselessness of this thing, although I care not to meddle with magic, lest I summon the Goddess of Evil. If Nitocris refuses me in spite of this charm then I will show her that the fate of Setos depends on her answer, and I will ask her to think again. If she still refuses I will denounce Setos at once."

He clasped the cold necklace around his brawny neck. "I, Mosû, wish for the willing consent of Nitocris, the adopted daughter of Ameni, to be my wife!"

Seating himself in an easy position to wait the allotted time, he mused upon his coming triumph over his rival Setos. The voices of some scantily clad boatmen on the Nile, fifty yards away on his right, came to him faintly on the soft warm air. Somewhere out of sight on the bank of the river a woman with a sweet voice was singing a gay love song.

The necklace clung tightly, but it no longer felt cold. On the contrary, it had become a warm, clinging, living thing, as the heat of his body awakened the dormant life of the subtle essence that Taia had mixed with the pigments before painting the beads, inducing a feeling of delicious restfulness. As the time passed on a drowsiness came over him, and the voices of the boatmen seemed to blend gradually with the voice of the singer as she began another song. Turning his head slowly, he looked towards the sun-bathed city, and noticed that its outlines had become indistinct.

"This is strange!" he muttered, trying to fix his gaze steadily on a tall watch-tower. "The city seems to be swaying to and fro, and now – what freak is this? – I am standing in the market-place! There is Taia, the old magician! All the people are gathered about her. Surely I have seen all this before! By the Goddess of Evil, I can see myself, standing on the outskirts of the crowd! What is the old impostor saying?

"'Listen, all who live on the soil and by the soil! Listen to the warning that is written by the gods in the stars! Save your grain, save your wine, lay up food in your houses, for next year there shall be little corn and little wine, and many shall wander starving through the land. So they shall wander until they die!'

"Some of the people are listening with frightened faces, some are whispering together. Now I remember! Taia's magic taught her that the Nile would not rise to its usual height, and so the crops and the grape-harvest failed."

For a space he was silent, his eyes closed. When he spoke again it was in a low, halting voice, for the essence was dominating his brain.

"Like a fool, I am jeering at her! The old woman turns her withered face and looks at me with her glittering eyes.

"'Listen, Mosû! O man of wealth! O man of many slaves and many golden ornaments! Taia is the servant of the mighty gods, and because of your unbelief they demand vengeance! The enemy of life shall come to you, Mosû, so quietly that you shall not hear his soft footsteps. Then, while he stands beside you, waiting, this scene shall pass before your eyes again, and you shall hear again your foolish words. In the Hall of Truth, Anubis, the Keeper of the Scales, shall say to Osiris, "This is the soul of a man who derided the gods!"'"

Mosû stirred uneasily on his sandy couch and opened his eyes. Again he saw dimly the city and the yellow desert. Then they vanished as swiftly as if a veil had been suddenly drawn before his face, and he fell asleep.

Later in the day the wandering Setos ventured near the city and found the body of Mosû under the date-palm, as Taia, the wise

woman of Memphis, had foreseen. But the necklace had disappeared, for, unknown to Mosû, Taia had followed him from the
house of Ameni after his interview with Nitocris. She had removed
the necklace from the neck of her enemy when she was sure that
it had done its work.

Taia, sitting alone in her upper room, was exulting in her revenge.
The wrath of the gods had been turned away! From time to time
she drew the necklace from its place of concealment in the cavity
of the chest, and looked at it lovingly.

"And the next shall be Setos!" she muttered, after she had sat
brooding in silence for a long time. "The vengeance of the gods is
swift and easy – too easy for the scoffing Mosû! Who shall give it
to Setos? Nitocris? No, I will give it to the ibis-slayer myself; but not
yet. There is no need for haste. Let the poor lovesick fools enjoy a
few more days together!"

She rose to her feet, and, moving into the middle of the room,
began a strange religious dance – a form of worship in which the
steps were slow and rhythmic, as if the dancer moved to the strains
of slow, sweet music. Snatching up the necklace, she clasped it
quickly around her thin, bony neck.

"Who dares to flirt with life and death, save Taia?" she cried,
and again she began to dance, her face wearing the strained look
of one listening to some half-heard, half-forgotten melody.

"It is enough," she said, breathlessly, after a few minutes. "I have
enticed Death from his cave of shadows, and, after teasing him, I
have sent him away disappointed. He has been waiting patiently,
so patiently, with uplifted spear – ready to strike! A little more, and
I should have seen the sheen of the blade." She looked fixedly at
a corner of the room that was in shadow. "So alert! So silent! So

remorseless! Even now he may be watching me with his cold eyes before he turns away!"

She was raising her hand to her throat to unclasp the necklace when her foot caught in the lion skin in front of the brazier. With a cry she tripped and fell, and, striking her head against the chest of sycamore wood, lay full length on the floor, half-stunned.

"The necklace!" she screamed, plucking wildly at her throat, and striving to overcome the dizziness caused by the blow. Then she lost consciousness.

The same evening Setos sought Nitocris and learnt from her the details of her interview with Taia, and that no charge had been preferred against him. All the city knew that Mosû and Taia had died mysteriously.

"Let us think no more of these things," said Setos, "since we can never understand them. Our bitter enemy can do us no more hurt, and we have life before us, Nitocris – a happy life."

She put her hands on his shoulders and looked at him as only a woman can look.

"And even when we reach the end of life, Setos," she whispered, "we shall still be together, you and I, in the beautiful gardens of Aahlu!"

III

The Professor's little daughter came into the room with a rush, and climbed on his knees.

"Time!" she exclaimed, in the tone of one who will stand no contradiction. She was punctual, for the clock at that moment struck half-past seven.

He did not move.

"Wake up and play bears!" shaking him energetically. "What's this pretty thing?"

She gave the necklace a little pull, with the result that the fine wire snapped. The beads flew about the floor.

Two days later the Professor was able to sit up in bed. Little Doris was playing on the floor with her doll.

"That was a near thing," he said, helping himself to some grapes. "Hassan could not have worn it. Doris, my dear, I am strongly of opinion that your habit of reaching out your hand for every pretty thing you see is a distinct virtue!"

He helped himself to some more grapes.

Doris stopped playing, and looked at him wonderingly.

"And when I get well, Doris, I am going to buy you a beautiful necklace of amber beads – *real* amber!"

Doris clapped her hands in glee and ran to the side of the bed.

"Hope you soon quite well!" she said, artlessly.

The Professor still has a little heap of perforated white stones in a velvet case, but they are quite harmless, for immersion in strong chemicals has removed the colouring matter, and with it the remainder of the essence. The case seldom sees the light of day, and it is only at rare intervals that he allows his thoughts to go back to that eventful evening when, but for Doris, he would have fallen a victim to the fatal "Necklace of Dreams".